AGATHA CHRISTIE'S POIROT

BOOK FOUR

Agatha Christie's Poirot

BOOK FOUR

Fontana
An Imprint of HarperCollins*Publishers*

Fontana
An Imprint of HarperCollins*Publishers*
77–85 Fulham Palace Road
Hammersmith, London W6 8JB

Published by Fontana 1993
9 8 7 6 5 4 3 2

'The Adventure of the Egyptian Tomb', 'The Adventure of the
Italian Nobleman', 'The Case of the Missing Will', 'The Jewel
Robbery at the Grand Metropolitan' were first published in the UK
in *Poirot Investigates*, 1924. 'Dead Man's Mirror' was first published
in *Murder in the Mews*, 1937. 'The Chocolate Box' was first
published in *Poirot's Early Cases*, 1974. 'The Under Dog' was first
published in *The Adventure of the Christmas Pudding*, 1960. 'Yellow
Iris' was first published in Strand Magazine in 1937, and in book
form in *Problem at Pollensa Bay and other stories*, 1991.

ISBN 0 00 647303 2

Set in Plantin

Printed in Great Britain by
HarperCollinsManufacturing, Glasgow

CONTENTS

THE ADVENTURE OF
THE EGYPTIAN TOMB

I have always considered that one of the most thrilling and dramatic adventures I have shared with Poirot was that of our investigation into the strange series of deaths which followed upon the discovery and opening of the Tomb of King Men-her-Ra.

Hard upon the discovery of the Tomb of TutankhAmen by Lord Carnarvon, Sir John Willard and Mr Bleibner of New York, pursuing their excavations not far from Cairo, in the vicinity of the Pyramids of Gizeh, came unexpectedly on a series of funeral chambers. The greatest interest was aroused by their discovery. The Tomb appeared to be that of King Men-her-Ra, one of those shadowy kings of the Eighth Dynasty, when the Old Kingdom was falling to decay. Little was known about this period, and the discoveries were fully reported in the newspapers.

An event soon occurred which took a profound hold on the public mind. Sir John Willard died suddenly of heart failure.

The more sensational newspapers immediately took the opportunity of reviving all the old superstitious stories connected with the ill luck of certain Egyptian treasures. The unlucky Mummy at the British Museum, that hoary old chestnut, was dragged out with fresh zest, was quietly denied by the Museum, but nevertheless enjoyed all its usual vogue.

A fortnight later Mr Bleibner died of acute blood poisoning, and a few days afterwards a nephew of his shot himself in New York. The 'Curse of Men-her-Ra' was the talk of the day, and the magic power of dead-and-gone Egypt was exalted to a fetish point.

It was then that Poirot reveived a brief note from Lady Willard, widow of the dead archaeologist, asking him to go and see her at her house in Kensington Square. I accompanied him.

Lady Willard was a tall, thin woman, dressed in deep mourning. Her haggard face bore eloquent testimony to her recent grief.

'It is kind of you to have come so promptly, Monsieur Poirot.'

'I am at your service, Lady Willard. You wished to consult me?'

'You are, I am aware, a detective, but it is not only as a detective that I wish to consult you. You are a man of original views, I know, you have imagination, experience of the world; tell me, Monsieur Poirot, what are your views on the supernatural?'

Poirot hesitated for a moment before he replied. He seemed to be considering. Finally he said:

'Let us not misunderstand each other, Lady Willard. It is not a general question that you are asking me there. It has a personal application, has it not? You are referring obliquely to the death of your late husband?'

'That is so,' she admitted.

'You want me to investigate the circumstances of his death?'

'I want you to ascertain for me exactly how much is newspaper chatter, and how much may be said to be founded on fact? Three deaths, Monsieur Poirot – each one explicable taken by itself, but taken together surely an almost unbelievable coincidence, and all within a month of the opening of the tomb! It may be mere superstition, it may be some potent curse from the past that operates in ways undreamed of by modern science. The fact remains

– three deaths! And I am afraid, Monsieur Poirot, horribly afraid. It may not yet be the end.'

'For whom do you fear?'

'For my son. When the news of my husband's death came I was ill. My son, who has just come down from Oxford, went out there. He brought the – the body home, but now he has gone out again, in spite of my prayers and entreaties. He is so fascinated by the work that he intends to take his father's place and carry on the system of excavations. You may think me a foolish, credulous woman, but, Monsieur Poirot, I am afraid. Supposing that the spirit of the dead King is not yet appeased? Perhaps to you I seem to be talking nonsense – '

'No, indeed, Lady Willard,' said Poirot quickly. 'I, too, believe in the force of superstition, one of the greatest forces the world has ever known.'

I looked at him in surprise. I should never have credited Poirot with being superstitious. But the little man was obviously in earnest.

'What you really demand is that I shall protect your son? I will do my utmost to keep him from harm.'

'Yes, in the ordinary way, but against an occult influence?'

'In volumes of the Middle Ages, Lady Willard, you will find many ways of counteracting black magic. Perhaps they knew more than we moderns with all our boasted science. Now let us come to facts, that I may have guidance. Your husband had always been a devoted Egyptologist, hadn't he?'

'Yes, from his youth upwards. He was one of the greatest living authorities upon the subject.'

'But Mr Bleibner, I understand, was more or less of an amateur?'

'Oh, quite. He was a very wealthy man who dabbled freely in any subject that happened to take his fancy. My husband managed to interest him in Egyptology, and it was his money that was so useful in financing the expedition.'

'And the nephew? What do you know of his tastes? Was he with the party at all?'

'I do not think so. In fact I never knew of his existence till I read of his death in the paper. I do not think he and Mr Bleibner can have been at all intimate. He never spoke of having any relations.'

'Who are the other members of the party?'

'Well, there's Dr Tosswill, a minor official connected with the British Museum; Mr Schneider of the Metropolitan Museum in New York; a young American secretary; Dr Ames, who accompanies the expedition in his professional capacity; and Hassan, my husband's devoted native servant.'

'Do you remember the name of the American secretary?'

'Harper, I think, but I cannot be sure. He had not been with Mr Bleibner very long, I know. He was a very pleasant young fellow.'

'Thank you, Lady Willard.'

'If there is anything else – '

'For the moment, nothing. Leave it now in my hands, and be assured that I will do all that is humanly possible to protect your son.'

They were not exactly reassuring words, and I observed Lady Willard wince as he uttered them. Yet, at the same time, the fact that he had not pooh-poohed her fears seemed in itself to be a relief to her.

For my part I had never before suspected that Poirot had so deep a vein of superstition in his nature. I tackled him on the subject as we went homewards. His manner was grave and earnest.

'But yes, Hastings. I believe in these things. You must not underrate the force of superstition.'

'What are we going to do about it?'

'*Toujours pratique*, the good Hastings! *Eh bien*, to begin with we are going to cable New York for fuller details of young Mr Bleibner's death.'

He duly sent off his cable. The reply was full and precise. Young Rupert Bleibner had been in low water for several years. He had been a beachcomber and a remittance man in several South Sea islands, but had returned to New York two years ago, where he had rapidly sunk lower and lower. The most significant thing, to my mind, was that he had recently managed to borrow enough money to take him to Egypt. 'I've a good friend there I can borrow from,' he had declared. Here, however, his plans had gone awry. He had returned to New York cursing his skinflint of an uncle who cared more for the bones of dead and gone kings than his own flesh and blood. It was during his sojourn in Egypt that the death of Sir John Willard had occurred. Rupert had plunged once more into his life of dissipation in New York, and then, without warning, he had committed suicide, leaving behind him a letter which contained some curious phrases. It seemed written in a sudden fit of remorse. He referred to himself as a leper and an outcast, and the letter ended by declaring that such as he were better dead.

A shadowy theory leapt into my brain. I had never really believed in the vengeance of a long dead Egyptian king. I saw here a more modern crime. Supposing this young man had decided to do away with his uncle – preferably by poison. By mistake Sir John Willard received the fatal dose. The young man returns to New York, haunted by his crime. The news of his uncle's death reaches him. He realizes how unnecessary his crime has been, and stricken with remorse takes his own life.

I outlined my solution to Poirot. He was interested.

'It is ingenious what you have thought of there – decidedly it is ingenious. It may even be true. But you leave out of count the fatal influence of the Tomb.'

I shrugged my shoulders.

'You still think that has something to do with it?'

'So much so, *mon ami*, that we start for Egypt tomorrow.'

'What?' I cried, astonished.

'I have said it.' An expression of conscious heroism spread over Poirot's face. Then he groaned. 'But oh,' he lamented, 'the sea! The hateful sea!'

It was a week later. Beneath our feet was the golden sand of the desert. The hot sun poured down overhead. Poirot, the picture of misery, wilted by my side. The little man was not a good traveller. Our four days' voyage from Marseilles had been one long agony to him. He had landed at Alexandria the wraith of his former self, even his usual neatness had deserted him. We had arrived in Cairo and had driven out at once to the Mena House Hotel, right in the shadow of the Pyramids.

The charm of Egypt had laid hold of me. Not so Poirot. Dressed precisely the same as in London, he carried a small clothes-brush in his pocket and waged an unceasing war on the dust which accumulated on his dark apparel.

'And my boots,' he wailed. 'Regard them, Hastings. My boots, of the neat patent leather, usually so smart and shining. See, the sand inside them, which is painful, and outside them, which outrages the eyesight. Also the heat, it causes my moustaches to become limp – but limp!'

'Look at the Sphinx,' I urged. 'Even I can feel the mystery and the charm it exhales.'

Poirot looked at it discontentedly.

'It has not the air happy,' he declared. 'How could it, half-buried in sand in that untidy fashion. Ah, this cursed sand!'

'Come, now, there's a lot of sand in Belgium,' I reminded him, mindful of a holiday spent at Knocke-sur-mer in the midst of '*Les dunes impeccables*' as the guide-book had phrased it.

'Not in Brussels,' declared Poirot. He gazed at the Pyramids thoughtfully. 'It is true that they, at least, are of a shape solid and geometrical, but their surface is of an unevenness most unpleasing. And the palm-trees I like them not. Not even do they plant them in rows!'

I cut short his lamentations, by suggesting that we should start for the camp. We were to ride there on camels, and the beasts were patiently kneeling, waiting for us to mount, in charge of several picturesque boys headed by a voluble dragoman.

I pass over the spectacle of Poirot on a camel. He started by groans and lamentations and ended by shrieks, gesticulations and invocations to the Virgin Mary and every Saint in the calendar. In the end, he descended ignominiously and finished the journey on a diminutive donkey. I must admit that a trotting camel is no joke for the amateur. I was stiff for several days.

At last we neared the scene of the excavations. A sunburnt man with a grey beard, in white clothes and wearing a helmet, came to meet us.

'Monsieur Poirot and Captain Hastings? We received your cable. I'm sorry that there was no one to meet you in Cairo. An unforseen event occurred which completely disorganized our plans.'

Poirot paled. His hand, which had stolen to his clothes-brush, stayed its course.

'Not another death?' he breathed.

'Yes.'

'Sir Guy Willard?' I cried.

'No, Captain Hastings. My American colleague, Mr Schneider.'

'And the cause?' demanded Poirot.

'Tetanus.'

I blanched. All around me I seemed to feel an atmosphere of evil, subtle and menacing. A horrible thought flashed across me. Supposing I were next?

'*Mon Dieu*,' said Poirot, in a very low voice, 'I do not understand this. It is horrible. Tell me, monsieur, there is no doubt that it was tetanus?'

'I believe not. But Dr Ames will tell you more than I can do.'

'Ah, of course, you are not the doctor.'

'My name is Tosswill.'

This, then, was the British expert described by Lady Willard as being a minor official the British Museum. There was something at once grave and steadfast about him that took my fancy.

'If you will come with me,' continued Dr Tosswill, 'I will take you to Sir Guy Willard. He was most anxious to be informed as soon as you should arrive.'

We were taken across the camp to a large tent. Dr Tosswill lifted up the flap and we entered. Three men were sitting inside.

'Monsieur Poirot and Captain Hastings have arrived, Sir Guy,' said Tosswill.

The youngest of the three men jumped up and came forward to greet us. There was a certain impulsiveness in his manner which reminded me of his mother. He was not nearly so sunburnt as the others, and that fact, coupled with a certain haggardness round the eyes, made him look older than his twenty-two years. He was clearly endeavouring to bear up under a severe mental strain.

He introduced his two companions, Dr Ames, a capable-looking man of thirty-odd, with a touch of greying hair at the temples, and Mr Harper, the secretary, a pleasant young man wearing the national insignia of horn-rimmed spectacles.

After a few minutes' desultory conversation the latter went out, and Dr Tosswill followed him. We were left alone with Sir Guy and Dr Ames.

'Please ask any questions you want to ask, Monsieur Poirot,' said Willard. 'We are utterly dumbfounded at this strange series of disasters, but it isn't – it can't be, anything but coincidence.'

There was a nervousness about his manner which rather belied the words. I saw that Poirot was studying him keenly.

'Your heart is really in this work, Sir Guy?'

'Rather. No matter what happens, or what comes of it, the work is going on. Make up your mind to that.'

Poirot wheeled round on the other.

'What have you to say to that, *monsieur le docteur*?'

'Well,' drawled the doctor, 'I'm not for quitting myself.'

Poirot made one of those expressive grimaces of his.

Then, *évidemment*, we must find out just how we stand. When did Mr Schneider's death take place?'

'Three days ago.'

'You are sure it was tetanus?'

'Dead sure.'

'It couldn't have been a case of strychnine poisoning, for instance?'

'No, Monsieur Poirot, I see what you are getting at. But it was a clear case of tetanus.'

'Did you not inject anti-serum?'

'Certainly we did,' said the doctor dryly. 'Every conceivable thing that could be done was tried.'

'Had you the anti-serum with you?'

'No. We procured it from Cairo.'

'Have there been any other cases of tetanus in the camp?'

'No, not one.'

'Are you certain that the death of Mr Bleibner was not due to tetanus?'

'Absolutely plumb certain. He had a scratch upon his thumb which became poisoned, and septicaemia set in. It sounds pretty much the same to a layman, I dare say, but the two things are entirely different.'

'Then we have four deaths – all totally dissimilar, one

heart failure, one blood poisoning, one suicide and one tetanus.'

'Exactly, Monsieur Poirot.'

'Are you certain that there is nothing which might link the four together?'

'I don't quite understand you?'

'I will put it plainly. Was any act committed by those four men which might seem to denote disrespect to the spirit of Men-her-Ra?'

The doctor gazed at Poirot in astonishment.

'You're talking through your hat, Monsieur Poirot. Surely you've not been guyed into believing all that fool talk?'

'Absolute nonsense,' muttered Willard angrily.

Poirot remained placidly immovable, blinking a little out of his green cat's eyes.

'So you do not believe it, *monsieur le docteur*?'

'No, sir, I do not,' declared the doctor emphatically. 'I am a scientific man, and I believe only what science teaches.'

'Was there no science then in Ancient Egypt?' asked Poirot softly. He did not wait for a reply, and indeed Dr Ames seemed rather at a loss for the moment. 'No, no, do not answer me, but tell me this. What do the native workmen think?'

'I guess,' said Dr Ames, 'that, where white folk lose their heads, natives aren't going to be far behind. I'll admit that they're getting what you might call scared – but they've no cause to be.'

'I wonder,' said Poirot non-committally.

Sir Guy leaned forward.

'Surely,' he cried incredulously, 'you cannot believe in – oh, but the thing's absurd! You can know nothing of Ancient Egypt if you think that.'

For an answer Poirot produced a little book from his pocket – an ancient tattered volume. As he held it out

I saw its title, *The Magic of the Egyptians and Chaldeans*. Then, wheeling round, he strode out of the tent. The doctor stared at me.

'What is his little idea?'

The phrase, so familiar on Poirot's lips, made me smile as it came from another.

'I don't know exactly,' I confessed. 'He's got some plan of exorcizing the evil spirits, I believe.'

I went in search of Poirot, and found him talking to the lean-faced young man who had been the late Mr Bleibner's secretary.

'No,' Mr Harper was saying, 'I've only been six months with the expedition. Yes, I knew Mr Bleibner's affairs pretty well.'

'Can you recount to me anything concerning his nephew?'

'He turned up here one day, not a bad-looking fellow. I'd never met him before, but some of the others had – Ames, I think, and Schneider. The old man wasn't at all pleased to see him. They were at it in no time, hammer and tongs. "Not a cent," the old man shouted. "Not one cent now or when I'm dead. I intend to leave my money to the furtherance of my life's work. I've been talking it over with Mr Schneider today." And a bit more of the same. Young Bleibner lit out for Cairo right away.'

'Was he in perfectly good health at the time?'

'The old man?'

'No, the young one.'

'I believe he did mention there was something wrong with him. But it couldn't have been anything serious, or I should have remembered.'

'One thing more, had Mr Bleibner left a will?'

'So far as we know, he has not.'

'Are you remaining with the expedition, Mr Harper?'

'No, sir, I am not. I'm for New York as soon as I can square up things here. You may laugh if you like, but I'm

not going to be this blasted Men-her-Ra's next victim.
He'll get me if I stop here.'

The young man wiped the perspiration from his brow.

Poirot turned away. Over his shoulder he said with a
peculiar smile:

'Remember, he got one of his victims in New York.'

'Oh, hell!' said Mr Harper forcibly.

'That young man is nervous,' said Poirot thoughtfully.
'He is on the edge, but absolutely on the edge.'

I glanced at Poirot curiously, but his enigmatical smile
told me nothing. In company with Sir Guy Willard and
Dr Tosswill we were taken round the excavations. The
principal finds had been removed to Cairo, but some of
the tomb furniture was extremely interesting. The
enthusiasm of the young baronet was obvious, but I
fancied that I detected a shade of nervousness in his
manner as though he could not quite escape from the
feeling of menace in the air. As we entered the tent which
had been assigned to us, for a wash before joining the
evening meal, a tall dark figure in white robes stood aside
to let us pass with a graceful gesture and a murmured
greeting in Arabic. Poirot stopped.

'You are Hassan, the late Sir John Willard's servant?'

'I served my Lord Sir John, now I serve his son.' He
took a step nearer to us and lowered his voice. 'You are
a wise one, they say, learned in dealing with evil spirits.
Let the young master depart from here. There is evil in
the air around us.'

And with an abrupt gesture, not waiting for a reply, he
strode away.

'Evil in the air,' muttered Poirot. 'Yes, I feel it.'

Our meal was hardly a cheerful one. The floor was left
to Dr Tosswill, who discoursed at length upon Egyptian
antiquities. Just as we were preparing to retire to rest, Sir
Guy caught Poirot by the arm and pointed. A shadowy
figure was moving amidst the tents. It was no human one:

I recognized distinctly the dog-headed figure I had seen carved on the walls of the tomb.

My blood froze at the sight.

'*Mon Dieu!*' murmured Poirot, crossing himself vigorously. 'Anubis, the jackal-headed, the god of departing souls.'

'Someone is hoaxing us,' cried Dr Tosswill, rising indignantly to his feet.

'It went into your tent, Harper,' muttered Sir Guy, his face dreadfully pale.

'No,' said Poirot, shaking his head, 'into that of the Dr Ames.'

The doctor stared at him incredulously; then, repeating Dr Tosswill's words, he cried:

'Someone is hoaxing us. Come, we'll soon catch the fellow.'

He dashed energetically in pursuit of the shadowy apparition. I followed him, but, search as we would, we could find no trace of any living soul having passed that way. We returned, somewhat disturbed in mind, to find Poirot taking energetic measures, in his own way, to ensure his personal safety. He was busily surrounding our tent with various diagrams and inscriptions which he was drawing in the sand. I recognized the five-pointed star or Pentagon many times repeated. As was his wont, Poirot was at the same time delivering an impromptu lecture on witchcraft and magic in general, White magic as opposed to Black, with various references to the Ka and the Book of the Dead thrown in.

It appeared to excite the liveliest contempt in Dr Tosswill, who drew me aside, literally snorting with rage.

'Balderdash, sir,' he exclaimed angrily. 'Pure balderdash. The man's an imposter. He doesn't know the difference between the superstitions of the Middle Ages and the beliefs of Ancient Egypt. Never have I heard such a hotch-potch of ignorance and credulity.'

I calmed the excited expert, and joined Poirot in the tent. My little friend was beaming cheerfully.

'We can now sleep in peace,' he declared happily. 'And I can do with some sleep. My head, it aches abominably. Ah, for a good *tisane*!'

As though in answer to a prayer, the flap of the tent was lifted and Hassan appeared, bearing a steaming cup which he offered to Poirot. It proved to be camomile tea, a beverage of which he is inordinately fond. Having thanked Hassan and refused his offer of another cup for myself, we were left alone once more. I stood at the door of the tent some time after undressing, looking out over the desert.

'A wonderful place,' I said aloud, 'and a wonderful work. I can feel the fascination. This desert life, this probing into the heart of a vanished civilization. Surely, Poirot, you, too, must feel the charm?'

I got no answer, and I turned, a little annoyed. My annoyance was quickly changed to concern. Poirot was lying back across the rude couch, his face horribly convulsed. Beside him was the empty cup. I rushed to his side, then dashed out and across the camp to Dr Ames's tent.

'Dr Ames!' I cried. 'Come at once.'

'What's the matter?' said the doctor, appearing in pyjamas.

'My friend. He's ill. Dying. The camomile tea. Don't let Hassan leave the camp.'

Like a flash the doctor ran to our tent. Poirot was lying as I left him.

'Extraordinary,' cried Ames. 'Looks like a seizure – or – what did you say about something he drank?' He picked up the empty cup.

'Only I did not drink it!' said a placid voice.

We turned in amazement. Poirot was sitting up on the bed. He was smiling.

20

'No,' he said gently. 'I did not drink it. While my good friend Hastings was apostrophizing the night, I took the opportunity of pouring it, not down my throat, but into a little bottle. That little bottle will go to the analytical chemist. No' — as the doctor made a sudden movement — 'as a sensible man, you will understand that violence will be of no avail. During Hastings' absence to fetch you, I have had time to put the bottle in safe keeping. Ah, quick, Hastings, hold him!'

I misunderstood Poirot's anxiety. Eager to save my friend, I flung myself in front of him. But the doctor's swift movement had another meaning. His hand went to his mouth, a smell of bitter almonds filled the air, and he swayed forward and fell.

'Another victim,' said Poirot gravely, 'but the last. Perhaps it is the best way. He has three deaths on his head.'

'Dr Ames?' I cried, stupefied. 'But I thought you believed in some occult influence?'

'You misunderstood me, Hastings. What I meant was that I believe in the terrific force of superstition. Once get it firmly established that a series of deaths are supernatural, and you might almost stab a man in broad daylight, and it would still be put down to the curse, so strongly is the instinct of the supernatural implanted in the human race. I suspected from the first that a man was taking advantage of that instinct. The idea came to him, I imagine, with the death of Sir John Willard. A fury of superstition arose at once. As far as I could see, nobody could derive any particular profit from Sir John's death. Mr Bleibner was a different case. He was a man of great wealth. The information I received from New York contained several suggestive points. To begin with, young Bleibner was reported to have said he had a good friend in Egypt from whom he could borrow. It was tacitly understood that he meant his uncle, but it seemed to me that in that case he would have said so outright. The words suggest some boon companion of his own. Another thing, he scraped up enough money to take him to Egypt, his uncle refused outright to advance him a penny, yet he was able to pay the return passage to New York. Someone must have lent him the money.'

'All that was very thin,' I objected.

'But there was more. Hastings, there occur often enough words spoken metaphorically which are taken literally. The opposite can happen too. In this case, words which were meant literally were taken metaphorically. Young Bleibner wrote plainly enough: "I am a leper," but nobody realized that he shot himself because he believed that he contracted the dread disease of leprosy.'

'What?' I ejaculated.

'It was the clever invention of a diabolical mind. Young Bleibner was suffering from some minor skin trouble; he had lived in the South Sea Islands, where the disease is common enough. Ames was a former friend of his, and a well-known medical man, he would never dream of doubting his word. When I arrived here, my suspicions were divided between Harper and Dr Ames, but I soon realized that only the doctor could have perpetrated and concealed the crimes, and I learn from Harper that he was previously acquainted with young Bleibner. Doubtless the latter at some time or another had made a will or had insured his life in favour of the doctor. The latter saw his chance of acquiring wealth. It was easy for him to inoculate Mr Bleibner with the deadly germs. Then the nephew, overcome with despair at the dread news his friend had conveyed to him, shot himself. Mr Bleibner, whatever his intentions, had made no will. His fortune would pass to his nephew and from him to the doctor.'

'And Mr Schneider?'

'We cannot be sure. He knew young Bleibner too, remember, and may have suspected something, or, again, the doctor may have thought that a further death motiveless and purposeless would strengthen the coils of superstition. Furthermore, I will tell you an interesting psychological fact, Hastings. A murderer has always a strong desire to repeat his successful crime, the performance of it grows upon him. Hence my fears for young Willard. The figure of Anubis you saw tonight was Hassan dressed up by my orders. I wanted to see if I could frighten the doctor. But it would take more than the supernatural to frighten him. I could see that he was not entirely taken in by my pretences of belief in the occult. The little comedy I played for him did not deceive him. I suspected that he would endeavour to make me the next victim. Ah, but in spite of *la mer maudite*, the heat abominable, and the annoyances of the sand, the little grey cells still functioned!'

Poirot proved to be perfectly right in his premises. Young Bleibner, some years ago, in a fit of drunken merriment, had made a jocular will, leaving 'my cigarette-case you admire so much and everything else of which I die possessed which will be principally debts, to my good friend Robert Ames who once saved my life from drowning.'

The case was hushed up as far as possible, and, to this day, people talk of the remarkable series of deaths in connection with the Tomb of Men-her-Ra as a triumphal proof of the vengeance of a bygone king upon the desecrators of his tomb – a belief which, as Poirot pointed out to me, is contrary to all Egyptian belief and thought.

YELLOW IRIS

Yellow Iris was first published in the UK in *Strand Magazine* in 1937. This story was expanded into the novel, *Sparkling Cyanide*, published by Collins in 1945, but did not feature Hercule Poirot.

Hercule Poirot stretched out his feet towards the electric radiator set in the wall. Its neat arrangement of red hot bars pleased his orderly mind.

'A coal fire,' he mused to himself, 'was always shapeless and haphazard! Never did it achieve the symmetry.'

The telephone bell rang. Poirot rose, glancing at his watch as he did so. The time was close on half past eleven. He wondered who was ringing him up at this hour. It might, of course, be a wrong number.

'And it might,' he murmured to himself with a whimsical smile, 'be a millionaire newspaper proprietor, found dead in the library of his country house, with a spotted orchid clasped in his left hand and a page torn from a cookbook pinned to his breast.'

Smiling at the pleasing conceit, he lifted the receiver.

Immediately a voice spoke – a soft husky woman's voice with a kind of desperate urgency about it.

'*Is that M. Hercule Poirot? Is that M. Hercule Poirot?*'

'Hercule Poirot speaks.'

'*M. Poirot – can you come at once – at once – I'm in danger – in great danger – I know it . . .*'

Poirot said sharply:

'Who are you? Where are you speaking from?'

The voice came more faintly but with an even greater urgency.

'*At once . . . it's life or death . . . the Jardin des Cygnes
. . . at once . . . table with yellow irises . . .*'

There was a pause – a queer kind of gasp – the line
went dead.

Hercule Poirot hung up. His face was puzzled. He
murmured between his teeth:

'There is something here very curious.'

In the doorway of the Jardin des Cygnes, fat Luigi hurried
forward.

'*Buona sera*, M. Poirot. You desire a table – yes?'

'No, no, my good Luigi. I seek here for some friends.
I will look round – perhaps they are not here yet. Ah,
let me see, that table there in the corner with the yellow
irises – a little question by the way, if it is not indiscreet.
On all the other tables there are tulips – pink tulips –
why on that one table do you have yellow irises?'

Luigi shrugged his expressive shoulders.

'A command, Monsieur! A special order! Without
doubt, the favourite flowers of one of the ladies. That table
it is the table of Mr Barton Russell – an American –
immensely rich.'

'Aha, one must study the whims of the ladies, must one
not, Luigi?'

'Monsieur has said it,' said Luigi.

'I see at that table an acquaintance of mine. I must go
and speak to him.'

Poirot skirted his way delicately round the dancing floor
on which couples were revolving. The table in question
was set for six, but it had at the moment only one
occupant, a young man who was thoughtfully, and it
seemed pessimistically, drinking champagne.

He was not at all the person that Poirot had expected
to see. It seemed impossible to associate the idea of danger
or melodrama with any party of which Tony Chapell was
a member.

Poirot paused delicately by the table.

'Ah, it is, is it not, my friend Anthony Chapell?'

'By all that's wonderful – Poirot, the police hound!' cried the young man. 'Not Anthony, my dear fellow – Tony to friends!'

He drew out a chair.

'Come, sit with me. Let us discourse of crime! Let us go further and drink to crime.' He poured champagne into an empty glass. 'But what are you doing in this haunt of song and dance and merriment, my dear Poirot? We have no bodies here, positively not a single body to offer you.'

Poirot sipped the champagne.

'You seem very gay, *mon cher?*'

'Gay? I am steeped in misery – wallowing in gloom. Tell me, you hear this tune they are playing. You recognize it?'

Poirot hazarded cautiously:

'Something perhaps to do with your baby having left you?'

'Not a bad guess,' said the young man. 'But wrong for once. ''There's nothing like love for making you miserable!'' That's what it's called.'

'Aha?'

'My favourite tune,' said Tony Chapell mournfully. 'And my favourite restaurant and my favourite band – and my favourite girl's here and she's dancing it with somebody else.'

'Hence the melancholy?' said Poirot.

'Exactly. Pauline and I, you see, have had what the vulgar call words. That is to say, she's had ninety-five words to five of mine out of every hundred. My five are: ''*But, darling – I can explain.*'' – Then she starts in on her ninety-five again and we get no further. I think,' added Tony sadly, 'that I shall poison myself.'

'Pauline?' murmured Poirot.

'Pauline Weatherby. Barton Russell's young sister-in-law. Young, lovely, disgustingly rich. Tonight Barton Russell gives a party. You know him? Big Business, clean-shaven American – full of pep and personality. His wife was Pauline's sister.'

'And who else is there at this party?'

'You'll meet 'em in a minute when the music stops. There's Lola Valdez – you know, the South American dancer in the new show at the Metropole, and there's Stephen Carter. D'you know Carter – he's in the diplomatic service. Very hush-hush. Known as silent Stephen. Sort of man who says, "*I am not at liberty to state, etc, etc.*" Hullo, here they come.'

Poirot rose. He was introduced to Barton Russell, to Stephen Carter, to Señora Lola Valdez, a dark and luscious creature, and to Pauline Weatherby, very young, very fair, with eyes like cornflowers.

Barton Russell said:

'What, is this the great M. Hercule Poirot? I am indeed pleased to meet you sir. Won't you sit down and join us? That is, unless –'

Tony Chapell broke in.

'He's got an appointment with a body, I believe, or is it an absconding financier, or the Rajah of Borrioboolagah's great ruby?'

'Ah, my friend, do you think I am never off duty? Can I not, for once, seek only to amuse myself?'

'Perhaps you've got an appointment with Carter here. The latest from the UN International situation now acute. The stolen plans *must* be found or war will be declared tomorrow!'

Pauline Weatherby said cuttingly:

'Must you be so *completely* idiotic, Tony?'

'Sorry, Pauline.'

Tony Chapell relapsed into crestfallen silence.

'How severe you are, Mademoiselle.'

'I hate people who play the fool all the time!'

'I must be careful, I see. I must converse only of serious matters.'

'Oh, no, M. Poirot. I didn't mean you.'

She turned a smiling face to him and asked:

'Are you really a kind of Sherlock Holmes and do wonderful deductions?'

'Ah, the deductions – they are not so easy in real life. But shall I try? Now then, I deduce – that yellow irises are your favourite flowers?'

'Quite wrong, M. Poirot. Lilies of the valley or roses.'

Poirot sighed.

'A failure. I will try once more. This evening, not very long ago, you telephoned to someone.'

Pauline laughed and clapped her hands.

'Quite right.'

'It was not long after you arrived here?'

'Right again. I telephoned the minute I got inside the doors.'

'Ah – that is not so good. You telephoned *before* you came to this table?'

'Yes.'

'Decidedly very bad.'

'Oh, no, I think it was very clever of you. How did you know I had telephoned?'

'That, Mademoiselle, is the great detective's secret. And the person to whom you telephoned – does the name begin with a P – or perhaps with an H?'

Pauline laughed.

'Quite wrong. I telephoned to my maid to post some frightfully important letters that I'd never sent off. Her name's Louise.'

'I am confused – quite confused.'

The music began again.

'What about it, Pauline?' asked Tony.

'I don't think I want to dance again so soon, Tony.'

'Isn't that too bad?' said Tony bitterly to the world at large.

Poirot murmured to the South American girl on his other side:

'Señora, I would not dare to ask you to dance with me. I am too much of the antique.'

Lola Valdez said:

'Ah, it ees nonsense that you talk there! You are steel young. Your hair, eet is still black!'

Poirot winced slightly.

'Pauline, as your brother-in-law and your guardian,' Barton Russell spoke heavily, 'I'm just going to force you onto the floor! This one's a waltz and a waltz is about the only dance I really can do.'

'Why, of course, Barton, we'll take the floor right away.'

'Good girl, Pauline, that's swell of you.'

They went off together. Tony tipped back his chair. Then he looked at Stephen Carter.

'Talkative little fellow, aren't you, Carter?' he remarked. 'Help to make a party go with your merry chatter, eh, what?'

'Really, Chapell, I don't know what you mean?'

'Oh, you don't – don't you?' Tony mimicked him.

'My dear fellow.'

'Drink, man, drink, if you won't talk.'

'No, thanks.'

'Then I will.'

Stephen Carter shrugged his shoulders.

'Excuse me, must just speak to a fellow I know over there. Fellow I was with at Eton.'

Stephen Carter got up and walked to a table a few places away.

Tony said gloomily:

'Somebody ought to drown old Etonians at birth.'

Hercule Poirot was still being gallant to the dark beauty beside him.

He murmured:

'I wonder, may I ask, what are the favourite flowers of mademoiselle?'

'Ah, now, why ees eet you want to know?'

Lola was arch.

'Mademoiselle, if I send flowers to a lady, I am particular that they should be flowers she likes.'

'That ees very charming of you, M. Poirot. I weel tell you – I adore the big dark red carnations – or the dark red roses.'

'Superb – yes, superb! You do not, then, like yellow irises?'

'Yellow flowers – no – they do not accord with my temperament.'

'How wise . . . Tell me, Mademoiselle, did you ring up a friend tonight, since you arrived here?'

'I? Ring up a friend? No, what a curious question!'

'Ah, but I, I am a very curious man.'

'I'm sure you are.' She rolled her dark eyes at him. 'A vairy *dan*gerous man.'

'No, no, not dangerous; say, a man who may be useful – in danger! You understand?'

Lola giggled. She showed white even teeth.

'No, no,' she laughed. 'You are dangerous.'

Hercule Poirot sighed.

'I see that you do not understand. All this is very strange.'

Tony came out of a fit of abstraction and said suddenly:

'Lola, what about a spot of swoop and dip? Come along.'

'I weel come – yes. Since M. Poirot ees not brave enough!'

Tony put an arm round her and remarked over his shoulder to Poirot as they glided off:

'You can meditate on crime yet to come, old boy!'

Poirot said: 'It is profound what you say there. Yes, it is profound . . .'

He sat meditatively for a minute or two, then he raised

a finger. Luigi came promptly, his wide Italian face wreathed in smiles.

'*Mon vieux*,' said Poirot. 'I need some information.'

'Always at your service, Monsieur.'

'I desire to know how many of these people at this table here have used the telephone tonight?'

'I can tell you, Monsieur. The young lady, the one in white, she telephoned at once when she got here. Then she went to leave her cloak and while she was doing that the other lady came out of the cloakroom and went into the telephone box.'

'So the Señora *did* telephone! Was that *before* she came into the restaurant?'

'Yes, Monsieur.'

'Anyone else?'

'No, Monsieur.'

'All this, Luigi, gives me furiously to think!'

'Indeed, Monsieur.'

'Yes. I think, Luigi, that *tonight of all nights*, I must have my wits about me! *Something* is going to happen, Luigi, and I am not at all sure what it is.'

'Anything I can do, Monsieur –'

Poirot made a sign. Luigi slipped discreetly away. Stephen Carter was returning to the table.

'We are still deserted, Mr Carter,' said Poirot.

'Oh – er – quite,' said the other.

'You know Mr Barton Russell well?'

'Yes, known him a good while.'

'His sister-in-law, little Miss Weatherby, is very charming.'

'Yes, pretty girl.'

'You know her well, too?'

'Quite.'

'Oh, quite, quite,' said Poirot.

Carter stared at him.

The music stopped and the others returned.

Barton Russell said to a waiter:

'Another bottle of champagne – quickly.'

Then he raised his glass.

'See here, folks. I'm going to ask you to drink a toast. To tell you the truth, there's an idea back of this little party tonight. As you know, I'd ordered a table for six. There were only five of us. That gave us an empty place. Then, by a very strange coincidence, M. Hercule Poirot happened to pass by and I asked him to join our party.

'You don't know yet what an apt coincidence that was. You see that empty seat tonight represents a lady – the lady in whose memory this party is being given. This party, ladies and gentlemen, is being held in memory of my dear wife – Iris – who died exactly four years ago on this very date!'

There was a startled movement round the table. Barton Russell, his face quietly impassive, raised his glass.

'I'll ask you to drink to her memory. *Iris!*'

'Iris?' said Poirot sharply.

He looked at the flowers. Barton Russell caught his glance and gently nodded his head.

There were little murmurs round the table.

'Iris – Iris . . .'

Everyone looked startled and uncomfortable.

Barton Russell went on, speaking with his slow monotonous American intonation, each word coming out weightily.

'It may seem odd to you all that I should celebrate the anniversary of a death in this way – by a supper party in a fashionable restaurant. But I have a reason – yes, I have a reason. For M. Poirot's benefit, I'll explain.'

He turned his head towards Poirot.

'Four years ago tonight, M. Poirot, there was a supper party held in New York. At it were my wife and myself, Mr Stephen Carter, who was attached to the Embassy in Washington, Mr Anthony Chapell, who had been a guest in our house for some weeks, and Señora Valdez, who was at that time enchanting New York City with her dancing. Little Pauline here –' he patted her shoulder ' – was only sixteen but she came to the supper party as a special treat. You remember, Pauline?'

'I remember – yes.' Her voice shook a little.

'M. Poirot, on that night a tragedy happened. There was a roll of drums and the cabaret started. The lights went down – all but a spotlight in the middle of the floor. When the lights went up again, M. Poirot, my wife was seen to have fallen forward on the table. She was dead – stone dead. There was potassium cyanide found in the dregs of her wine glass, and the remains of the packet was discovered in her handbag.'

'She had committed suicide?' said Poirot.

'That was the accepted verdict . . . It broke me up, M. Poirot. There was, perhaps, a possible reason for such an action – the police thought so. I accepted their decision.'

He pounded suddenly on the table.

'But I was not satisfied . . . No, for four years I've been thinking and brooding – and I'm not satisfied: I don't believe Iris killed herself. I believe, M. Poirot, that she was murdered – by one of those people at the table.'

'Look here, sir –'

Tony Chapell half sprang to his feet.

'Be quiet, Tony,' said Russell. 'I haven't finished. One of them did it – I'm sure of that now. Someone who, under cover of the darkness, slipped the half emptied packet of cyanide into her handbag. I think I know which of them it was. I mean to know the truth –'

Lola's voice rose sharply.

'You are mad – crazee – who would have harmed her? No, you are mad. Me, I will not stay –'

She broke off. There was a roll of drums.

Barton Russell said:

'The cabaret. Afterwards we will go on with this. Stay

where you are, all of you. I've got to go and speak to the dance band. Little arrangement I've made with them.'

He got up and left the table.

'Extraordinary business,' commented Carter. 'Man's mad.'

'He ees crazee, yes,' said Lola.

The lights were lowered.

'For two pins I'd clear out,' said Tony.

'No!' Pauline spoke sharply. Then she murmured, 'Oh, dear – oh, dear –'

'What is it, Mademoiselle?' murmured Poirot.

She answered almost in a whisper.

'It's horrible! It's just like it was that night –'

'Sh! Sh!' said several people.

Poirot lowered his voice.

'A little word in your ear.' He whispered, then patted her shoulder. 'All will be well,' he assured her.

'My God, listen,' cried Lola.

'What is it, Señora?'

'*It's the same tune* – the same song that they played that night in New York. Barton Russell must have fixed it. I don't like this.'

'Courage – courage –'

There was a fresh hush.

A girl walked out into the middle of the floor, a coal black girl with rolling eyeballs and white glistening teeth. She began to sing in a deep hoarse voice – a voice that was curiously moving.

> I've forgotten you
> I never think of you
> The way you walked
> The way you talked
> The things you used to say
> I've forgotten you
> I never think of you

I couldn't say
For sure today
Whether your eyes were blue or grey
I've forgotten you
I never think of you.

I'm through
Thinking of you
I tell you I'm through
Thinking of you . . .
You . . . you . . . you . . .

The sobbing tune, the deep golden Negro voice had a powerful effect. It hypnotized – cast a spell. Even the waiters felt it. The whole room stared at her, hypnotized by the thick cloying emotion she distilled.

A waiter passed softly round the table filling up glasses, murmuring 'champagne' in an undertone but all attention was on the one glowing spot of light – the black woman whose ancestors came from Africa, singing in her deep voice:

I've forgotten you
I never think of you

Oh, what a lie
I shall think of you, think of you, think of you

till I die . . .

The applause broke out frenziedly. The lights went up. Barton Russell came back and slipped into his seat.

'She's great, that girl –' cried Tony.

But his words were cut short by a low cry from Lola. '*Look – look . . .*'

And then they all saw. Pauline Weatherby dropped forward onto the table.

35

Lola cried:

'She's dead — just like Iris — like Iris in New York.'

Poirot sprang from his seat, signing to the others to keep back. He bent over the huddled form, very gently lifted a limp hand and felt for a pulse.

His face was white and stern. The others watched him. They were paralysed, held in a trance.

Slowly, Poirot nodded his head.

'Yes, she is dead — *la pauvre petite*. And I sitting by her! Ah! but this time the murderer shall not escape.'

Barton Russell, his face grey, muttered:

'Just like Iris . . . She saw something — Pauline saw something that night — Only she wasn't sure — she told me she wasn't sure . . . We must get the police . . . Oh, God, little Pauline.'

Poirot said:

'Where is her glass?' He raised it to his nose. 'Yes, I can smell the cyanide. A smell of bitter almonds . . . the same method, the same poison . . .'

He picked up her handbag.

'Let us look in her handbag.'

Barton Russell cried out:

'You don't believe this is suicide, too? Not on your life.'

'Wait,' Poirot commanded. 'No, there is nothing here. The lights went up, you see, too quickly, the murderer had not time. Therefore, the poison is still on him.'

'Or her,' said Carter.

He was looking at Lola Valdez.

She spat out:

'What do you mean — what do you say? That I killed her — eet is not true — not true — why should I do such a thing?'

'You had rather a fancy for Barton Russell yourself in New York. That's the gossip I heard. Argentine beauties are notoriously jealous.'

'That ees a pack of lies. And I do not come from the

Argentine. I come from Peru. Ah – I spit upon you. I –' She lapsed into Spanish.

'I demand silence,' cried Poirot. 'It is for me to speak.'

Barton Russell said heavily:

'Everyone must be searched.'

Poirot said calmly.

'*Non, non,* it is not necessary.'

'What d'you mean, not necessary?'

'I, Hercule Poirot, know. I see with the eyes of the mind. And I will speak! M. Carter, *will you show us the packet in your breast pocket?*'

'There's nothing in my pocket. What the hell –'

'Tony, my good friend, if you will be so obliging.'

Carter cried out:

'Damn you –'

Tony flipped the packet neatly out before Carter could defend himself.

'There you are, M. Poirot, just as you said!'

'IT'S A DAMNED LIE,' cried Carter.

Poirot picked up the packet, read the label.

'Cyanide potassium. The case is complete.'

Barton Russell's voice came thickly.

'Carter! I always thought so. Iris was in love with you. She wanted to go away with you. You didn't want a scandal for the sake of your precious career so you poisoned her. You'll hang for this, you dirty dog.'

'Silence!' Poirot's voice rang out, firm and authoritative. 'This is not finished yet. I, Hercule Poirot, have something to say. My friend here, Tony Chapell, he says to me when I arrive, that I have come in search of crime. That, it is partly true. There *was* crime in my mind – but it was to prevent a crime that I came. And I have prevented it. The murderer, he planned well – but Hercule Poirot he was one move ahead. He had to think fast, and to whisper quickly in Mademoiselle's ear when the lights went down. She is very quick and clever, Mademoiselle Pauline, she played her part well. Mademoiselle, will you be so kind as to show us that you are not dead after all?'

Pauline sat up. She gave an unsteady laugh.

'Resurrection of Pauline,' she said.

'Pauline – darling.'

'Tony!'

'My sweet!'

'Angel.'

Barton Russell gasped.

'I – I don't understand . . .'

'I will help you to understand, Mr Barton Russell. Your plan has miscarried.'

'My plan?'

'Yes, your plan. Who was the only man who had an *alibi* during the darkness? The man who left the table – you, Mr Barton Russell. But you returned to it under cover of the darkness, circling round it, with a champagne bottle, filling up glasses, putting cyanide in Pauline's glass and dropping the half empty packet in Carter's pocket as you bent over him to remove a glass. Oh, yes, it is easy to play the part of a waiter in darkness when the attention of everyone is elsewhere. That was the real reason for your party tonight. The safest place to commit a murder is in the middle of a crowd.'

'What the – why the hell should I want to kill Pauline?'

'It might be, perhaps, a question of money. Your wife left you guardian to her sister. You mentioned that fact tonight. Pauline is twenty. At twenty-one or on her marriage you would have to render an account of your stewardship. I suggest that you could not do that. You have speculated with it. I do not know, Mr Barton Russell, whether you killed your wife in the same way, or whether her suicide suggested the idea of this crime to you, but I do know that tonight you have been guilty of attempted murder. It rests with Miss Pauline whether you are prosecuted for that.'

'No,' said Pauline. 'He can get out of my sight and out of this country. I don't want a scandal.'

'You had better go quickly, Mr Barton Russell, and I advise you to be careful in future.'

Barton Russell got up, his face working.

'To hell with you, you interfering little Belgian jackanapes.'

He strode out angrily.

Pauline sighed.

'M. Poirot, you've been wonderful . . .'

'You, Mademoiselle, you have been the marvellous one. To pour away the champagne, to act the dead body so prettily.'

'Ugh,' she shivered, 'you give me the creeps.'

He said gently:

'It was you who telephoned me, was it not?'

'Yes.'

'Why?'

'I don't know. I was worried and – frightened without knowing quite why I was frightened. Barton told me he was having this party to commemorate Iris' death. I realized he had some scheme on – but he wouldn't tell me what it was. He looked so – so queer and so excited that I felt something terrible might happen – only, of course, I never dreamed that he meant to – to get rid of *me*.'

'And so, Mademoiselle?'

'I'd heard people talking about you. I thought if I could only get you here perhaps it would stop anything happening. I thought that being a – a foreigner – if I rang up and pretended to be in danger and – and made it sound mysterious –'

'You thought the melodrama, it would attract me? That is what puzzled me. The message itself – definitely it was what you call "bogus" – it did not ring true. But the fear in the voice – that was real. Then I came – and you

39

denied very categorically having sent me a message.'

'I had to. Besides, I didn't want you to know it was me.'

'Ah, but I was fairly sure of that! Not at first. But I soon realized that the only two people who could know about the yellow irises on the table were you or Mr Barton Russell.'

Pauline nodded.

'I heard him ordering them to be put on the table,' she explained. 'That, and his ordering a table for six when I knew only five were coming, made me suspect –' She stopped, biting her lip.

'What did you suspect, Mademoiselle?'

She said slowly:

'I was afraid – of something happening – to Mr Carter.'

Stephen Carter cleared his throat. Unhurriedly but quite decisively he rose from the table.

'Er – h'm – I have to – er – thank you, M. Poirot. I owe you a great deal. You'll excuse me, I'm sure, if I leave you. Tonight's happenings have been – rather upsetting.'

Looking after his retreating figure, Pauline said violently:

'I hate him. I've always thought it was – because of him that Iris killed herself. Or perhaps – Barton killed her. Oh, it's all so hateful . . .'

Poirot said gently:

'Forget, Mademoiselle . . . forget . . . Let the past go . . . Think only of the present . . .'

Pauline murmured, 'Yes – you're right . . .'

Poirot turned to Lola Valdez.

'Señora, as the evening advances I become more brave. If you would dance with me now –'

'Oh, yes, indeed. You are – you are ze cat's whiskers, M. Poirot. I inseest on dancing with you.'

'You are too kind, Señora.'

Tony and Pauline were left. They leant towards each other across the table.

'Darling Pauline.'

'Oh, Tony, I've been such a nasty spiteful spitfiring little cat to you all day. Can you ever forgive me?'

'Angel! This is Our Tune again. Let's dance.'

They danced off, smiling at each other and humming softly:

There's nothing like Love for making you miserable
There's nothing like Love for making you blue
Depressed
Possessed
Sentimental
Temperamental
There's nothing like Love
For getting you down.

There's nothing like Love for driving you crazy
There's nothing like Love for making you mad
Abusive
Allusive
Suicidal
Homicidal
There's nothing like Love
There's nothing like Love . . .

THE ADVENTURE OF
THE ITALIAN NOBLEMAN

Poirot and I had many friends and acquaintances of an informal nature. Amongst these was to be numbered Dr Hawker, a near neighbour of ours, and a member of the medical profession. It was the genial doctor's habit to drop in sometimes of an evening and have a chat with Poirot, of whose genius he was an ardent admirer. The doctor himself, frank and unsuspicious to the last degree, admired the talents so far removed from his own.

On one particular evening in early June, he arrived about half past eight and settled down to a comfortable discussion on the cheery topic of the prevalence of arsenical poisoning in crimes. It must have been about a quarter of an hour later when the door of our sitting room flew open, and a distracted female precipitated herself into the room.

'Oh, doctor, you're wanted! Such a terrible voice. It gave me a turn, it did indeed.'

I recognized in our new visitor Dr Hawker's house-keeper, Miss Rider. The doctor was a bachelor, and lived in a gloomy old house a few streets away. The usually placid Miss Rider was now in a state bordering on incoherence.

'What terrible voice? Who is it, and what's the trouble?'

'It was the telephone, doctor. I answered it – and a voice spoke. "Help," it said. "Doctor – help. They've killed me!" Then it sort of tailed away. "Who's speaking?" I said. "Who's speaking?" Then I got a reply, just a whisper, it seemed "Foscatine" – something like that – "Regent's Court." '

The doctor uttered an exclamation.

'Count Foscatini. He has a flat in Regent's Court. I must go at once. What can have happened?'

'A patient of yours?' asked Poirot.

'I attended him for some slight ailment a few weeks ago. An Italian, but he speaks English perfectly. Well, I must wish you good night, Monsieur Poirot, unless – ' He hesitated.

'I perceive the thought in your mind,' said Poirot, smiling. 'I shall be delighted to accompany you. Hastings, run down and get hold of a taxi.'

Taxis always make themselves sought for when one is particularly pressed for time, but I captured one at last, and we were soon bowling along in the direction of Regent's Park. Regent's Court was a new block of flats, situated just off St John's Wood Road. They had only recently been built, and contained the latest service devices.

There was no one in the hall. The doctor pressed the lift-bell impatiently, and when the lift arrived questioned the uniformed attendant sharply.

'Flat 11. Count Foscatini. There's been an accident there, I understand.'

The man stared at him.

'First I've heard of it. Mr Graves – that's Count Foscatini's man – went out about half an hour ago, and he said nothing.'

'Is the Count alone in the flat?'

'No, sir, he's got two gentlemen dining with him.'

'What are they like?' I asked eagerly.

We were in the lift now, ascending rapidly to the second floor, on which Flat 11 was situated.

'I didn't see them myself, sir, but I understand they were foreign gentlemen.'

He pulled back the iron door, and we stepped out on the landing. No 11 was opposite to us. The doctor rang the bell. There was no reply, and we could hear no sound from within. The doctor rang again and again; we could hear the bell trilling within, but no sign of life rewarded us.

'This is getting serious,' muttered the doctor. He turned to the lift attendant.

'Is there any pass-key to this door?'

'There's one in the porter's office downstairs.'

'Get it, then, and, look here, I think you'd better send for the police.'

Poirot approved with a nod of the head.

The man returned shortly, with him came the manager.

'Will you tell me, gentlemen, what is the meaning of all this?'

'Certainly. I received a telephone message from Count Foscatini stating that he had been attacked and was dying. You can understand that we must lose no time – if we are not already too late.'

The manager produced the key without more ado, and we all entered the flat.

We passed first into the small square lounge hall. A door on the right of it was half open. The manager indicated it with a nod.

'The dining room.'

Dr Hawker led the way. We followed close on his heels. As we entered the room I gave a gasp. The round table in the centre bore the remains of a meal; three chairs were pushed back, as though their occupants had just risen. In the corner, to the right of the fireplace, was a big writing-table, and sitting at it was a man – or what had been a man. His right hand still grasped the base of the telephone, but he had fallen forward, struck down by a terrific blow on the head from behind. The weapon was not far to seek. A marble statue stood where it had been hurriedly put down, the base of it stained with blood.

The doctor's examination did not take a minute. 'Stone dead. Must have been almost instantaneous. I wonder he even managed to telephone. It will be better not to move him until the police arrive.'

On the manager's suggestion we searched the flat, but the result was a foregone conclusion. It was not likely that the murderers would be concealed there when all they had to do was walk out.

We came back to the dining room. Poirot had not accompanied us in our tour. I found him studying the centre table with close attention. I joined him. It was a well-polished round mahogany table. A bowl of roses decorated the centre, and white lace mats reposed on the gleaming surface. There was a dish of fruit, but the three dessert plates were untouched. There were three coffee-cups with remains of coffee in them – two black, one with milk. All three men had taken port, and the decanter, half-full, stood before the centre plate. One of the men had smoked a cigar, the other two cigarettes. A tortoiseshell-and-silver box, holding cigars and cigarettes, stood open upon the table.

I enumerated all these facts to myself, but I was forced to admit that they did not shed any brilliant light on the situation. I wondered what Poirot saw in them to make him so intent. I asked him.

'*Mon ami*, he replied, 'you miss the point. I am looking for something that I do *not* see.'

'What is that?'

'A mistake – even a little mistake – on the part of the murderer.'

He stepped swiftly to the small adjoining kitchen, looked in, and shook his head.

'Monsieur,' he said to the manager, 'explain to me, I pray, your system of serving meals here.'

The manager stepped to a small hatch in the wall.

'This is the service lift,' he explained. 'It runs to the kitchens at the top of the building. You order through this telephone, and the dishes are sent down in the lift, one course at a time. The dirty plates and dishes are sent up in the same manner. No domestic worries, you understand, and at the same time you avoid the wearying publicity of always dining in a restaurant.'

Poirot nodded.

'Then the plates and dishes that were used tonight are on high in the kitchen. You permit that I mount there?'

'Oh, certainly, if you like! Roberts, the lift man, will take you up and introduce you; but I'm afraid you won't find anything that's of any use. They're handling hundreds of plates and dishes, and they'll be all lumped together.'

Poirot remained firm, however, and together we visited the kitchens and questioned the man who had taken the order from Flat 11.

'The order was given for the à la carte menu – for three,' he explained. 'Soup julienne, filet de sole normande, tournedos of beef, and a rice soufflé. What time? Just about eight o'clock, I should say. No, I'm afraid the plates and dishes have been all washed up by now. Unfortunate. You were thinking of fingerprints, I suppose?'

'Not exactly,' said Poirot, with an enigmatical smile. 'I am more interested in Count Foscatini's appetite. Did he partake of every dish?'

'Yes; but of course I can't say how much of each he ate. The plates were all soiled, and the dishes empty – that is to say, with the exception of the rice soufflé. There was a fair amount of that left.'

'Ah!' said Poirot, and seemed satisfied with the fact.

As we descended to the flat again he remarked in a low tone:

'We have decidedly to do with a man of method.'

'Do you mean the murderer, or Count Foscatini?'

'The latter was undoubtedly an orderly gentleman. After imploring help and announcing his approaching demise, he carefully hung up the telephone receiver.'

I stared at Poirot. His words now and his recent inquiries gave me a glimmering of an idea.

'You suspect poison?' I breathed. 'The blow on the head was a blind.'

Poirot merely smiled.

We re-entered the flat to find the local inspector of police had arrived with two constables. He was inclined to resent our appearance, but Poirot calmed him with the mention of our Scotland Yard friend, Inspector Japp, and we were accorded a grudging permission to remain. It was a lucky thing we were, for we had not been back five minutes before an agitated middle-aged man came rushing into the room with every appearance of grief and agitation.

This was Graves, valet-butler to the late Count Foscatini. The story he had to tell was a sensational one.

On the previous morning, two gentlemen had called to see his master. They were Italians, and the elder of the two, a man about forty, gave his name as Signor Ascanio. The younger was a well-dressed lad of about twenty-four.

Count Foscatini was evidently prepared for their visit and immediately sent Graves out upon some trivial errand. Here the man paused and hesitated in his story. In the end, however, he admitted that, curious as to the purport of the interview, he had not obeyed immediately, but had lingered about endeavouring to hear something of what was going on.

The conversation was carried on in so low a tone that he was not as successful as he had hoped; but he gathered enough to make it clear that some kind of monetary proposition was being discussed, and that the basis of it was a threat. The discussion was anything but amicable. In the end, Count Foscatini raised his voice slightly, and the listener heard these words clearly:

'I have not time to argue further now, gentlemen. If

47

you will dine with me tomorrow night at eight o'clock, we will resume the discussion.'

Afraid of being discovered listening, Graves had then hurried out to do his master's errand. This evening the two men had arrived punctually at eight. During dinner they had talked of indifferent matters – politics, the weather, and the theatrical world. When Graves had placed the port upon the table and brought in the coffee his master told him that he might have the evening off.

'Was that a usual proceeding of his when he had guests?' asked the inspector.

'No, sir, it wasn't. That's what made me think it must be some business of a very unusual kind that he was going to discuss with these gentlemen.'

That finished Graves's story. He had gone out about 8.30, and meeting a friend, had accompanied him to the Metropolitan Music Hall in Edgware Road.

Nobody had seen the two men leave, but the time of the murder was fixed clearly enough at 8.47. A small clock on the writing-table had been swept off by Foscatini's arm, and had stopped at that hour, which agreed with Miss Rider's telephone summons.

The police surgeon had made his examination of the body, and it was now lying on the couch. I saw the face for the first time – the olive complexion, the long nose, the luxuriant black moustache, and the full red lips drawn back from the dazzlingly white teeth. Not altogether a pleasant face.

'Well,' said the inspector, refastening his notebook. 'The case seems clear enough. The only difficulty will be to lay our hands on this Signor Ascanio. I suppose his address is not in the dead man's pocket-book by any chance?'

As Poirot had said, the late Foscatini was an orderly man. Neatly written in small, precise handwriting was the inscription, 'Signor Paolo Ascanio, Grosvenor Hotel.'

The inspector busied himself with the telephone, then turned to us with a grin.

'Just in time. Our fine gentleman was off to catch the boat train to the Continent. Well, gentlemen, that's about all we can do here. It's a bad business, but straightforward enough. One of these Italian vendetta things, as likely as not.'

Thus airily dismissed, we found our way downstairs. Dr Hawker was full of excitement.

'Like the beginning of a novel, eh? Real exciting stuff. Wouldn't believe it if you read about it.'

Poirot did not speak. He was very thoughtful. All the evening he had hardly opened his lips.

'What says the master detective, eh?' asked Hawker, clapping him on the back. 'Nothing to work your grey cells over this time.'

'You think not?'

'What could there be?'

'Well, for example, there is the window.'

'The window? But it was fastened. Nobody could have got out or in that way. I noticed it specially.'

'And why were you able to notice it?'

The doctor looked puzzled. Poirot hastened to explain.

'It is to the curtains that I refer. They were not drawn. A little odd, that. And then there was the coffee. It was very black coffee.'

'Well, what of it?'

'Very black,' repeated Poirot. 'In conjunction with that let us remember that very little of the rice soufflé was eaten, and we get – what?'

'Moonshine,' laughed the doctor. 'You're pulling my leg.'

'Never do I pull the leg. Hastings here knows that I am perfectly serious.'

'I don't know what you are getting at, all the same,'

I confessed. 'You don't suspect the manservant, do you? He might have been in with the gang, and put some dope in the coffee. I suppose they'll test his alibi?'

'Without doubt, my friend; but it is the alibi of Signor Ascanio that interests me.'

'You think he has an alibi?'

'That is just what worries me. I have no doubt that we shall soon be enlightened on that point.'

The *Daily Newsmonger* enabled us to become conversant with succeeding events.

Signor Ascanio was arrested and charged with the murder of Count Foscatini. When arrested, he denied knowing the Count, and declared he had never been near Regent's Court either on the evening of the crime or on the previous morning. The younger man had disappeared entirely. Signor Ascanio had arrived alone at the Grosvenor Hotel from the Continent two days before the murder. All efforts to trace the second man failed.

Ascanio, however, was not sent for trial. No less a personage than the Italian Ambassador himself came forward and testified at the police-court proceedings that Ascanio had been with him at the Embassy from eight till nine that evening. The prisoner was discharged. Naturally, a lot of people thought that the crime was a political one, and was being deliberately hushed up.

Poirot had taken a keen interest in all these points. Nevertheless, I was somewhat surprised when he suddenly informed me one morning that he was expecting a visitor at eleven o'clock, and that the visitor was none other than Ascanio himself.

'He wishes to consult you?'

'*Du tout*, Hastings, I wish to consult him.'

'What about?'

'The Regent's Court murder.'

'You are going to prove that he did it?'

'A man cannot be tried twice for murder, Hastings.

Endeavour to have the common sense. Ah, that is our friend's ring.'

A few minutes later Signor Ascanio was ushered in – a small, thin man with a secretive and furtive glance in his eyes. He remained standing, darting suspicious glances from one to the other of us.

'Monsieur Poirot?'

My little friend tapped himself gently on the chest.

'Be seated, signor. You received my note. I am determined to get to the bottom of this mystery. In some small measure you can aid me. Let us commence. You – in company with a friend – visited the late Count Foscatini on the morning of Tuesday the 9th – '

The Italian made an angry gesture.

'I did nothing of the sort. I have sworn in court – '

'*Précisément* – and I have a little idea that you have sworn falsely.'

'You threaten me? Bah! I have nothing to fear from you. I have been acquitted.'

'Exactly; and as I am not an imbecile, it is not with the gallows I threaten you – but with publicity. Publicity! I see that you do not like the word. I had an idea that you would not. My little ideas, you know, they are very valuable to me. Come, signor, your only chance is to be frank with me. I do not ask to know whose indiscretions brought you to England. I know this much, you came for the special purpose of seeing Count Foscatini.'

'He was not a count,' growled the Italian.

'I have already noted the fact that his name does not appear in the *Almanach de Gotha*. Never mind, the title of count is often useful in the profession of blackmailing.'

'I suppose I might as well be frank. You seem to know a good deal.'

'I have employed my grey cells to some advantage. Come, Signor Ascanio, you visited the dead man on the Tuesday morning – that is so, is it not?'

'Yes; but I never went there on the following evening. There was no need. I will tell you all. Certain information concerning a man of great position in Italy had come into this scoundrel's possession. He demanded a big sum of money in return for the papers. I came over to England to arrange the matter. I called upon him by appointment that morning. One of the young secretaries of the Embassy was with me. The Count was more reasonable than I had hoped, although even then the sum of money I paid him was a huge one.'

'Pardon, how was it paid?'

'In Italian notes of comparatively small denomination. I paid over the money then and there. He handed me the incriminating papers. I never saw him again.'

'Why did you not say all this when you were arrested?'

'In my delicate position I was forced to deny any association with the man.'

'And how do you account for the events of the evening then?'

'I can only think that someone must have deliberately impersonated me. I understand that no money was found in the flat.'

Poirot looked at him and shook his head.

'Strange,' he murmured. 'We all have the little grey cells. And so few of us know how to use them. Good morning, Signor Ascanio. I believe your story. It is very much as I had imagined. But I had to make sure.'

After bowing his guest out, Poirot returned to his armchair and smiled at me.

'Let us hear M. le Capitaine Hastings on the case.'

'Well, I suppose Ascanio is right – somebody impersonated him.'

'Never, never will you use the brains the good God has given you. Recall to yourself some words I uttered after leaving the flat that night. I referred to the window-curtains not being drawn. We are in the month of June.

It is still light at eight o'clock. The light is failing by half-past. *Ça vous dit quelque chose?* I perceive a struggling impression that you will arrive some day. Now let us continue. The coffee was, as I said, very black. Count Foscatini's teeth were magnificently white. Coffee stains the teeth. We reason from that that Count Foscatini did not drink any coffee. Yet there was coffee in all three cups. Why should anyone pretend Count Foscatini had drunk coffee when he had not done so?'

I shook my head, utterly bewildered.

'Come, I will help you. What evidence have we that Ascanio and his friend, or two men posing as them, ever came to the flat that night? Nobody saw them go in; nobody saw them go out. We have the evidence of one man and a host of inanimate objects.'

'You mean?'

'I mean knives and forks and plates and empty dishes. Ah, but it was a clever idea! Graves is a thief and a scoundrel, but what a man of method! He overhears a portion of the conversation in the morning, enough to realize that Ascanio will be in an awkward position to defend himself. The following evening, about eight o'clock, he tells his master he is wanted on the telephone. Foscatini sits down, stretches out his hand to the telephone, and from behind Graves strikes him down with the marble figure. Then quickly to the service telephone – dinner for three! It comes, he lays the table, dirties the plates, knives, and forks, etc. But he has to get rid of the food too. Not only is he a man of brain; he has a resolute and capacious stomach! But after eating three tournedos, the rice soufflé is too much for him! He even smokes a cigar and two cigarettes to carry out the illusion. Ah, but it was magnificently thorough! Then, having moved on the hands of the clock to 8.47, he smashes it and stops it. The one thing he does not do is to draw the curtains. But if there had been a real dinner party the curtains would have been drawn as soon as the light began to fail. Then he hurries out, mentioning the guests to the lift man in passing. He hurries to a telephone box, and as near as possible to 8.47 rings up the doctor with his master's dying cry. So successful is his idea that no one ever inquires if a call was put through from Flat 11 at that time.'

'Except Hercule Poirot, I suppose?' I said sarcastically.

'Not even Hercule Poirot,' said my friend, with a smile. 'I am about to inquire now. I had to prove my point to you first. But you will see, I shall be right; and then Japp, to whom I have already given a hint, will be able to arrest the respectable Graves. I wonder how much of the money he has spent.'

Poirot *was* right. He always is, confound him!

THE CASE OF THE MISSING WILL

The problem presented to us by Miss Violet Marsh made rather a pleasant change from our usual routine work. Poirot had received a brisk and businesslike note from the lady asking for an appointment, and had replied asking her to call upon him at eleven o'clock the following day.

She arrived punctually – a tall, handsome young woman, plainly but neatly dressed, with an assured and businesslike manner. Clearly a young woman who meant to get on in the world. I am not a great admirer of the so-called New Woman myself, and, in spite of her good looks, I was not particularly prepossessed in her favour.

'My business is of a somewhat unusual nature, Monsieur Poirot,' she began, after she had accepted a chair. 'I had better begin at the beginning and tell you the whole story.'

'If you please, mademoiselle.'

'I am an orphan. My father was one of two brothers, sons of a small yeoman farmer in Devonshire. The farm was a poor one, and the elder brother, Andrew, emigrated to Australia, where he did very well indeed, and by means of successful speculation in land became a very rich man. The younger brother, Roger (my father), had no leanings towards the agricultural life. He managed to educate himself a little, and obtained a post as a clerk with a small firm. He married slightly above him; my mother was the daughter of a poor artist. My father died when I was six years old. When I was fourteen, my mother followed him to the grave. My only living relation then was my uncle Andrew, who had recently returned from Australia and

bought a small place, Crabtree Manor, in his native county.
He was exceedingly kind to his brother's orphan child,
he took me to live with him, and treated me in every way
as though I was his own daughter.

'Crabtree Manor, in spite of its name, is really only an
old farmhouse. Farming was in my uncle's blood, and he
was intensely interested in various modern farming
experiments. Although kindness itself to me, he had
certain peculiar and deeply-rooted ideas as to the
upbringing of women. Himself a man of little or no
education, though possessing remarkable shrewdness, he
placed little value on what he called "Book knowledge".
He was especially opposed to the education of women. In
his opinion, girls should learn practical housework and
dairy-work, be useful about the home, and have as little
to do with book learning as possible. He proposed to bring
me up on these lines, to my bitter disappointment and
annoyance. I rebelled frankly. I knew that I possessed a
good brain, and had absolutely no talent for domestic
duties. My uncle and I had many bitter arguments on the
subject, for, though much attached to each other, we were
both self-willed. I was lucky enough to win a scholarship,
and up to a certain point was successful in getting my own
way. The crisis arose when I resolved to go to Girton. I
had a little money of my own, left me by my mother, and
I was quite determined to make the best use of the gifts
God had given me. I had one long, final argument with
my uncle. He put the facts plainly before me. He had no
other relations, and he had intended me to be his sole
heiress. As I have told you, he was a very rich man. If
I persisted in these "new-fangled notions" of mine,
however, I need look for nothing from him. I remained
polite, but firm. I should always be deeply attached to him,
I told him, but I must lead my own life. We parted on
that note. "You fancy your brains, my girl," were his last
words. "I've no book learning, but, for all that, I'll pit

mine against yours any day. Well see what we shall see." '

'That was nine years ago. I have stayed with him for a weekend occasionally, and our relations were perfectly amicable, though his views remained unaltered. He never referred to my having matriculated, nor to my BSc. For the last three years his health had been failing, and a month ago he died.

'I am now coming to the point of my visit. My uncle left a most extraordinary will. By its terms, Crabtree Manor and its contents are to be at my disposal for a year from his death − "during which time my clever niece may prove her wits", the actual words run. At the end of that period, "my wits having been proved better than hers", the house and all my uncle's large fortune pass to various charitable institutions.'

'That is a little hard on you, mademoiselle, seeing that you were Mr Marsh's only blood relation.'

'I do not look on it in that way. Uncle Andrew warned me fairly, and I chose my own path. Since I would not fall in with his wishes, he was at perfect liberty to leave his money to whom he pleased.'

'Was the will drawn up by a lawyer?'

'No; it was written on a printed will-form and witnessed by the man and his wife who live at the house and do for my uncle.'

'There might be a possibility of upsetting such a will?'

'I would not even attempt to do such a thing.'

'You regard it then as a sporting challenge on the part of your uncle?'

'That is exactly how I look upon it.'

'It bears that interpretation, certainly,' said Poirot thoughtfully. 'Somewhere in this rambling old manor-house your uncle has concealed either a sum of money in notes or possibly a second will, and has given you a year in which to exercise your ingenuity to find it.'

'Exactly, Monsieur Poirot; and I am paying you the

compliment of assuming that your ingenuity will be greater than mine.'

'Eh! eh! but that is very charming of you. My grey cells are at your disposal. You have made no search yourself?'

'Only a cursory one; but I have too much respect for my uncle's undoubted abilities to fancy that the task will be an easy one.'

'Have you the will or a copy of it with you?'

Miss Marsh handed a document across the table. Poirot ran through it, nodding to himself.

'Made three years ago. Dated March 25; and the time is given also – 11 A.M. – that is very suggestive. It narrows the field of search. Assuredly it is another will we have to seek for. A will made even half an hour later would upset this. *Eh bien*, mademoiselle, it is a problem charming and ingenious that you have presented to me here. I shall have all the pleasure in the world in solving it for you. Granted that your uncle is a man of ability, his grey cells cannot have been the quality of Hercule Poirot's!'

(Really, Poirot's vanity is blatant!)

'Fortunately, I have nothing of moment on hand at the minute. Hastings and I will go down to Crabtree Manor tonight. The man and wife who attended on your uncle are still there, I presume?'

'Yes, their name is Baker.'

The following morning saw us started on the hunt proper. We had arrived late the night before. Mr and Mrs Baker, having received a telegram from Miss Marsh, were expecting us. They were a pleasant couple, the man gnarled and pink-cheeked, like a shrivelled pippin, and his wife a woman of vast proportion and true Devonshire calm.

Tired with our journey and the eight-mile drive from the station, we had retired at once to bed after a supper of roast chicken, apple pie, and Devonshire cream. We had now disposed of an excellent breakfast, and were sitting in a small panelled room which had been the late Mr Marsh's study and living room. A roll-top desk stuffed with papers, all neatly docketed, stood against the wall, and a big leather armchair showed plainly that it had been its owner's constant resting-place. A big chintz-covered settee ran along the opposite wall, and the deep low window seats were covered with the same faded chintz of an old-fashioned pattern.

'*Eh bien, mon ami,*' said Poirot, lighting one of his tiny cigarettes, 'we must map out our plan of campaign. Already I have made a rough survey of the house, but I am of the opinion that any clue will be found in this room. We shall have to go through the documents in the desk with meticulous care. Naturally, I do not expect to find the will amongst them, but it is likely that some apparently innocent paper may conceal the clue to its hiding-place. But first we must have a little information. Ring the bell, I pray of you.'

I did so. While we were waiting for it to be answered, Poirot walked up and down, looking about him approvingly.

'A man of method, this Mr Marsh. See how neatly the packets of papers are docketed; then the key to each drawer has its ivory label – so has the key of the china cabinet on the wall; and see with what precision the china within is arranged. It rejoices the heart. Nothing here offends the eye – '

He came to an abrupt pause, as his eye was caught by the key of the desk itself, to which a dirty envelope was affixed. Poirot frowned at it and withdrew it from the lock. On it were scrawled the words: 'Key of Roll Top Desk,' in a crabbed handwriting, quite unlike the neat superscriptions on the other keys.

'An alien note,' said Poirot, frowning. 'I could swear

that here we have no longer the personality of Mr Marsh. But who else has been in the house? Only Miss Marsh, and she, if I mistake it not, is also a young lady of method and order.'

Baker came in answer to the bell.

'Will you fetch madame your wife, and answer a few questions?'

Baker departed, and in a few moments returned with Mrs Baker, wiping her hands on her apron and beaming all over her face.

In a few clear words Poirot set forth the object of his mission. The Bakers were immediately sympathetic.

'Us don't want to see Miss Violet done out of what's hers,' declared the woman. 'Cruel hard 'twould be for hospitals to get it all.'

Poirot proceeded with his questions. Yes, Mr and Mrs Baker remembered perfectly witnessing the will. Baker had previously been sent into the neighbouring town to get two printed will-forms.

'Two?' said Poirot sharply.

'Yes, sir, for safety like, I suppose, in case he should spoil one – and sure enough, so he did do. Us had signed one – '

'What time of day was that?'

Baker scratched his head, but his wife was quicker.

'Why, to be sure, I'd just put the milk on for the cocoa at eleven. Don't ee remember? It had boiled over on the stove when us got back to the kitchen.'

'And afterwards?'

''Twould be about an hour later. Us had to go in again. ''I've made a mistake,'' said old master, ''had to tear the whole thing up. I'll trouble you to sign again,'' and us did. And afterwards master gave us a tidy sum of money each. ''I've left you nothing in my will,'' says he, ''but each year I live you'll have this to be a nestegg when I'm gone'': and sure enough, so he did.'

Poirot reflected.

'After you had signed the second time, what did Mr Marsh do? Do you know?'

'Went out to the village to pay tradesmen's books.'

That did not seem very promising. Poirot tried another tack. He held out the key of the desk.

'Is that your master's writing?'

I may have imagined it, but I fancied that a moment or two elapsed before Baker replied: 'Yes, sir, it is.'

'He's lying,' I thought. 'But why?'

'Has your master let the house? – have there been any strangers in it during the last three years?'

'No, sir.'

'No visitors?'

'Only Miss Violet.'

'No strangers of any kind been inside this room?'

'No, sir.'

'You forget the workmen, Jim,' his wife reminded him.

'Workmen?' Poirot wheeled round on her. 'What workmen?'

The woman explained that about two years and a half ago workmen had been in the house to do certain repairs. She was quite vague as to what the repairs were. Her view seemed to be that the whole thing was a fad of her master's quite unnecessary. Part of the time the workmen had been in the study; but what they had done there she could not say, as her master had not let either of them into the room whilst the work was in progress. Unfortunately, they could not remember the name of the firm employed, beyond the fact that it was a Plymouth one.

'We progress, Hastings,' said Poirot, rubbing his hands as the Bakers left the room. 'Clearly he made a second will and then had workmen from Plymouth in to make a suitable hiding-place. Instead of wasting time taking up the floor and tapping the walls, we will go to Plymouth.'

With a little trouble, we were able to get the information

we wanted. After one or two essays we found the firm employed by Mr Marsh.

Their employees had all been with them many years, and it was easy to find the two men who had worked under Mr Marsh's orders. They remembered the job perfectly. Amongst various other minor jobs, they had taken up one of the bricks of the old-fashioned fireplace, made a cavity beneath, and so cut the brick that it was impossible to see the join. By pressing on the second brick from the end, the whole thing was raised. It had been quite a complicated piece of work, and the old gentleman had been very fussy about it. Our informant was a man called Coghan, a big, gaunt man with a grizzled moustache. He seemed an intelligent fellow.

We returned to Crabtree Manor in high spirits, and, locking the study door, proceeded to put our newly acquired knowledge into effect. It was impossible to see any sign on the bricks, but when we pressed in the manner indicated, a deep cavity was at once disclosed.

Eagerly Poirot plunged in his hand. Suddenly his face fell from complacent elation to consternation. All he held was a charred fragment of stiff paper. But for it, the cavity was empty.

Sacré!' cried Poirot angrily. 'Someone has been before us.'

We examined the scrap of paper anxiously. Clearly it was a fragment of what we sought. A portion of Baker's signature remained, but no indication of what the terms of the will had been.

Poirot sat back on his heels. His expression would have been comical if we had not been so overcome. 'I understand it not,' he growled. 'Who destroyed this? And what was their object?'

'The Bakers?' I suggested.

'*Pourquoi?* Neither will makes any provision for them, and they are more likely to be kept on with Miss Marsh than if the place became the property of a hospital. How could it be to anyone's advantage to destroy the will? The hospitals benefit – yes; but one cannot suspect institutions.'

'Perhaps the old man changed his mind and destroyed it himself,' I suggested.

Poirot rose to his feet, dusting his knees with his usual care.

'That may be,' he admitted. 'One of your more sensible observations, Hastings. Well, we can do no more here. We have done all that mortal man can do. We have successfully pitted our wits against the late Andrew Marsh's; but, unfortunately, his niece is not better off for our success.'

By driving to the station at once, we were just able to catch a train to London, though not the principal express. Poirot was sad and dissatisfied. For my part, I was tired and dozed in a corner. Suddenly, as we were just moving out of Taunton, Poirot uttered a piercing squeal.

'*Vite*, Hastings! Awake and jump! But jump I say!'

Before I knew where I was we were standing on the platform, bareheaded and minus our valises, whilst the train disappeared into the night. I was furious. But Poirot paid no attention.

'Imbecile that I have been!' he cried. 'Triple imbecile! Not again will I vaunt my little grey cells!'

'That's a good job at any rate,' I said grumpily. 'But what is this all about?'

As usual, when following out his own ideas, Poirot paid absolutely no attention to me.

'The tradesmen's books – I have left them entirely out of account? Yes, but where? Where? Never mind, I cannot be mistaken. We must return at once.'

Easier said than done. We managed to get a slow train to Exeter, and there Poirot hired a car. We arrived back at Crabtree Manor in the small hours of the morning. I pass over the bewilderment of the Bakers when we had at last aroused them. Paying no attention to anybody, Poirot strode at once to the study.

'I have been, not a triple imbecile, but thirty-six times one, my friend,' he deigned to remark. 'Now, behold!'

Going straight to the desk he drew out the key, and detached the envelope from it. I stared at him stupidly. How could he possibly hope to find a big will-form in that tiny envelope? With great care he cut open the envelope, laying it out flat. Then he lighted the fire and held the plain inside surface of the envelope to the flame. In a few minutes faint characters began to appear.

'Look, *mon ami!*' cried Poirot in triumph.

I looked. There were just a few lines of faint writing stating briefly that he left everything to his niece, Violet Marsh. It was dated March 25 12.30 P.M., and witnessed by Albert Pike, confectioner, and Jessie Pike, married woman.

'But is it legal?' I gasped.

'As far as I know, there is no law against writing your will in a blend of disappearing and sympathetic ink. The intention of the testator is clear, and the beneficiary is his only living relation. But the cleverness of him! He foresaw every step that a searcher would take – that I, miserable imbecile, took. He gets two will-forms, makes the servants sign twice, then sallies out with his will written on the inside of a dirty envelope and a fountain-pen containing his little ink mixture. On some excuse he gets the confectioner and his wife to sign their names under his own signature, then he ties it to the key of his desk and chuckles to himself. If his niece sees through his little ruse, she will have justified her choice of life and elaborate education and be thoroughly welcome to his money.'

'She didn't see through it, did she?' I said slowly. 'It seems rather unfair. The old man really won.'

'But no, Hastings. It is *your* wits that go astray. Miss

Marsh proved the astuteness of her wits and the value of the higher education for women by at once putting the matter in *my* hands. Always employ the expert. She has amply proved her right to the money.'

I wonder – I very much wonder – what old Andrew Marsh would have thought!

THE JEWEL ROBBERY AT
THE GRAND METROPOLITAN

'Poirot,' I said, 'a change of air would do you good.'

'You think so, *mon ami*?'

'I am sure of it.'

'Eh –eh?' said my friend, smiling. 'Is it all arranged, then?'

'You will come?'

'Where do you propose to take me?'

'Brighton. As a matter of fact, a friend of mine in the City put me on to a very good thing, and – well, I have money to burn, as the saying goes. I think a weekend at the Grand Metropolitan would do us all the good in the world.'

'Thank you, I accept most gratefully. You have the good heart to think of an old man. And the good heart, it is in the end worth all the little grey cells. Yes, yes, I who speak to you am in danger of forgetting that sometimes.'

I did not relish the implication. I fancy that Poirot is sometimes a little inclined to underestimate my mental capabilities. But his pleasure was so evident that I put my slight annoyance aside.

'Then, that's all right,' I said hastily.

Saturday evening saw us dining at the Grand Metropolitan in the midst of a gay throng. All the world and his wife seemed to be at Brighton. The dresses were marvellous, and the jewels – worn sometimes with more love of display than good taste – were something magnificent.

'*Hein*, it is a good sight, this!' murmured Poirot. 'This

is the home of the Profiteer, is it not so, Hastings?'

'Supposed to be,' I replied. 'But we'll hope they aren't all tarred with the Profiteering brush.'

Poirot gazed round him placidly.

'The sight of so many jewels makes me wish I had turned my brains to crime, instead of to its detection. What a magnificent opportunity for some thief of distinction! Regard, Hastings, that stout woman by the pillar. She is, as you would say, plastered with gems.'

I followed his eyes.

'Why,' I exclaimed, 'it's Mrs Opalsen.'

'You know her?'

'Slightly. Her husband is a rich stockbroker who made a fortune in the recent oil boom.'

After dinner we ran across the Opalsens in the lounge, and I introduced Poirot to them. We chatted for a few minutes, and ended by having our coffee together.

Poirot said a few words in praise of some of the costlier gems displayed on the lady's ample bosom, and she brightened up at once.

'It's a perfect hobby of mine, Mr Poirot. I just *love* jewellery. Ed knows my weakness, and every time things go well he brings me something new. You are interested in precious stones?'

'I have had a good deal to do with them one time and another, madame. My profession has brought me into contact with some of the most famous jewels in the world.'

He went on to narrate, with discreet pseudonyms, the story of the historic jewels of a reigning house, and Mrs Opalsen listened with bated breath.

'There now,' she exclaimed, as he ended. 'If it isn't just like a play! You know, I've got some pearls of my own that have a history attached to them. I believe it's supposed to be one of the finest necklaces in the world – the pearls are so beautifully matched and so perfect in colour. I declare I really must run up and get it!'

'Oh, madame,' protested Poirot, 'you are too amiable. Pray do not derange yourself!'

'Oh, but I'd like to show it to you.'

The buxom dame waddled across to the lift briskly enough. Her husband, who had been talking to me, looked at Poirot inquiringly.

'Madame your wife is so amiable as to insist on showing me her pearl necklace,' explained the latter.

'Oh, the pearls!' Opalsen smiled in a satisfied fashion. 'Well, they *are* worth seeing. Cost a pretty penny too! Still, the money's there all right; I could get what I paid for them any day – perhaps more. May have to, too, if things go on as they are now. Money's confoundedly tight in the City. All this infernal EPD.' He rambled on, launching into technicalities where I could not follow him.

He was interrupted by a small page-boy who approached him and murmured something in his ear.

'Eh – what? I'll come at once. Not taken ill, is she? Excuse me, gentlemen.'

He left us abruptly, Poirot leaned back and lit one of his tiny Russian cigarettes. Then, carefully and meticulously, he arranged the empty coffee-cups in a neat row, and beamed happily on the result.

The minutes passed. The Opalsens did not return.

'Curious,' I remarked, at length. 'I wonder when they will come back.'

Poirot watched the ascending spirals of smoke, and then said thoughtfully:

'They will not come back.'

'Why?'

'Because, my friend, something has happened.'

'What sort of thing? How do you know?' I asked curiously.

Poirot smiled.

'A few minutes ago the manager came hurriedly out of his office and ran upstairs. He was much agitated. The liftboy is deep in talk with one of the pages. The lift-bell has rung three times, but he heeds it not. Thirdly, even the waiters are *distrait*; and to make a waiter *distrait* – ' Poirot shook his head with an air of finality. 'The affair must indeed be of the first magnitude. Ah, it is as I thought! Here come the police.'

Two men had just entered the hotel – one in uniform, the other in plain clothes. They spoke to a page, and were immediately ushered upstairs. A few minutes later, the same boy descended and came up to where we were sitting.

'Mr Opalsen's compliments, and would you step upstairs?'

Poirot sprang nimbly to his feet. One would have said that he awaited the summons. I followed with no less alacrity.

The Opalsens' apartments were situated on the first floor. After knocking on the door, the page-boy retired, and we answered the summons. 'Come in!' A strange scene met our eyes. The room was Mrs Opalsen's bedroom, and in the centre of it, lying back in an armchair, was the lady herself, weeping violently. She presented an extraordinary spectacle, with the tears making great furrows in the powder with which her complexion was liberally coated. Mr Opalsen was striding up and down angrily. The two police officials stood in the middle of the room, one with a notebook in hand. An hotel chambermaid, looking frightened to death, stood by the fireplace; and on the other side of the room a Frenchwoman, obviously Mrs Opalsen's maid, was weeping and wringing her hands, with an intensity of grief that rivalled that of her mistress.

Into this pandemonium stepped Poirot, neat and smiling. Immediately, with an energy surprising in one of her bulk, Mrs Opalsen sprang from her chair towards him.

'There now; Ed may say what he likes, but I believe in luck, I do. It was fated I should meet you the way I did this evening, and I've a feeling that if you can't get my pearls back for me nobody can.'

'Calm yourself, I pray of you, madame.' Poirot patted her hand soothingly. 'Reassure yourself. All will be well. Hercule Poirot will aid you!'

Mr Opalsen turned to the police inspector.

'There will be no objection to my – er – calling in this gentleman, I suppose?'

'None at all, sir,' replied the man civilly, but with complete indifference. 'Perhaps now your lady's feeling better she'll just let us have the facts?'

Mrs Opalsen looked helplessly at Poirot. He led her back to her chair.

'Seat yourself, madame, and recount to us the whole history without agitating yourself!' .

Thus abjured, Mrs Opalsen dried her eyes gingerly, and began.

'I came upstairs after dinner to fetch my pearls for Mr Poirot here to see. The chambermaid and Célestine were both in the room as usual – '

'Excuse me, madame, but what do you mean by "as usual"?'

Mr Opalsen explained.

'I make it a rule that no one is to come into this room unless Célestine, the maid, is there also. The chambermaid does the room in the morning while Célestine is present, and comes in after dinner to turn down the beds under the same conditions; otherwise she never enters the room.'

'Well, as I was saying,' continued Mrs Opalsen, 'I came up. I went to the drawer here' – she indicated the bottom right-hand drawer of the knee-hole dressing-table – 'took out my jewel-case and unlocked it. It seemed quite as usual – but the pearls were not there!'

The inspector had been busy with his notebook. 'When had you last seen them?' he asked.

'They were there when I went down to dinner.'

'You are sure?'

'Quite sure. I was uncertain whether to wear them or not, but in the end I decided on the emeralds, and put them back in the jewel-case.'

'Who locked up the jewel-case?'

'I did. I wear the key on a chain round my neck.' She held it up as she spoke.

The inspector examined it, and shrugged his shoulders.

'The thief must have had a duplicate key. No difficult matter. The lock is quite a simple one. What did you do after you'd locked the jewel-case?'

'I put it back in the bottom drawer where I always keep it.'

'You didn't lock the drawer?'

'No, I never do. My maid remains in the room till I come up, so there's no need.'

The inspector's face grew greyer.

'Am I to understand that the jewels were there when you went down to dinner, and that since then *the maid has not left the room*?'

Suddenly, as though the horror of her own situation for the first time burst upon her, Célestine uttered a piercing shriek, and, flinging herself upon Poirot, poured out a torrent of incoherent French.

The suggestion was infamous! That she should be suspected of robbing Madame! The police were well known to be of a stupidity incredible! But Monsieur, who was a Frenchman — '

'A Belgian,' interjected Poirot, but Célestine paid no attention to the correction.

Monsieur would not stand by and see her falsely accused, while that infamous chambermaid was allowed to go scot-free. She had never liked her — a bold, red-faced thing — a born thief. She had said from the first that she was not honest. And had kept a sharp watch over her too, when she was doing Madame's room! Let those idiots of policemen search her, and if they did not find Madame's pearls on her it would be very surprising!

Although this harangue was uttered in rapid and virulent French, Célestine had interlarded it with a wealth of gesture, and the chambermaid realized at least a part of her meaning. She reddened angrily.

'If that foreign woman's saying I took the pearls, it's a lie!' she declared heatedly. 'I never so much as saw them.'

'Search her!' screamed the other. 'You will find it is as I say.'

'You're a liar – do your hear?' said the chambermaid, advancing upon her. 'Stole 'em yourself, and want to put it on me. Why, I was only in the room about three minutes before the lady came up, and then you were sitting here the whole time, as you always do, like a cat watching a mouse.'

The inspector looked across inquiringly at Célestine. 'Is that true? Didn't you leave the room at all?'

'I did not actually leave her alone,' admitted Célestine reluctantly, 'but I went into my own room through the door here twice – once to fetch a reel of cotton, and once for my scissors. She must have done it then.'

'You wasn't gone a minute,' retorted the chambermaid angrily. 'Just popped out and in again. I'd be glad if the police *would* search me. *I've* nothing to be afraid of.'

At this moment there was a tap at the door. The inspector went to it. His face brightened when he saw who it was.

'Ah!' he said. 'That's rather fortunate. I sent for one of our female searchers, and she's just arrived. Perhaps if you wouldn't mind going into the room next door.'

He looked at the chambermaid, who stepped across the threshold with a toss of her head, the searcher following closely.

The French girl had sunk sobbing into a chair. Poirot

was looking round the room, the main features of which
I have made clear by a sketch.

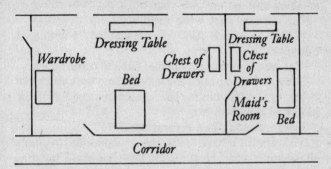

'Where does that door lead?' he inquired, nodding his
head towards the one by the window.

'Into the next apartment, I believe,' said the inspector.
'It's bolted, anyway, on this side.'

Poirot walked across to it, tried it, then drew back the
bolt and tried it again.

'And on the other side as well,' he remarked. 'Well, that
seems to rule out that.'

He walked over to the windows, examining each of them
in turn.

'And again – nothing. Not even a balcony outside.'

'Even if there were,' said the imspector impatiently, 'I
don't see how that would help us, if the maid never left
the room.'

'*Évidemment*,' said Poirot, not disconcerted. 'As
Mademoiselle is positive she did not leave the room – '

He was interrupted by the reappearance of the
chambermaid and the police searcher.

'Nothing,' said the latter laconically.

'I should hope not, indeed,' said the chambermaid
virtuously. 'And that French hussy ought to be ashamed
of herself taking away an honest girl's character.'

'There, there, my girl; that's all right,' said the inspector, opening the door. 'Nobody suspects you. You go along and get on with your work.'

The chambermaid went unwillingly.

'Going to search *her*?' she demanded, pointing at Célestine.

'Yes, yes!' He shut the door on her and turned the key.

Célestine accompanied the searcher into the small room in her turn. A few minutes later she also returned. Nothing had been found on her.

The inspector's face grew graver.

'I'm afraid I'll have to ask you to come along with me all the same, miss.' He turned to Mrs Opalsen. 'I'm sorry, madam, but all the evidence points that way. If she's not got them on her, they're hidden somewhere about the room.'

Célestine uttered a piercing shriek, and clung to Poirot's arm. The latter bent and whispered something in the girl's ear. She looked up at him doubtfully.

'*Si, si, mon enfant* – I assure you it is better not to resist.' Then he turned to the inspector. 'You permit, monsieur? A little experiment – purely for my own satisfaction.'

'Depends on what it is,' replied the police officer non-committally.

Poirot addressed Célestine once more.

'You have told us that you went into your room to fetch a reel of cotton. Whereabouts was it?'

'On top of the chest of drawers, monsieur.'

'And the scissors?'

'They also.'

'Would it be troubling you too much, mademoiselle, to ask you to repeat those two actions? You were sitting here with your work, you say?'

Célestine sat down, and then, at a sign from Poirot, rose, passed into the adjoining room, took up an object from the chest of drawers, and returned.

Poirot divided his attention between her movements and a large turnip of a watch which he held in the palm of his hand.

'Again, if you please, mademoiselle.'

At the conclusion of the second performance, he made a note in his pocket-book, and returned the watch to his pocket.

'Thank you, mademoiselle. And you, monsieur' – he bowed to the inspector – 'for your courtesy.'

The inspector seemed somewhat entertained by this excessive politeness. Célestine departed in a flood of tears, accompanied by the woman and the plain-clothes official.

Then, with a brief apology to Mrs Opalsen, the inspector set to work to ransack the room. He pulled out drawers, opened cupboards, completely unmade the bed, and tapped the floor. Mr Opalsen looked on sceptically.

'You really think you will find them?'

'Yes, sir. It stands to reason. She hadn't time to take them out of the room. The lady's discovering the robbery so soon upset her plans. No, they're here right enough. One of the two must have hidden them – and it's very unlikely for the chambermaid to have done so.'

'More than unlikely – impossible!' said Poirot quietly.

'Eh?' The inspector stared.

Poirot smiled modestly.

'I will demonstrate. Hastings, my good friend, take my watch in your hand – with care. It is a family heirloom! Just now I timed Mademoiselle's movements – her first absence from the room was of twelve seconds, her second of fifteen. Now observe my actions. Madame will have the kindness to give me the key of the jewel-case. I thank you. My friend Hastings will have the kindness to say "Go!"'

'Go!' I said.

With almost incredible swiftness, Poirot wrenched open the drawer of the dressing-table, extracted the jewel-case, fitted the key in the lock, opened the case, selected a piece of jewellery, shut and locked the case, and returned it to the drawer, which he pushed to again. His movements were like lightning.

'Well, *mon ami*?' he demanded of me breathlessly.

'Forty-six seconds,' I replied.

'You see?' He looked round. 'There would not have been time for the chambermaid even to take the necklace out, far less hide it.'

'Then that settles it on the maid,' said the inspector with satisfaction, and returned to his search. He passed into the maid's bedroom next door.

Poirot was frowning thoughtfully. Suddenly he shot a question at Mr Opalsen.

'This necklace – it was, without doubt, insured?'

Mr Opalsen looked a trifle surprised at the question.

'Yes,' he said hesitatingly, 'that is so.'

'But what does that matter?' broke in Mrs Opalsen tearfully. 'It's my necklace I want. It was unique. No money could be the same.'

'I comprehend, madame,' said Poirot soothingly. 'I comprehend perfectly. To *la femme* sentiment is everything – is it not so? But, monsieur, who has not the so fine susceptibility, will doubtless find some slight consolation in the fact.'

'Of course, of course,' said Mr Opalsen rather uncertainly. 'Still – '

He was interrupted by a shout of triumph from the inspector. He came in dangling something from his fingers.

With a cry, Mrs Opalsen heaved herself up from her chair. She was a changed woman.

'Oh, oh, my necklace!'

She clasped it to her breast with both hands. We crowded round.

'Where was it?' demanded Opalsen.

'Maid's bed. In among the springs of the wire mattress.

She must have stolen it and hidden it there before the chambermaid arrived on the scene.'

'You permit, madame?' said Poirot gently. He took the necklace from her and examined it closely; then handed it back with a bow.

'I'm afraid, madame, you'll have to hand it over to us for the time being,' said the inspector. 'We shall want it for the charge. But it shall be returned to you as soon as possible.'

Mr Opalsen frowned.

'Is that necessary?'

'I'm afraid so, sir. Just a formality.'

'Oh, let him take it, Ed!' cried his wife. 'I'd feel safer if he did. I shouldn't sleep a wink thinking someone else might try to get hold of it. That wretched girl! And I would never have believed it of her.'

'There, there, my dear, don't take on so.'

I felt a gentle pressure on my arm. It was Poirot.

'Shall we slip away, my friend? I think our services are no longer needed.'

Once outside, however, he hesitated, and then, much to my surprise, he remarked:

'I should rather like to see the room next door.'

The door was not locked, and we entered. The room, which was a large double one, was unoccupied. Dust lay about rather noticeably, and my sensitive friend gave a characteristic grimace as he ran his finger round a rectangular mark on a table near the window.

'The *service* leaves to be desired,' he observed dryly.

He was staring thoughtfully out of the window, and seemed to have fallen into a brown study.

'Well?' I demanded impatiently. 'What did we come in here for?'

He started.

'*Je vous demande pardon, mon ami*. I wished to see if the door was really bolted on this side also.'

'Well,' I said, glancing at the door which communicated with the room we had just left, 'it *is* bolted.'

Poirot nodded. He still seemed to be thinking.

'And anyway,' I continued, 'what does it matter? The case is over. I wish you'd had more chance of distinguishing yourself. But it was the kind of case that even a stiff-backed idiot like that inspector couldn't go wrong over.'

Poirot shook his head.

'The case is not over, my friend. It will not be over until we find out who stole the pearls.'

'But the maid did!'

'Why do you say that?'

'Why,' I stammered, 'they were found – actually in her mattress.'

'Ta, ta, ta!' said Poirot impatiently. 'Those were not the pearls.'

'What?'

'Imitation, *mon ami*.'

The statement took my breath away. Poirot was smiling placidly.

'The good inspector obviously knows nothing of jewels. But presently there will be a fine hullabaloo!'

'Come!' I cried, dragging at his arm.

'Where?'

'We must tell the Opalsens at once.'

'I think not.'

'But that poor woman – '

'*Eh bien*; that poor woman, as you call her, will have a much better night believing the jewels to be safe.'

'But the thief may escape with them!'

'As usual, my friend, you speak without reflection. How do you know that the pearls Mrs Opalsen locked up so carefully tonight were not the false ones, and that the real robbery did not take place at a much earlier date?'

'Oh!' I said, bewildered.

'Exactly,' said Poirot, beaming. 'We start again.'

He led the way out of the room, paused a moment as though considering, and then walked down to the end of the corridor, stopping outside the small den where the chambermaids and valets of the respective floors congregated. Our particular chambermaid appeared to be holding a small court there, and to be retailing her late experiences to an appreciative audience. She stopped in the middle of a sentence. Poirot bowed with his usual politeness.

'Excuse that I derange you, but I shall be obliged if you will unlock for me the door of Mr Opalsen's room.'

The woman rose willingly, and we accompanied her down the passage again. Mr Opalsen's room was on the other side of the corridor, its door facing that of his wife's room. The chambermaid unlocked it with her pass-key, and we entered.

As she was about to depart Poirot detained her.

'One moment; have you ever seen among the effects of Mr Opalsen a card like this?'

He held out a plain white card, rather highly glazed and uncommon in appearance. The maid took it and scrutinized it carefully.

'No, sir, I can't say I have. But, anyway, the valet has most to do with the gentlemen's rooms.'

'I see. Thank you.'

Poirot took back the card. The woman departed. Poirot appeared to reflect a little. Then he gave a short, sharp nod of the head.

'Ring the bell, I pray you, Hastings. Three times for the valet.'

I obeyed, devoured with curiosity. Meanwhile Poirot had emptied the waste-paper basket on the floor, and was swiftly going through its contents.

In a few moments the valet answered the bell. To him Poirot put the same question, and handed him the card to examine. But the response was the same. The valet had never seen a card of that particular quality among Mr Opalsen's belongings. Poirot thanked him, and he withdrew, somewhat unwillingly, with an inquisitive glance at the overturned waste-paper basket and the litter on the floor. He could hardly have helped overhearing Poirot's thoughtful remark as he bundled the torn papers back again:

'And the necklace was heavily insured . . .'

'Poirot,' I cried, 'I see – '

'You see nothing, my friend,' he replied quickly. 'As usual, nothing at all! It is incredible – but there it is. Let us return to our own apartments.'

We did so in silence. Once there, to my intense surprise, Poirot effected a rapid change of clothing.

'I go to London tonight,' he explained. 'It is imperative.'

'What?'

'Absolutely. The real work, that of the brain (ah, those brave little grey cells), it is done. I go to seek the confirmation. I shall find it! Impossible to deceive Hercule Poirot!'

'You'll come a cropper one of these days,' I observed, rather disgusted by his vanity.

'Do not be enraged, I beg of you, *mon ami*. I count on you to do me a service – of your friendship.'

'Of course,' I said eagerly, rather ashamed of my moroseness. 'What is it?'

'The sleeve of my coat that I have taken off – will you brush it? See you, a little white powder has clung to it. You without doubt observed me run my finger round the drawer of the dressing-table?'

'No, I didn't.'

'You should observe my actions, my friend. Thus I obtained the powder on my finger, and, being a little overexcited, I rubbed it on my sleeve; an action without method which I deplore – false to all my principles.'

'But what was the powder?' I asked, not particularly interested in Poirot's principles.

'Not the poison of the Borgias,' replied Poirot with a twinkle. 'I see your imagination mounting. I should say it was French chalk.'

'French chalk?'

'Yes, cabinet-makers use it to make drawers run smoothly.'

I laughed.

'You old sinner! I thought you were working up to something exciting.'

'Au revoir, my friend. I save myself. I fly!'

The door shut behind him. With a smile, half of derision, half of affection, I picked up the coat and stretched out my hand for the clothes brush.

The next morning, hearing nothing from Poirot, I went out for a stroll, met some old friends, and lunched with them at their hotel. In the afternoon we went for a spin. A punctured tyre delayed us, and it was past eight when I got back to the Grand Metropolitan.

The first sight that met my eyes was Poirot, looking even more diminutive than usual, sandwiched between the Opalsens, beaming in a state of placid satisfaction.

'*Mon ami* Hastings!' he cried, and sprang to meet me. 'Embrace me, my friend; all has marched to a marvel!'

Luckily, the embrace was merely figurative – not a thing one is always sure of with Poirot.

'Do you mean – ' I began.

'Just wonderful, I call it!' said Mrs Opalsen, smiling all over her fat face. 'Didn't I tell you, Ed, that if he couldn't get back my pearls nobody could?'

'You did, my dear, you did. And you were right.'

I looked helplessly at Poirot, and he answered the glance.

'My friend Hastings is, as you say in England, all at the

seaside. Seat yourself, and I will recount to you all the affair that has so happily ended.'

'Ended?'

'But yes. They are arrested.'

'Who are arrested?'

'The chambermaid and the valet, *parbleu*! You did not supect? Not with my parting hint about the French chalk?'

'You said cabinet-makers used it.'

'Certainly they do – to make drawers slide easily. Somebody wanted the drawer to slide in and out without any noise. Who could that be? Obviously, only the chambermaid. The plan was so ingenious that it did not at once leap to the eye – not even to the eye of Hercule Poirot.

'Listen, this was how it was done. The valet was in the empty room next door, waiting. The French maid leaves the room. Quick as a flash the chambermaid whips open the drawer, takes out the jewel-case and, slipping back the bolt, passes it through the door. The valet opens it at his leisure with the duplicate key with which he has provided himself, extracts the necklace, and waits his time. Célestine leaves the room again, and – pst! – in a flash the case is passed back again and replaced in the drawer.

'Madame arrives, the theft is discovered. The chambermaid demands to be searched, with a good deal of righteous indignation, and leaves the room without a stain on her character. The imitation necklace with which they have provided themselves has been concealed in the French girl's bed that morning by the chambermaid – a master stroke, *ça*!'

'But what did you go to London for?'

'You remember the card?'

'Certainly. It puzzled me – puzzles me still. I thought – '

I hesitated delicately, glancing at Mr Opalsen.

Poirot laughed heartily.

'*Une blague*! For the benefit of the valet. The card was one with a specially prepared surface – for fingerprints. I went straight to Scotland Yard, asked for our old friend Inspector Japp, and laid all the facts before him. As I had suspected, the fingerprints proved to be those of two well-known jewel thieves who have been "wanted" for some time. Japp came down with me, the thieves were arrested, and the necklace discovered in the valet's possession. A clever pair, but they failed in *method*. Have I not told you, Hastings, at least thirty-six times, that without method –'

'At least thirty-six thousand times!' I interrupted. 'But where did their "method" break down?'

'*Mon ami*, it is a good plan to take a place as chambermaid or valet – but you must not shirk your work. They left an empty room undusted; and therefore, when the man put down the jewel-case on the little table near the communicating door, it left a square mark – '

'I remember,' I cried.

'Before, I was undecided. Then – I *knew*!'

There was a moment's silence.

'And I've got my pearls,' said Mrs Opalsen as a sort of Greek chorus.

'Well,' I said, 'I'd better have some dinner.'

Poirot accompanied me.

'This ought to mean kudos for you,' I observed.

'*Pas du tout*,' replied Poirot tranquilly. 'Japp and the local inspector will divide the credit between them. But' – he tapped his pocket – 'I have a cheque here, from Mr Opalsen, and, how you say, my friend? This weekend has not gone according to plan. Shall we return here next weekend – at my expense this time?'

THE CHOCOLATE BOX

It was a wild night. Outside, the wind howled malevolently, and the rain beat against the windows in great gusts.

Poirot and I sat facing the hearth, our legs stretched out to the cheerful blaze. Between us was a small table. On my side of it stood some carefully brewed hot toddy; on Poirot's was a cup of thick, rich chocolate which I would not have drunk for a hundred pounds! Poirot sipped the thick brown mess in the pink china cup, and sighed with contentment.

'*Quelle belle vie!*' he murmured.

'Yes, it's a good old world,' I agreed. 'Here am I with a job, and a good job too! And here are you, famous –'

'Oh, *mon ami*!' protested Poirot.

'But you are. And rightly so! When I think back on your long line of successes, I am positively amazed. I don't believe you know what failure is!'

'He would be a droll kind of original who could say that!'

'No, but seriously, *have* you ever failed?'

'Innumerable times, my friend. What would you? *La bonne chance*, it cannot always be on your side. I have been called in too late. Very often another, working towards the same goal, has arrived there first. Twice have I been stricken down with illness just as I was on the point of success. One must take the downs with the ups, my friend.'

'I didn't quite mean that,' I said. 'I meant, had you ever been completely down and out over a case through your own fault?'

'Ah, I comprehend! You ask if I have ever made the complete prize ass of myself, as you say over here? Once, my friend –' A slow, reflective smile hovered over his face. 'Yes, once I made a fool of myself.'

He sat up suddenly in his chair.

'See here, my friend, you have, I know, kept a record of my little successes. You shall add one more story to the collection, the story of a failure!'

He leaned forward and placed a log on the fire. Then, after carefully wiping his hands on a little duster that hung on a nail by the fireplace, he leaned back and commenced his story.

That of which I tell you (said M. Poirot) took place in Belgium many years ago. It was at the time of the terrible struggle in France between church and state. M. Paul Déroulard was a French deputy of note. It was an open secret that the portfolio of a Minister awaited him. He was among the bitterest of the anti-Catholic party, and it was certain that on his accession to power, he would have to face violent enmity. He was in many ways a peculiar man. Though he neither drank nor smoked, he was nevertheless not so scrupulous in other ways. You comprehend, Hastings, *c'était des femmes – toujours des femmes*!

He had married some years earlier a young lady from Brussels who had brought him a substantial *dot*. Undoubtedly the money was useful to him in his career, as his family was not rich, though on the other hand he was entitled to call himself M. le Baron if he chose. There were no children of the marriage, and his wife died after two years – the result of a fall downstairs. Among the property which she bequeathed to him was a house on the Avenue Louise in Brussels.

It was in this house that his sudden death took place, the event coinciding with the resignation of the Minister whose portfolio he was to inherit. All the papers printed long notices of his career. His death, which had taken place

85

quite suddenly in the evening after dinner, was attributed to heart-failure.

At that time, *mon ami*, I was, as you know, a member of the Belgian detective force. The death of M. Paul Déroulard was not particularly interesting to me. I am, as you also know, *bon catholique*, and his demise seemed to me fortunate.

It was some three days afterwards, when my vacation had just begun, that I received a visitor at my own apartments – a lady, heavily veiled, but evidently quite young; and I perceived at once that she was a *jeune fille tout à fait comme il faut*.

'You are Monsieur Hercule Poirot?' she asked in a low sweet voice.

I bowed.

'Of the detective service?'

Again I bowed. 'Be seated, I pray of you, mademoiselle,' I said.

She accepted a chair and drew aside her veil. Her face was charming, though marred with tears, and haunted as though with some poignant anxiety.

'Monsieur,' she said, 'I understand that you are now taking a vacation. Therefore you will be free to take up a private case. You understand that I do not wish to call in the police.'

I shook my head. 'I fear what you ask is impossible, mademoiselle. Even though on vacation, I am still of the police.'

She leaned forward. '*Ecoutez, monsieur*. All that I ask of you is to investigate. The result of your investigations you are at perfect liberty to report to the police. If what I believe to be true *is* true, we shall need all the machinery of the law.'

That placed a somewhat different complexion on the matter, and I placed myself at her service without more ado.

A slight colour rose in her cheeks. 'I thank you, monsieur. It is the death of M. Paul Déroulard that I ask you to investigate.'

'*Comment?*' I exclaimed, surprised.

'Monsieur, I have nothing to go upon – nothing but my woman's instinct, but I am convinced – *convinced*, I tell you – that M. Déroulard did not die a natural death!'

'But surely the doctors –'

'Doctors may be mistaken. He was so robust, so strong. Ah, Monsieur Poirot, I beseech of you to help me –'

The poor child was almost beside herself. She would have knelt to me. I soothed her as best I could.

'I will help you, mademoiselle. I feel almost sure that your fears are unfounded, but we will see. First, I will ask you to describe to me the inmates of the house.'

'There are the domestics, of course, Jeannette, Félice, and Denise the cook. She has been there many years; the others are simple country girls. Also there is François, but he too is an old servant. Then there is Monsieur Déroulard's mother who lived with him, and myself. My name is Virginie Mesnard. I am a poor cousin of the late Madame Déroulard, M. Paul's wife, and I have been a member of their ménage for over three years. I have now described to you the household. There were also two guests staying in the house.'

'And they were?'

'M. de Saint Alard, a neighbour of M. Déroulard's in France. Also an English friend, Mr John Wilson.'

'Are they still with you?'

'Mr Wilson, yes, but M. de Saint Alard departed yesterday.'

'And what is your plan, Mademoiselle Mesnard?'

'If you will present yourself at the house in half an hour's time, I will have arranged some story to account for your presence. I had better represent you to be connected with journalism in some way. I shall say you have come from

Paris, and that you have brought a card of introduction from M. de Saint Alard. Madame Déroulard is very feeble in health, and will pay little attention to details.'

On mademoiselle's ingenious pretext I was admitted to the house, and after a brief interview with the dead deputy's mother, who was a wonderfully imposing and aristocratic figure though obviously in failing health, I was made free of the premises.

I wonder, my friend (continued Poirot), whether you can possibly figure to yourself the difficulties of my task? Here was a man whose death had taken place three days previously. If there *had* been foul play, only one possibility was admittable – *poison*! And I had no chance of seeing the body, and there was no possibility of examining, or analysing, any medium in which the poison could have been administered. There were no clues, false or otherwise, to consider. Had the man been poisoned? Had he died a natural death? I, Hercule Poirot, with nothing to help me, had to decide.

First, I interviewed the domestics, and with their aid, I recapitulated the evening. I paid especial notice to the food at dinner, and the method of serving it. The soup had been served by M. Déroulard himself from a tureen. Next a dish of cutlets, then a chicken. Finally, a compote of fruits. And all placed on the table, and served by Monsieur himself. The coffee was brought in a big pot to the dinner-table. Nothing there, *mon ami* – impossible to poison one without poisoning all!

After dinner Madame Déroulard had retired to her own apartments and Mademoiselle Virginie had accompanied her. The three men had adjourned to M. Déroulard's study. Here they had chatted amicably for some time, when suddenly, without any warning, the deputy had fallen heavily to the ground. M. de Saint Alard had rushed out and told François to fetch the doctor immediately. He said it was without doubt an apoplexy, explained the man. But when the doctor arrived, the patient was past help.

Mr John Wilson, to whom I was presented by Mademoiselle Virginie, was what was known in those days as a regular John Bull Englishman, middle-aged and burly. His account, delivered in very British French, was substantially the same.

'Déroulard went very red in the face, and down he fell.'

There was nothing further to be found out there. Next I went to the scene of the tragedy, the study, and was left alone there at my own request. So far there was nothing to support Mademoiselle Mesnard's theory. I could not but believe that it was a delusion on her part. Evidently she had entertained a romantic passion for the dead man which had not permitted her to take a normal view of the case. Nevertheless, I searched the study with meticulous care. It was just possible that a hypodermic needle might have been introduced into the dead man's chair in such a way as to allow of a fatal injection. The minute puncture it would cause was likely to remain unnoticed. But I could discover no sign to support the theory. I flung myself down in the chair with a gesture of despair.

'*Enfin*, I abandon it?' I said aloud. 'There is not a clue anywhere! Everything is perfectly normal.'

As I said the words, my eyes fell on a large box of chocolates standing on a table near by, and my heart gave a leap. It might not be a clue to M. Déroulard's death, but here at least was something that was *not* normal. I lifted the lid. The box was full, untouched; not a chocolate was missing – but that only made the peculiarity that had caught my eye more striking. For, see you, Hastings, while the box itself was pink, the lid was *blue*. Now, one often sees a blue ribbon on a pink box, and vice versa, but a box of one colour, and a lid of another – no, decidedly – *ça ne se voit jamais!*

I did not as yet see that this little incident was of any

use to me, yet I determined to investigate it as being out of the ordinary. I rang the bell for François, and asked him if his late master had been fond of sweets. A faint melancholy smile came to his lips.

'Passionately fond of them, monsieur. He would always have a box of chocolates in the house. He did not drink wine of any kind, you see.'

'Yet this box has not been touched?' I lifted the lid to show him.

'Pardon, monsieur, but that was a new box purchased on the day of his death, the other being nearly finished.'

'Then the other box was finished on the day of his death,' I said slowly.

'Yes, monsieur, I found it empty in the morning and threw it away.'

'Did M. Déroulard eat sweets at all hours of the day?'

'Usually after dinner, monsieur.'

I began to see light.

'François,' I said, 'you can be discreet?'

'If there is need, monsieur.'

'*Bon*! Know, then, that I am of the police. Can you find me that other box?'

'Without doubt, monsieur. It will be in the dustbin.'

He departed, and returned in a few minutes with a dust-covered object. It was the duplicate of the box I held, save for the fact that this time the box was *blue* and the lid was *pink*. I thanked François, recommended him once more to be discreet, and left the house in the Avenue Louise without more ado.

Next I called upon the doctor who had attended M. Déroulard. With him I had a difficult task. He entrenched himself prettily behind a wall of learned phraseology, but I fancied that he was not quite as sure about the case as he would like to be.

'There have been many curious occurrences of the kind,' he observed, when I had managed to disarm him

somewhat. 'A sudden fit of anger, a violent emotion –
after a heavy dinner, *c'est entendu* – then with an access
of rage, the blood flies to the head, and *pst*! – there you
are!'

'But M. Déroulard had had no violent emotion.'

'No? I made sure that he had been having a stormy
altercation with M. de Saint Alard.'

'Why should he?'

'*C'est évident!*' The doctor shrugged his shoulders. 'Was
not M. de Saint Alard a Catholic of the most fanatical?
Their friendship was being ruined by this question of
church and state. Not a day passed without discussions.
To M. de Saint Alard, Déroulard appeared almost as
Antichrist.'

This was unexpected, and gave me food for thought.

'One more question, Doctor: would it be possible to
introduce a fatal dose of poison into a chocolate?'

'It would be possible, I suppose,' said the doctor slowly.
'Pure prussic acid would meet the case if there were no
chance of evaporation, and a tiny globule of anything might
be swallowed unnoticed – but it does not seem a very
likely supposition. A chocolate full of morphine or
strychnine –' He made a wry face. 'You comprehend, M.
Poirot – one bite would be enough! The unwary one
would not stand upon ceremony.'

'Thank you, M. le Docteur.'

I withdrew. Next I made enquiries of the chemists,
especially those in the neighbourhood of the Avenue
Louise. It is good to be of the police. I got the information
I wanted without any trouble. Only in one case could I
hear of any poison having been supplied to the house in
question. This was some eye drops of atropine sulphate
for Madame Déroulard. Atropine is a potent poison, and
for the moment I was elated, but the symptoms of atropine
poisoning are closely allied to those of ptomaine, and bear
no resemblance to those I was studying. Besides, the

prescription was an old one. Madame Déroulard had suffered from cataract in both eyes for many years.

I was turning away discouraged when the chemist's voice called me back.

'*Un moment, M. Poirot.* I remember, the girl who brought that prescription, she said something about having to go on to the *English* chemist. You might try there.'

I did. Once more enforcing my official status, I got the information I wanted. On the day before M. Déroulard's death they had made up a prescription for Mr John Wilson. Not that there was any making up about it. They were simply little tablets of trinitrine. I asked if I might see some. He showed me them, and my heart beat faster – for the tiny tablets were of *chocolate*.

'Is it a poison?' I asked.

'No, monsieur.'

'Can you describe to me its effect?'

'It lowers the blood-pressure. It is given for some forms of heart trouble – angina pectoris for instance. It relieves the arterial tension. In arteriosclerosis –'

I interrupted him. '*Ma foi*! This rigmarole says nothing to me. Does it cause the face to flush?'

'Certainly it does.'

'And supposing I ate ten – twenty of your little tablets, what then?'

'I should not advise you to attempt it,' he replied drily.

'And yet you say it is not poison?'

'There are many things not called poison which can kill a man,' he replied as before.

I left the shop elated. At last, things had begun to march!

I now knew that John Wilson had the means for the crime – but what about the motive? He had come to Belgium on business, and had asked M. Déroulard, whom he knew slightly, to put him up. There was apparently no way in which Déroulard's death could benefit him. Moreover, I discovered by inquiries in England that he had suffered for some years from that painful form of heart disease known as angina. Therefore he had a genuine right to have those tablets in his possession. Nevertheless, I was convinced that someone had gone to the chocolate box, opening the full one first by mistake, and had abstracted the contents of the last chocolate, cramming in instead as many little trinitrine tablets as it would hold. The chocolates were large ones. Between twenty or thirty tablets, I felt sure, could have been inserted. But who had done this?

There were two guests in the house. John Wilson had the means. Saint Alard had the motive. Remember, he was a fanatic, and there is no fanatic like a religious fanatic. Could he, by any means, have got hold of John Wilson's trinitrine?

Another little idea came to me. Ah, you smile at my little ideas! Why had Wilson run out of trinitrine? Surely he would bring an adequate supply from England. I called once more at the house in the Avenue Louise. Wilson was out, but I saw the girl who did his room, Félicie. I demanded of her immediately whether it was not true that M. Wilson had lost a bottle from his washstand some little time ago. The girl responded eagerly. It was quite true. She, Félicie, had been blamed for it. The English gentleman had evidently thought that she had broken it, and did not like to say so. Whereas she had never even touched it. Without doubt it was Jeannette – always nosing round where she had no business to be –

I calmed the flow of words, and took my leave. I knew now all that I wanted to know. It remained for me to be sure that Saint Alard had removed the bottle of trinitrine from John Wilson's washstand, but to convince others, I would have to produce evidence. And I had none to produce!

Never mind. I *knew* – that was the great thing. You remember our difficulty in the Styles case, Hastings?

There again, I *knew* — but it took me a long time to find the last link which made my chain of evidence against the murderer complete.

I asked for an interview with Mademoiselle Mesnard. She came at once. I demanded of her the address of M. de Saint Alard. A look of trouble came over her face.

'Why do you want it, monsieur?'

'Mademoiselle, it is necessary.'

She seemed doubtful — troubled.

'He can tell you nothing. He is a man whose thoughts are not in this world. He hardly notices what goes on around him.'

'Possibly, mademoiselle. Nevertheless, he was an old friend of M. Déroulard's. There may be things he can tell me — things of the past — old grudges — old love-affairs.'

The girl flushed and bit her lip. 'As you please — but — but I feel sure now that I have been mistaken. It was good of you to accede to my demand, but I was upset — almost distraught at the time. I see now that there is no mystery to solve. Leave it, I beg of you, monsieur.'

I eyed her closely.

'Mademoiselle,' I said, 'it is sometimes difficult for a dog to find a scent, but once he *has* found it, nothing on earth will make him leave it! That is if he is a good dog! And I, mademoiselle, I, Hercule Poirot, am a very good dog.'

Without a word she turned away. A few minutes later she returned with the address written on a sheet of paper. I left the house. François was waiting for me outside. He looked at me anxiously.

'There is no news, monsieur?'

'None as yet, my friend.'

'Ah! *Pauvre* Monsieur Déroulard!' he sighed. 'I too was of his way of thinking. I do not care for priests. Not that I would say so in the house. The women are all devout — a good thing perhaps. *Madame est très pieuse — et Mademoiselle Virginie aussi.*'

Mademoiselle Virginie? Was she '*très pieuse?*' Thinking of the tear-stained passionate face I had seen that first day, I wondered.

Having obtained the address of M. de Saint Alard, I wasted no time. I arrived in the neighbourhood of his château in the Ardennes but it was some days before I could find a pretext for gaining admission to the house. In the end I did – how do you think – as a plumber, *mon ami*! It was the affair of a moment to arrange a neat little gas leak in his bedroom. I departed for my tools, and took care to return with them at an hour when I knew I should have the field pretty well to myself. What I was searching for, I hardly knew. The one thing needful, I could not believe there was any chance of finding. He would never have run the risk of keeping it.

Still when I found the little cupboard above the washstand locked, I could not resist the temptation of seeing what was inside it. The lock was quite a simple one to pick. The door swung open. It was full of old bottles. I took them up one by one with a trembling hand. Suddenly, I uttered a cry. Figure to yourself, my friend, I held in my hand a little phial with an English chemist's label. On it were the words: '*Trinitrine Tablets. One to be taken when required. Mr John Wilson.*'

I controlled my emotion, closed the cupboard, slipped the bottle into my pocket, and continued to repair the gas leak! One must be methodical. Then I left the château, and took the train for my own country as soon as possible. I arrived in Brussels late that night. I was writing out a report for the préfet in the morning, when a note was brought to me. It was from old Madame Déroulard, and it summoned me to the house in the Avenue Louise without delay.

François opened the door to me.

'Madame la Baronne is awaiting you.'

He conducted me to her apartments. She sat in state in

a large armchair. There was no sign of Mademoiselle Virginie.

'M. Poirot,' said the old lady, 'I have just learned that you are not what you pretend to be. You are a police officer.'

'That is so, madame.'

'You came here to inquire into the circumstances of my son's death?'

Again I replied: 'That is so, madame.'

'I should be glad if you would tell me what progress you have made.'

I hesitated.

'First I would like to know how you have learned all this, madame.'

'From one who is no longer of this world.'

Her words, and the brooding way she uttered them, sent a chill to my heart. I was incapable of speech.

'Therefore, monsieur, I would beg of you most urgently to tell me exactly what progress you have made in your investigation.'

'Madame, my investigation is finished.'

'My son?'

'Was killed deliberately.'

'You know by whom?'

'Yes, madame.'

'Who, then?'

'M. de Saint Alard.'

'You are wrong. M. de Saint Alard is incapable of such a crime.'

'The proofs are in my hands.'

'I beg of you once more to tell me all.'

This time I obeyed, going over each step that had led me to the discovery of the truth. She listened attentively. At the end she nodded her head.

'Yes, yes, it is all as you say, all but one thing. It was not M. de Saint Alard who killed my son. It was I, his mother.'

I stared at her. She continued to nod her head gently.

'It is well that I sent for you. It is the providence of the good God that Virginie told me, before she departed for the convent, what she had done. Listen, M. Poirot! My son was an evil man. He persecuted the church. He led a life of mortal sin. He dragged down the other souls beside his own. But there was worse than that. As I came out of my room in this house one morning, I saw my daughter-in-law standing at the head of the stairs. She was reading a letter. I saw my son steal up behind her. One swift push, and she fell, striking her head on the marble steps. When they picked her up she was dead. My son was a murderer, and only I, his mother, knew it.'

She closed her eyes for a moment. 'You cannot conceive, monsieur, of my agony, my despair. What was I to do? Denounce him to the police? I could not bring myself to do it. It was my duty, but my flesh was weak. Besides, would they believe me? My eyesight had been failing for some time – they would say I was mistaken. I kept silence. But my conscience gave me no peace. By keeping silence I too was a murderer. My son inherited his wife's money. He flourished as the green bay tree. And now he was to have a Minister's portfolio. His persecution of the church would be redoubled. And there was Virginie. She, poor child, beautiful, naturally pious, was fascinated by him. He had a strange and terrible power over women. I saw it coming. I was powerless to prevent it. He had no intention of marrying her. The time came when she was ready to yield everything to him.

'Then I saw my path clear. He was my son. I had given him life. I was responsible for him. He had killed one woman's body, now he would kill another's soul! I went to Mr Wilson's room, and took the bottle of tablets. He had once said laughingly that there were enough in it to kill a man! I went into the study and opened the big box of chocolates that always stood on the table. I opened a new box by mistake. The other was on the table also. There was just one chocolate left in it. That simplified things. No one ate chocolates except my son and Virginie. I would keep her with me that night. All went as I had planned –'

She paused, closing her eyes a minute then opened them again.

'M. Poirot, I am in your hands. They tell me I have not many days to live. I am willing to answer for my action before the good God. Must I answer for it on earth also?'

I hesitated. 'But the empty bottle, madame,' I said to gain time. 'How came that into M. de Saint Alard's possession?'

'When he came to say goodbye to me, monsieur, I slipped it into his pocket. I did not know how to get rid of it. I am so infirm that I cannot move about much without help, and finding it empty in my rooms might have caused suspicion. You understand, monsieur –' she drew herself up to her full height – 'it was with no idea of casting suspicion on M. de Saint Alard! I never dreamed of such a thing. I thought his valet would find an empty bottle and throw it away without question.'

I bowed my head. 'I comprehend, madame,' I said.

'And your decision, monsieur?'

Her voice was firm and unfaltering, her head held as high as ever.

I rose to my feet.

'Madame,' I said, 'I have the honour to wish you good day. I have made my investigations – and failed! The matter is closed.'

He was silent for a moment, then said quietly: 'She died just a week later. Mademoiselle Virginie passed through her novitiate, and duly took the veil. That, my friend, is the story. I must admit that I do not make a fine figure in it.'

'But that was hardly a failure,' I expostulated. 'What

else could you have thought under the circumstances?'

'Ah, sacré, mon ami,' cried Poirot, becoming suddenly animated. 'Is it that you do not see? But I was thirty-six times an idiot! My grey cells, they functioned not at all. The whole time I had the clue in my hands.'

'What clue?'

'*The chocolate box*! Do you not see? Would anyone in possession of their full eyesight make such a mistake? I knew Madame Déroulard had cataract – the atropine drops told me that. There was only one person in the household whose eyesight was such that she could not see which lid to replace. It was the chocolate box that started me on the track, and yet up to the end I failed consistently to perceive its real significance!

'Also my psychology was at fault. Had M. de Saint Alard been the criminal, he would never have kept an incriminating bottle. Finding it was a proof of his innocence. I had learned already from Mademoiselle Virginie that he was absentminded. Altogether it was a miserable affair that I have recounted to you there! Only to you have I told the story. You comprehend, I do not figure well in it! An old lady commits a crime in such a simple and clever fashion that I, Hercule Poirot, am completely deceived. *Sapristi*! It does not bear thinking of! Forget it. Or no – remember it, and if you think at any time that I am growing conceited – it is not likely, but it might arise.'

I concealed a smile.

'*Eh bien*, my friend, you shall say to me, "Chocolate box". Is it agreed?'

'It's a bargain!'

'After all,' said Poirot reflectively, 'it was an experience! I, who have undoubtedly the finest brain in Europe at present, can afford to be magnanimous!'

'Chocolate box,' I murmured gently.

'*Pardon, mon ami?*'

99

I looked at Poirot's innocent face, as he bent forward inquiringly, and my heart smote me. I had suffered often at his hands, but I, too, though not possessing the finest brain in Europe, could afford to be magnanimous!

'Nothing,' I lied, and lit another pipe, smiling to myself.

DEAD MAN'S MIRROR

Chapter 1

The flat was a modern one. The furnishings of the room were modern, too. The armchairs were squarely built, the upright chairs were angular. A modern writing-table was set squarely in front of the window, and at it sat a small, elderly man. His head was practically the only thing in the room that was not square. It was egg-shaped.

M. Hercule Poirot was reading a letter:

Station: Whimperley.   Hamborough Close,
Telegrams: Hamborough St Mary
  Hamborough St John.   Westshire.
                         September 24th, 1936.

M. Hercule Poirot.

Dear Sir, – A matter has arisen which requires handling with great delicacy and discretion. I have heard good accounts of you, and have decided to entrust the matter to you. I have reason to believe that I am the victim of fraud, but for family reasons I do not wish to call in the police. I am taking certain measures of my own to deal with the business, but you must be prepared to come down here immediately on receipt of a telegram. I should be obliged if you will not answer this letter.

　　　　　　　Yours faithfully,
　　　　　　　　GERVASE CHEVENIX-GORE

The eyebrows of M. Hercule Poirot climbed slowly up his forehead until they nearly disappeared into his hair.

'And who, then,' he demanded of space, 'is this Gervase Chevenix-Gore?'

He crossed to a bookcase and took out a large, fat book. He found what he wanted easily enough.

Chevenix-Gore, Sir Gervase Francis Xavier, 10th Bt. cr. 1694; formerly Captain 17th Lancers; b. 18th May, 1878; e.s. of Sir Guy Chevenix-Gore, 9th Bt., and Lady Claudia Bretherton, 2nd. d. of 8th Earl of Wallingford. S. father, 1911; m. 1912, Vanda Elizabeth, e.d. of Colonel Frederick Arbuthnot, q.v.; educ. Eton. Served European War, 1914–18. Recreations: travelling, big-game hunting. Address: Hamborough St Mary, Westshire, and 218 Lowndes Square, S.W.1. Clubs: Cavalry. Travellers.

Poirot shook his head in a slightly dissatisfied manner. For a moment or two he remained lost in thought, then he went to the desk, pulled open a drawer and took out a little pile of invitation cards.

His face brightened.

'*A la bonne heure!* Exactly my affair! He will certainly be there.'

A duchess greeted M. Hercule Poirot in fulsome tones.

'So you could manage to come after all, M. Poirot! Why, that's splendid.'

'The pleasure is mine, madame,' murmured Poirot, bowing.

He escaped from several important and splendid beings – a famous diplomat, an equally famous actress and a well-known sporting peer – and found at last the person he had come to seek, that invariably 'also present' guest, Mr Satterthwaite.

Mr Satterthwaite twittered amiably.

'The dear duchess – I always enjoy her parties . . . Such a *personality*, if you know what I mean. I saw a lot of her in Corsica some years ago . . .'

Mr Satterthwaite's conversation was apt to be unduly burdened by mentions of his titled acquaintances. It is possible that he *may* sometimes have found pleasure in the company of Messrs Jones, Brown or Robinson, but, if so, he did not mention the fact. And yet, to describe Mr Satterthwaite as a mere snob and leave it at that would have been to do him an injustice. He was a keen observer of human nature, and if it is true that the looker-on knows most of the game, Mr Satterthwaite knew a good deal.

'You know, my dear fellow, it is really ages since I saw you. I always feel myself privileged to have seen you work at close quarters in the Crow's Nest business. I feel since then that I am in the know, so to speak. I saw Lady Mary only last week, by the way. A charming creature – pot-pourri and lavender!'

After passing lightly on one or two scandals of the moment – the indiscretions of an earl's daughter, and the lamentable conduct of a viscount – Poirot succeeded in introducing the name of Gervase Chevenix-Gore.

Mr Satterthwaite responded immediately.

'Ah, now, there *is* a character, if you like! The Last of the Baronets – that's his nickname.'

'*Pardon*, I do not quite comprehend.'

Mr Satterthwaite unbent indulgently to the lower comprehension of a foreigner.

'It's a joke, you know – a *joke*. Naturally, he's not *really* the last baronet in England – but he *does* represent the end of an era. The Bold Bad Baronet – the mad harum-scarum baronet so popular in the novels of the last century – the kind of fellow who laid impossible wagers and won 'em.'

He went on to expound what he meant in more detail.

In younger years, Gervase Chevenix-Gore had sailed round the world in a windjammer. He had been on an expedition to the Pole. He had challenged a racing peer to a duel. For a wager he had ridden his favourite mare up the staircase of a ducal house. He had once leapt from a box to the stage and carried off a well-known actress in the middle of her rôle.

The anecdotes of him were innumerable.

'It's an old family,' went on Mr Satterthwaite. 'Sir Guy de Chevenix went on the first crusade. Now, alas, the line looks like coming to an end. Old Gervase is the last Chevenix-Gore.'

'The estate, it is impoverished?'

'Not a bit of it. Gervase is fabulously wealthy. Owns valuable house property – coalfields – and in addition he staked out a claim to some mine in Peru or somewhere in South America, when he was a young man, which has yielded him a fortune. An amazing man. Always lucky in everything he's undertaken.'

'He is now an elderly man, of course?'

'Yes, poor old Gervase.' Mr Satterthwaite sighed, shook his head. 'Most people would describe him to you as mad as a hatter. It's true, in a way. He *is* mad – not in the sense of being certifiable or having delusions – but mad in the sense of being abnormal. He's always been a man of great originality of character.'

'And originality becomes eccentricity as the years go by?' suggested Poirot.

'Very true. That's exactly what's happened to poor old Gervase.'

'He has perhaps, a swollen idea of his own importance?'

'Absolutely. I should imagine that, in Gervase's mind, the world has always been divided into two parts – there are the Chevenix-Gores, and the other people!'

'An exaggerated sense of family!'

'Yes. The Chevenix-Gores are all arrogant as the devil

– a law unto themselves. Gervase, being the last of them, has got it badly. He is – well, really, you know, to hear him talk, you might imagine him to be – er, the Almighty!'

Poirot nodded his head slowly and thoughtfully.

'Yes, I imagined that. I have had, you see, a letter from him. It was an unusual letter. It did not demand. It summoned!'

'A royal command,' said Mr Satterthwaite, tittering a little.

'Precisely. It did not seem to occur to this Sir Gervase that I, Hercule Poirot, am a man of importance, a man of infinite affairs! That it was extremely unlikely that I should be able to fling everything aside and come hastening like an obedient dog – like a mere nobody, gratified to receive a commission!'

Mr Satterthwaite bit his lip in an effort to suppress a smile. It may have occurred to him that where egoism was concerned, there was not much to choose between Hercule Poirot and Gervase Chevenix-Gore.

He murmured:

'Of course, if the cause of the summons was urgent –?'

'It was not!' Poirot's hands rose in the air in an emphatic gesture. 'I was to hold myself at his disposition, that was all, *in case* he should require me! *Enfin, je vous demande!*'

Again the hands rose eloquently, expressing better than words could do M. Hercule Poirot's sense of utter outrage.

'I take it,' said Mr Satterthwaite, 'that you refused?'

'I have not yet had the opportunity,' said Poirot slowly.

'But you will refuse?'

A new expression passed over the little man's face. His brow furrowed itself perplexedly.

He said:

'How can I express myself? To refuse – yes, that was my first instinct. But I do not know . . . One has, sometimes, a feeling. Faintly, I seem to smell the fish . . .'

Mr Satterthwaite received this last statement without any sign of amusement.

'Oh?' he said. 'That is interesting . . .'

'It seems to me,' went on Hercule Poirot, 'that a man such as you have described might be very vulnerable –'

'Vulnerable?' queried Mr Satterthwaite. For the moment he was surprised. The word was not one that he would naturally have associated with Gervase Chevenix-Gore. But he was a man of perception, quick in observation. He said slowly:

'I think I see what you mean.'

'Such a one is encased, is he not, in an armour – such an armour! The armour of the crusaders was nothing to it – an armour of arrogance, of pride, of complete self-esteem. This armour, it is in some ways a protection, the arrows, the everyday arrows of life glance off it. But there is this danger; *Sometimes a man in armour might not even know he was being attacked.* He will be slow to see, slow to hear – slower still to feel.'

He paused, then asked with a change of manner:

'Of what does the family of this Sir Gervase consist?'

'There's Vanda – his wife. She was an Arbuthnot – very handsome girl. She's still quite a handsome woman. Frightfully vague, though. Devoted to Gervase. She's got a leaning towards the occult, I believe. Wears amulets and scarabs and gives out that she's the reincarnation of an Egyptian Queen . . . Then there's Ruth – she's their adopted daughter. They've no children of their own. Very attractive girl in the modern style. That's all the family. Except, of course, for Hugo Trent. He's Gervase's nephew. Pamela Chevenix-Gore married Reggie Trent and Hugo was their only child. He's an orphan. He can't inherit the title, of course, but I imagine he'll come in for most of Gervase's money in the end. Good-looking lad, he's in the Blues.'

Poirot nodded his head thoughtfully. Then he asked:

'It is a grief to Sir Gervase, yes, that he has no son to inherit his name?'

'I should imagine that it cuts pretty deep.'

'The family name, it is a passion with him?'

'Yes.'

Mr Satterthwaite was silent a moment or two. He was very intrigued. Finally he ventured:

'You see a definite reason for going down to Hamborough Close?'

Slowly, Poirot shook his head.

'No,' he said. 'As far as I can see, there is no reason at all. But, all the same, I fancy I shall go.'

Chapter 2

Hercule Poirot sat in the corner of a first-class carriage speeding through the English countryside.

Meditatively he took from his pocket a neatly-folded telegram, which he opened and re-read:

> Take four-thirty from St Pancras instruct guard
> have express stopped at Whimperley.
>
> CHEVENIX-GORE

He folded up the telegram again and put it back in his pocket.

The guard on the train had been obsequious. The gentleman was going to Hamborough Close? Oh, yes, Sir Gervase Chevenix-Gore's guests always had the express stopped at Whimperley. 'A special kind of prerogative, I think it is, sir.'

Since then the guard had paid two visits to the carriage – the first in order to assure the traveller that everything would be done to keep the carriage for himself, the second to announce that the express was running ten minutes late.

The train was due to arrive at 7.50, but it was exactly two minutes past eight when Hercule Poirot descended on to the platform of the little country station and pressed the expected half-crown into the attentive guard's hand.

There was a whistle from the engine, and the Northern Express began to move once more. A tall chauffeur in dark green uniform stepped up to Poirot.

'Mr Poirot? For Hamborough Close?'

He picked up the detective's neat valise and led the way out of the station. A big Rolls was waiting. The chauffeur held the door open for Poirot to get in, arranged a sumptuous fur rug over his knees, and they drove off.

After some ten minutes of cross-country driving, round sharp corners and down country lanes, the car turned in at a wide gateway flanked with huge stone griffons.

They drove through a park and up to the house. The door of it was opened as they drew up, and a butler of imposing proportions showed himself upon the front step.

'Mr Poirot? This way, sir.'

He led the way along the hall and threw open a door half-way along it on the right.

'Mr Hercule Poirot,' he announced.

The room contained a number of people in evening dress, and as Poirot walked in his quick eyes perceived at once that his appearance was not expected. The eyes of all present rested on him in unfeigned surprise.

Then a tall woman, whose dark hair was threaded with grey, made an uncertain advance towards him.

Poirot bowed over her hand.

'My apologies, madame,' he said. 'I fear that my train was late.'

'Not at all,' said Lady Chevenix-Gore vaguely. Her eyes still stared at him in a puzzled fashion. 'Not at all, Mr – er – I didn't quite hear –'

'Hercule Poirot.'

He said the name clearly and distinctly.

Somewhere behind him he heard a sudden sharp intake of breath.

At the same time he realized that clearly his host could not be in the room. He murmured gently:

'You knew I was coming, madame?'

'Oh – oh, yes . . .' Her manner was not convincing. 'I think – I mean I suppose so, but I am so terribly impractical, M. Poirot. I forget everything.' Her tone held a melancholy pleasure in the fact. 'I am told things. I appear to take them in – but they just pass through my brain and are gone! Vanished! As though they had never been.'

Then, with a slight air of performing a duty long overdue, she glanced round her vaguely and murmured:

'I expect you know everybody.'

Though this was patently not the case, the phrase was clearly a well-worn formula by means of which Lady Chevenix-Gore spared herself the trouble of introduction and the strain of remembering people's right names.

Making a supreme effort to meet the difficulties of this particular case, she added:

'My daughter – Ruth.'

The girl who stood before him was also tall and dark, but she was of a very different type. Instead of the flattish, indeterminate features of Lady Chevenix-Gore, she had a well-chiselled nose, slightly aquiline, and a clear, sharp line of jaw. Her black hair swept back from her face into a mass of little tight curls. Her colouring was of carnation clearness and brilliance, and owed little to make-up. She was, so Hercule Poirot thought, one of the loveliest girls he had seen.

He recognized, too, that she had brains as well as beauty, and guessed at certain qualities of pride and temper. Her voice, when she spoke, came out with a slight drawl that struck him as deliberately put on.

'How exciting,' she said, 'to entertain M. Hercule

Poirot! The old man arranged a little surprise for us, I suppose.'

'So you did not know I was coming, mademoiselle?' he said quickly.

'I hadn't an idea of it. As it is, I must postpone getting my autograph book until after dinner.'

The notes of a gong sounded from the hall, then the butler opened the door and announced:

'Dinner is served.'

And then, almost before the last word, 'served', had been uttered, something very curious happened. The pontifical domestic figure became, just for one moment, a highly-astonished human being . . .

The metamorphosis was so quick and the mask of the well-trained servant was back again so soon, that anyone who had not happened to be looking would not have noticed the change. Poirot, however, *had* happened to be looking. He wondered.

The butler hesitated in the doorway. Though his face was again correctly expressionless, an air of tension hung about his figure.

Lady Chevenix-Gore said uncertainly:

'Oh, dear – this is most extraordinary. Really, I – one hardly knows what to do.'

Ruth said to Poirot:

'This singular consternation, M. Poirot, is occasioned by the fact that my father, for the first time for at least twenty years, is late for dinner.'

'It is most extraordinary –' wailed Lady Chevenix-Gore. 'Gervase never –'

An elderly man of upright soldierly carriage came to her side. He laughed genially.

'Good old Gervase! Late at last! Upon my word, we'll rag him over this. Elusive collar-stud, d'you think? Or is Gervase immune from our common weaknesses?'

Lady Chevenix-Gore said in a low, puzzled voice:

'But Gervase is *never* late.'

It was almost ludicrous, the consternation caused by this simple *contretemps*. And yet, to Hercule Poirot, it was *not* ludicrous . . . Behind the consternation he felt uneasiness – perhaps even apprehension. And he, too, found it strange that Gervase Chevenix-Gore should not appear to greet the guest he had summoned in such a mysterious manner.

In the meantime, it was clear that nobody knew quite what to do. An unprecedented situation had arisen with which nobody knew how to deal.

Lady Chevenix-Gore at last took the initiative, if initiative it can be called. Certainly her manner was vague in the extreme.

'Snell,' she said, 'is your master –?'

She did not finish the sentence, merely looked at the butler expectantly.

Snell, who was clearly used to his mistress's methods of seeking information, replied promptly to the unspecified question:

'Sir Gervase came downstairs at five minutes to eight, m'lady, and went straight to the study.'

'Oh, I see –' Her mouth remained open, her eyes seemed far away. 'You don't think – I mean – he heard the gong?'

'I think he must have done so, m'lady, the gong being immediately outside the study door. I did not, of course, know that Sir Gervase was still in the study, otherwise I should have announced to him that dinner was ready. Shall I do so now, m'lady?'

Lady Chevenix-Gore seized on the suggestion with manifest relief.

'Oh, thank you, Snell. Yes, please do. Yes, certainly.'

She said, as the butler left the room:

'Snell is such a treasure. I rely on him absolutely. I really don't know what I should *do* without Snell.'

Somebody murmured a sympathetic assent, but nobody spoke. Hercule Poirot, watching that room full of people with suddenly sharpened attention, had an idea that one and all were in a state of tension. His eyes ran quickly over them, tabulating them roughly. Two elderly men, the soldierly one who had spoken just now, and a thin, spare, grey-haired man with closely pinched legal lips. Two youngish men – very different in type from each other. One with a moustache and an air of modest arrogance, he guessed to be possibly Sir Gervase's nephew, the one in the Blues. The other, with sleek brushed-back hair and a rather obvious style of good looks, he put down as of a definitely inferior social class. There was a small middle-aged woman with pince-nez and intelligent eyes, and there was a girl with flaming red hair.

Snell appeared at the door. His manner was perfect, but once again the veneer of the impersonal butler showed signs of the perturbed human being beneath the surface.

'Excuse me, m'lady, the study door is locked.'

'Locked?'

It was a man's voice – young, alert, with a ring of excitement in it. It was the good-looking young man with the slicked-back hair who had spoken. He went on, hurrying forward:

'Shall I go and see –?'

But very quietly Hercule Poirot took command. He did it so naturally that no one thought it odd that this stranger, who had just arrived, should suddenly assume charge of the situation.

'Come,' he said. 'Let us go to the study.'

He continued, speaking to Snell:

'Lead the way, if you please.'

Snell obeyed. Poirot followed close behind him, and, like a flock of sheep, everyone else followed.

Snell led the way through the big hall, past the great branching curve of the staircase, past an enormous grandfather clock and a recess in which stood a gong, along a narrow passage which ended in a door.

Here Poirot passed Snell and gently tried the handle. It turned, but the door did not open. Poirot rapped gently with his knuckles on the panel of the door. He rapped louder and louder. Then, suddenly desisting, he dropped to his knees and applied his eye to the keyhole.

Slowly he rose to his feet and looked round. His face was stern.

'Gentlemen!' he said. 'This door must be broken open immediately!'

Under his direction the two young men, who were both tall and powerfully built, attacked the door. It was no easy matter. The doors of Hamborough Close were solidly built.

At last, however, the lock gave, and the door swung inwards with a noise of splintering, rending wood.

And then, for a moment, everyone stood still, huddled in the doorway looking at the scene inside. The lights were on. Along the left-hand wall was a big writing-table, a massive affair of solid mahogany. Sitting, not at the table, but sideways to it, so that his back was directly towards them, was a big man slouched down in a chair. His head and the upper part of his body hung down over the right side of the chair, and his right hand and arm hung limply down. Just below it on the carpet was a small, gleaming pistol . . .

There was no need of speculation. The picture was clear. Sir Gervase Chevenix-Gore had shot himself.

Chapter 3

For a moment or two the group in the doorway stood motionless, staring at the scene. Then Poirot strode forward.

At the same moment Hugo Trent said crisply:

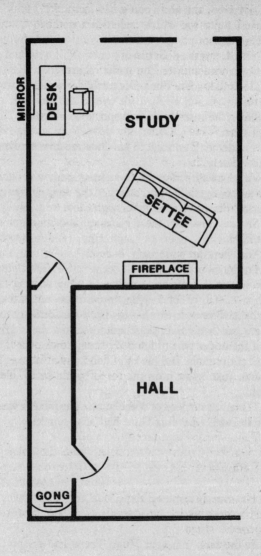

'My God, the Old Man's shot himself!'

And there was a long, shuddering moan from Lady Chevenix-Gore.

'Oh, Gervase – Gervase!'

Over his shoulder Poirot said sharply:

'Take Lady Chevenix-Gore away. She can do nothing here.'

The elderly soldierly man obeyed. He said:

'Come, Vanda. Come, my dear. You can do nothing. It's all over. Ruth, come and look after your mother.'

But Ruth Chevenix-Gore had pressed into the room and stood close by Poirot's side as he bent over the dreadful sprawled figure in the chair – the figure of a man of Herculean build with a Viking beard.

She said in a low, tense voice, curiously restrained and muffled:

'You're quite sure he's – dead?'

Poirot looked up.

The girl's face was alive with some emotion – an emotion sternly checked and repressed – that he did not quite understand. It was not grief – it seemed more like a kind of half-fearful excitement.

The little woman in the pince-nez murmured:

'Your mother, my dear – don't you think –?'

In a high, hysterical voice the girl with the red hair cried out:

'Then it *wasn't* a car or a champagne cork! It was a *shot* we heard . . .'

Poirot turned and faced them all.

'Somebody must communicate with the police –'

Ruth Chevenix-Gore cried out violently:

'No!'

The elderly man with the legal face said:

'Unavoidable, I am afraid. Will you see to that, Burrows? Hugo –'

Poirot said:

'You are Mr Hugo Trent?' to the tall young man with the moustache. 'It would be well, I think, if everyone except you and I were to leave this room.'

Again his authority was not questioned. The lawyer shepherded the others away. Poirot and Hugo Trent were left alone.

The latter said, staring:

'Look here – who *are* you? I mean, I haven't the foggiest idea. What are you doing here?'

Poirot took a card-case from his pocket and selected a card.

Hugo Trent said, staring at it:

'Private detective – eh? Of course, I've heard of you . . . But I still don't see what you are doing *here*.'

'You did not know that your uncle – he was your uncle, was he not – ?'

Hugo's eyes dropped for a fleeting moment to the dead man.

'The Old Man? Yes, he was my uncle all right.'

'You did not know that he had sent for me?'

Hugo shook his head. He said slowly:

'I'd no idea of it.'

There was an emotion in his voice that was rather hard to classify. His face looked wooden and stupid – the kind of expression, Poirot thought, that made a useful mask in times of stress.

Poirot said quietly:

'We are in Westshire, are we not? I know your Chief Constable, Major Riddle, very well.'

Hugo said:

'Riddle lives about half a mile away. He'll probably come over himself.'

'That,' said Poirot, 'will be very convenient.'

He began prowling gently round the room. He twitched aside the window curtain and examined the french windows, trying them gently. They were closed.

On the wall behind the desk there hung a round mirror. The mirror was shivered. Poirot bent down and picked up a small object.

'What's that?' asked Hugo Trent.

'The bullet.'

'It passed straight through his head and struck the mirror?'

'It seems so.'

Poirot replaced the bullet meticulously where he had found it. He came up to the desk. Some papers were arranged neatly stacked in heaps. On the blotting-pad itself there was a loose sheet of paper with the word SORRY printed across it in large, shaky handwriting.

Hugo said: 'He must have written that just before he – did it.'

Poirot nodded thoughtfully.

He looked again at the smashed mirror, then at the dead man. His brow creased itself a little as though in perplexity. He went over to the door, where it hung crookedly with its splintered lock. There was no key in the door, as he knew – otherwise he would not have been able to see through the keyhole. There was no sign of it on the floor. Poirot leaned over the dead man and ran his fingers over him.

'Yes,' he said. 'The key is in his pocket.'

Hugo drew out a cigarette-case and lighted a cigarette. He spoke rather hoarsely.

'It seems all quite clear,' he said. 'My uncle shut himself up in here, scrawled that message on a piece of paper, and then shot himself.'

Poirot nodded meditatively. Hugo went on:

'But I don't understand why he sent for you. What was it all about?'

'That is rather more difficult to explain. While we are waiting, Mr Trent, for the authorities to take charge, perhaps you will tell me exactly who all the people are whom I saw tonight when I arrived?'

'Who they are?' Hugo spoke almost absently. 'Oh, yes, of course. Sorry. Shall we sit down?' He indicated a settee in the farthest corner of the room from the body. He went on, speaking jerkily: 'Well, there's Vanda – my aunt, you know. And Ruth, my cousin. But you know them. Then the other girl is Susan Cardwell. She's just staying here. And there's Colonel Bury. He's an old friend of the family. And Mr Forbes. He's an old friend, too, besides being the family lawyer and all that. Both the old boys had a passion for Vanda when she was young, and they still hang round in a faithful, devoted sort of way. Ridiculous, but rather touching. Then there's Godfrey Burrows, the Old Man's – I mean my uncle's – secretary, and Miss Lingard, who's here to help him write a history of the Chevenix-Gores. She mugs up historical stuff for writers. That's the lot, I think.'

Poirot nodded. Then he said:

'And I understand you actually heard the shot that killed your uncle?'

'Yes, we did. Thought it was a champagne cork – at least, I did. Susan and Miss Lingard thought it was a car backfiring outside – the road runs quite near, you know.'

'When was this?'

'Oh, about ten past eight. Snell had just sounded the first gong.'

'And where were you when you heard it?'

'In the hall. We – we were laughing about it – arguing, you know, as to where the sound came from. I said it came from the dining-room, and Susan said it came from the direction of the drawing-room, and Miss Lingard said it sounded like upstairs, and Snell said it came from the road outside, only it came through the upstairs windows. And Susan said, "Any more theories?" And I laughed and said there was always murder! Seems pretty rotten to think of it now.'

His face twitched nervously.

'It did not occur to anyone that Sir Gervase might have shot himself?'

'No, of course not.'

'You have, in fact, no idea why he should have shot himself?'

Hugo said slowly:

'Oh, well, I shouldn't say that –'

'You *have* an idea?'

'Yes – well – it's difficult to explain. Naturally I didn't expect him to commit suicide, but all the same I'm not frightfully surprised. The truth of it is that my uncle was as mad as a hatter, M. Poirot. Everyone knew that.'

'That strikes you as a sufficient explanation?'

'Well, people do shoot themselves when they're a bit barmy.'

'An explanation of an admirable simplicity.'

Hugo stared.

Poirot got up again and wandered aimlessly round the room. It was comfortably furnished, mainly in a rather heavy Victorian style. There were massive bookcases, huge armchairs, and some upright chairs of genuine Chippendale. There were not many ornaments, but some bronzes on the mantelpiece attracted Poirot's attention and apparently stirred his admiration. He picked them up one by one, carefully examining them before replacing them with care. From the one on the extreme left he detached something with a fingernail.

'What's that?' asked Hugo without much interest.

'Nothing very much. A tiny sliver of looking-glass.'

Hugo said:

'Funny the way that mirror was smashed by the shot. A broken mirror means bad luck. Poor old Gervase . . . I suppose his luck had held a bit too long.'

'Your uncle was a lucky man?'

Hugo gave a short laugh.

'Why, his luck was proverbial! Everything he touched

119

turned to gold! If he backed an outsider, it romped home! If he invested in a doubtful mine, they struck a vein of ore at once! He's had the most amazing escapes from the tightest of tight places. His life's been saved by a kind of miracle more than once. He was rather a fine old boy, in his way, you know. He'd certainly "been places and seen things" – more than most of his generation.'

Poirot murmured in a conversational tone:

'You were attached to your uncle, Mr Trent?'

Hugo Trent seemed a little startled by the question.

'Oh – er – yes, of course,' he said rather vaguely. 'You know, he was a bit difficult at times. Frightful strain to live with, and all that. Fortunately I didn't have to see much of him.'

'*He* was fond of *you?*'

'Not so that you'd notice it! As a matter of fact, he rather resented my existence, so to speak.'

'How was that, Mr Trent?'

'Well, you see, he had no son of his own – and he was pretty sore about it. He was mad about family and all that sort of thing. I believe it cut him to the quick to know that when he died the Chevenix-Gores would cease to exist. They've been going ever since the Norman Conquest, you know. The Old Man was the last of them. I suppose it *was* rather rotten from his point of view.'

'You yourself do not share that sentiment?'

Hugo shrugged his shoulders.

'All that sort of thing seems to me rather out of date.'

'What will happen to the estate?'

'Don't really know. I might get it. Or he may have left it to Ruth. Probably Vanda has it for her lifetime.'

'Your uncle did not definitely declare his intentions?'

'Well, he had his pet idea.'

'And what was that?'

'His idea was that Ruth and I should make a match of it.'

'That would doubtless have been very suitable.'

'Eminently suitable. But Ruth – well, Ruth has very decided views of her own about life. Mind you, she's an extremely attractive young woman, and she knows it. She's in no hurry to marry and settle down.'

Poirot leaned forward.

'But you yourself would have been willing, M. Trent?'

Hugo said in a bored tone of voice:

'I really can't see it makes a ha'p'orth of difference who you marry nowadays. Divorce is so easy. If you're not hitting it off, nothing is easier than to cut the tangle and start again.'

The door opened and Forbes entered with a tall, spruce-looking man.

The latter nodded to Trent.

'Hallo, Hugo. I'm extremely sorry about this. Very rough on all of you.'

Hercule Poirot came forward.

'How do you do, Major Riddle? You remember me?'

'Yes, indeed.' The chief constable shook hands. 'So *you're* down here?'

There was a meditative note in his voice. He glanced curiously at Hercule Poirot.

Chapter 4

'Well?' said Major Riddle.

It was twenty minutes later. The chief constable's interrogative 'Well?' was addressed to the police surgeon, a lank elderly man with grizzled hair.

The latter shrugged his shoulders.

'He's been dead over half an hour – but not more than an hour. You don't want technicalities, I know, so I'll spare you them. The man was shot through the head, the pistol being held a few inches from the right temple. Bullet passed right through the brain and out again.'

'Perfectly compatible with suicide?'

'Oh, perfectly. The body then slumped down in the chair, and the pistol dropped from his hand.'

'You've got the bullet?'

'Yes.' The doctor held it up.

'Good,' said Major Riddle. 'We'll keep it for comparison with the pistol. Glad it's a clear case and no difficulties.'

Hercule Poirot asked gently:

'You are sure there *are* no difficulties, Doctor?'

The doctor replied slowly:

'Well, I suppose you might call one thing a little odd. When he shot himself he must have been leaning slightly over to the right. Otherwise the bullet would have hit the wall *below* the mirror, instead of plumb in the middle.'

'An uncomfortable position in which to commit suicide,' said Poirot.

The doctor shrugged his shoulders.

'Oh, well – comfort – if you're going to end it all –' He left the sentence unfinished.

Major Riddle said:

'The body can be moved now?'

'Oh, yes. I've done with it until the P.-M.'

'What about you, Inspector?' Major Riddle spoke to a tall impassive-faced man in plain clothes.

'O.K., sir. We've got all we want. Only the deceased's fingerprints on the pistol.'

'Then you can get on with it.'

The mortal remains of Gervase Chevenix-Gore were removed. The chief constable and Poirot were left together.

'Well,' said Riddle, 'everything seems quite clear and above-board. Door locked, window fastened, key of door in dead man's pocket. Everything according to Cocker – but for one circumstance.'

'And what is that, my friend?' inquired Poirot.

'*You!*' said Riddle bluntly. 'What are *you* doing down here?'

By way of reply, Poirot handed to him the letter he had received from the dead man a week ago, and the telegram which had finally brought him there.

'Humph,' said the chief constable. 'Interesting. We'll have to get to the bottom of this. I should say it had a direct bearing upon his suicide.'

'I agree.'

'We must check up on who is in the house.'

'I can tell you their names. I have just been making inquiries of Mr Trent.'

He repeated the list of names.

'Perhaps you, Major Riddle, know something about these people?'

'I know something of them, naturally. Lady Chevenix-Gore is quite as mad in her own way as old Sir Gervase. They were devoted to each other – and both quite mad. She's the vaguest creature that ever lived, with an occasional uncanny shrewdness that strikes the nail on the head in the most surprising fashion. People laugh at her a good deal. I think she knows it, but she doesn't care. She's absolutely no sense of humour.'

'Miss Chevenix-Gore is only their adopted daughter, I understand?'

'Yes.'

'A very handsome young lady.'

'She's a devilishly attractive girl. Has played havoc with most of the young fellows round here. Leads them all on and then turns round and laughs at them. Good seat on a horse, and wonderful hands.'

'That, for the moment, does not concern us.'

'Er – no, perhaps not . . . Well, about the other people. I know old Bury, of course. He's here most of the time. Almost a tame cat about the house. Kind of A.D.C. to Lady Chevenix-Gore. He's a very old friend. They've known him all their lives. I think he and Sir Gervase were both interested in some company of which Bury was a director.'

'Oswald Forbes, do you know anything of him?'

'I rather believe I've met him once.'

'Miss Lingard?'

'Never heard of her.'

'Miss Susan Cardwell?'

'Rather a good-looking girl with red hair? I've seen her about with Ruth Chevenix-Gore the last few days.'

'Mr Burrows?'

'Yes, I know him. Chevenix-Gore's secretary. Between you and me, I don't take to him much. He's good-looking, and knows it. Not quite out of the top drawer.'

'Had he been with Sir Gervase long?'

'About two years, I fancy.'

'And there is no one else –?'

Poirot broke off.

A tall, fair-haired man in a lounge suit came hurrying in. He was out of breath and looked disturbed.

'Good evening, Major Riddle. I heard a rumour that Sir Gervase had shot himself, and I hurried up here. Snell tells me it's true. It's incredible! I can't believe it!'

'It's true enough, Lake. Let me introduce you. This is Captain Lake, Sir Gervase's agent for the estate. M. Hercule Poirot, of whom you may have heard.'

Lake's face lit up with what seemed a kind of delighted incredulity.

'M. Hercule Poirot? I'm most awfully pleased to meet you. At least –' He broke off, the quick charming smile vanished – he looked disturbed and upset. 'There isn't anything – fishy – about this suicide, is there, sir?'

'Why should there be anything "fishy," as you call it?' asked the chief constable sharply.

'I mean, because M. Poirot is here. Oh, and because the whole business seems so incredible!'

'No, no,' said Poirot quickly. 'I am not here on account of the death of Sir Gervase. I was already in the house – as a guest.'

'Oh, I see. Funny, he never told me you were coming when I was going over accounts with him this afternoon.'

Poirot said quietly:

'You have twice used the word "incredible," Captain Lake. Are you, then, so surprised to hear of Sir Gervase committing suicide?'

'Indeed I am. Of course, he was mad as a hatter; everyone would agree about that. But all the same, I simply can't imagine his thinking the world would be able to get on without him.'

'Yes,' said Poirot. 'It is a point, that.' And he looked with appreciation at the frank, intelligent countenance of the young man.

Major Riddle cleared his throat.

'Since you are here, Captain Lake, perhaps you will sit down and answer a few questions.'

'Certainly, sir.'

Lake took a chair opposite the other two.

'When did you last see Sir Gervase?'

'This afternoon, just before three o'clock. There were some accounts to be checked, and the question of a new tenant for one of the farms.'

'How long were you with him?'

'Perhaps half an hour.'

'Think carefully, and tell me whether you noticed anything unusual in his manner.'

The young man considered.

'No, I hardly think so. He was, perhaps, a trifle excited – but that wasn't unusual with him.'

'He was not depressed in any way?'

'Oh, no, he seemed in good spirits. He was enjoying himself very much just now, writing up a history of the family.'

'How long had he been doing this?'

'He began it about six months ago.'

'Is that when Miss Lingard came here?'

'No. She arrived about two months ago when he had discovered that he could not manage the necessary research work by himself.'

'And you consider he was enjoying himself?'

'Oh, simply enormously! He really didn't think that anything else mattered in the world except his family.'

There was a momentary bitterness in the young man's tone.

'Then, as far as you know, Sir Gervase had no worries of any kind?'

There was a slight – a very slight – pause before Captain Lake answered.

'No.'

Poirot suddenly interposed a question:

'Sir Gervase was not, you think, worried about his daughter in any way?'

'His daughter?'

'That is what I said.'

'Not as far as I know,' said the young man stiffly.

Poirot said nothing further. Major Riddle said:

'Well, thank you, Lake. Perhaps you'd stay around in case I might want to ask you anything.'

'Certainly, sir.' He rose. 'Anything I can do?'

'Yes, you might send the butler here. And perhaps you'd find out for me how Lady Chevenix-Gore is, and if I could have a few words with her presently, or if she's too upset.'

The young man nodded and left the room with a quick, decisive step.

'An attractive personality,' said Hercule Poirot.

'Yes, nice fellow, and good at his job. Everyone likes him.'

Chapter 5

'Sit down, Snell,' said Major Riddle in a friendly tone. 'I've a good many questions to ask you, and I expect this has been a shock to you.'

'Oh, it has indeed, sir. Thank you, sir.' Snell sat down with such a discreet air that it was practically the same as though he had remained on his feet.

'Been here a good long time, haven't you?'

'Sixteen years, sir, ever since Sir Gervase – er – settled down, so to speak.'

'Ah, yes, of course, your master was a great traveller in his day.'

'Yes, sir. He went on an expedition to the Pole and many other interesting places.'

'Now, Snell, can you tell me when you last saw your master this evening?'

'I was in the dining-room, sir, seeing that the table arrangements were all complete. The door into the hall was open, and I saw Sir Gervase come down the stairs, cross the hall and go along the passage to the study.'

'That was at what time?'

'Just before eight o'clock. It might have been as much as five minutes before eight.'

'And that was the last you saw of him?'

'Yes, sir.'

'Did you hear a shot?'

'Oh, yes, indeed, sir; but of course I had no idea at the time – how should I have had?'

'What did you think it was?'

'I thought it was a car, sir. The road runs quite near the park wall. Or it might have been a shot in the woods – a poacher, perhaps. I never dreamed –'

Major Riddle cut him short.

'What time was that?'

'It was exactly eight minutes past eight, sir.'

The chief constable said sharply:

'How is it you can fix the time to a minute?'

'That's easy, sir. I had just sounded the first gong.'

'The first gong?'

'Yes, sir. By Sir Gervase's orders, a gong was always to be sounded seven minutes before the actual dinner gong. Very particular he was, sir, that everyone should be assembled ready in the drawing-room when the second gong went. As soon as I had sounded the second gong, I went to the drawing-room and announced dinner, and everyone went in.'

'I begin to understand,' said Hercule Poirot, 'why you looked so surprised when you announced dinner this evening. It was usual for Sir Gervase to be in the drawing-room?'

'I'd never known him not be there before, sir. It was quite a shock, I little thought – '

Again Major Riddle interrupted adroitly:

'And were the others also usually there?'

Snell coughed.

'Anyone who was late for dinner, sir, was never asked to the house again.'

'H'm, very drastic.'

'Sir Gervase, sir, employed a chef who was formerly with the Emperor of Moravia. He used to say, sir, that dinner was as important as a religious ritual.'

'And what about his own family?'

'Lady Chevenix-Gore was always very particular not to upset him, sir, and even Miss Ruth dared not be late for dinner.'

'Interesting,' murmured Hercule Poirot.

'I see,' said Riddle. 'So, dinner being at a quarter past eight, you sounded the first gong at eight minutes past as usual?'

'That is so, sir – but it wasn't as usual. Dinner was usually at eight. Sir Gervase gave orders that dinner was to be a quarter of an hour later this evening, as he was expecting a gentleman by the late train.'

Snell made a little bow towards Poirot as he spoke.

'When your master went to the study, did he look upset or worried in any way?'

'I could not say, sir. It was too far for me to judge of his expression. I just noticed him, that was all.'

'Was he left alone when he went to the study?'

'Yes, sir.'

'Did anyone go to the study after that?'

'I could not say, sir. I went to the butler's pantry after that, and was there until I sounded the first gong at eight minutes past eight.'

'That was when you heard the shot?'

'Yes, sir.'

Poirot gently interposed a question.

'There were others, I think, who also heard the shot?'

'Yes, sir. Mr Hugo and Miss Cardwell. And Miss Lingard.'

'These people were also in the hall?'

'Miss Lingard came out from the drawing-room, and Miss Cardwell and Mr Hugo were just coming down the stairs.'

Poirot asked:

'Was there any conversation about the matter?'

'Well, sir, Mr Hugo asked if there was champagne for dinner. I told him that sherry, hock and burgundy were being served.'

'He thought it was a champagne cork?'

'Yes, sir.'

'But nobody took it seriously?'

'Oh, no, sir. They all went into the drawing-room talking and laughing.'

'Where were the other members of the household?'

'I could not say, sir.'

Major Riddle said:

'Do you know anything about this pistol?' He held it out as he spoke.

'Oh, yes, sir. That belonged to Sir Gervase. He always kept it in the drawer of his desk in here.'

'Was it usually loaded?'

'I couldn't say, sir.'

Major Riddle laid down the pistol and cleared his throat.

'Now, Snell, I'm going to ask you a rather important question. I hope you will answer it as truthfully as you can. *Do you know of any reason which might lead your master to commit suicide?*'

'No, sir. I know of nothing.'

'Sir Gervase had not been odd in his manner of late? Not depressed? Or worried?'

Snell coughed apologetically.

'You'll excuse my saying it, sir, but Sir Gervase was always what might have seemed to strangers a little odd in his manner. He was a highly original gentleman, sir.'

'Yes, yes, I am quite aware of that.'

'Outsiders, sir, did not always Understand Sir Gervase.'

Snell gave the phrase a definite value of capital letter.

'I know. I know. But there was nothing that *you* would have called unusual?'

The butler hesitated.

'I think, sir, that Sir Gervase was worried about something,' he said at last.

'Worried and depressed?'

'I shouldn't say depressed, sir. But worried, yes.'

'Have you any idea of the cause of that worry?'

'No, sir.'

'Was it connected with any particular person, for instance?'

'I could not say at all, sir. In any case, it is only an impression of mine.'

Poirot spoke again.

'You were surprised at his suicide?'

'Very surprised, sir. It has been a terrible shock to me. I never dreamed of such a thing.'

Poirot nodded thoughtfully.

Riddle glanced at him, then he said:

'Well, Snell, I think that is all we want to ask you. You are quite sure that there is nothing else you can tell us – no unusual incident, for instance, that has happened in the last few days?'

The butler, rising to his feet, shook his head.

'There is nothing, sir, nothing whatever.'

'Then you can go.'

'Thank you, sir.'

Moving towards the doorway, Snell drew back and stood aside. Lady Chevenix-Gore floated into the room.

She was wearing an oriental-looking garment of purple and orange silk wound tightly round her body. Her face was serene and her manner collected and calm.

'Lady Chevenix-Gore.' Major Riddle sprang to his feet.

She said:

'They told me you would like to talk to me, so I came.'

'Shall we go into another room? This must be painful for you in the extreme.'

Lady Chevenix-Gore shook her head and sat down on one of the Chippendale chairs. She murmured:

'Oh, no, what does it matter?'

'It is very good of you, Lady Chevenix-Gore, to put your feelings aside. I know what a frightful shock this must have been and –'

She interrupted him.

'It was rather a shock at first,' she admitted. Her tone was easy and conversational. 'But there is no such thing as Death, really, you know, only Change.' She added: 'As a matter of fact, Gervase is standing just behind your left shoulder now. I can see him distinctly.'

Major Riddle's left shoulder twitched slightly. He looked at Lady Chevenix-Gore rather doubtfully.

She smiled at him, a vague, happy smile.

'You don't believe, of course! So few people will. To me, the spirit world is quite as real as this one. But please ask me anything you like, and don't worry about distressing me. I'm not in the least distressed. Everything, you see, is Fate. One cannot escape one's Karma. It all fits in – the mirror – everything.'

'The mirror, madame?' asked Poirot.

She nodded her head towards it vaguely.

'Yes. It's splintered, you see. A symbol! You know Tennyson's poem? I used to read it as a girl – though, of course, I didn't realise then the esoteric side of it. "*The mirror cracked from side to side. 'The curse is come upon me!' cried the Lady of Shalott.*" That's what happened to Gervase. The Curse came upon him suddenly. I think, you know, most very old families have a curse . . . the mirror cracked. He knew that he was doomed! *The Curse had come!*'

'But, madame, it was not a curse that cracked the mirror – it was a bullet!'

Lady Chevenix-Gore said, still in the same sweet vague manner:

'It's all the same thing, really . . . It was Fate.'

'But your husband shot himself.'

Lady Chevenix-Gore smiled indulgently.

'He shouldn't have done that, of course. But Gervase was always impatient. He could never wait. His hour had come – he went forward to meet it. It's all so simple, really.'

Major Riddle, clearing his throat in exasperation, said sharply:

'Then you weren't surprised at your husband's taking his own life? Had you been expecting such a thing to happen?'

'Oh, no.' Her eyes opened wide. 'One can't always

foresee the future. Gervase, of course, was a very strange man, a very unusual man. He was quite unlike anyone else. He was one of the Great Ones born again. I've known that for some time. I think he knew it himself. He found it very hard to conform to the silly little standards of the everyday world.' She added, looking over Major Riddle's shoulder, 'He's smiling now. He's thinking how foolish we all are. So we are really. Just like children. Pretending that life is real and that it matters . . . Life is only one of the Great Illusions.'

Feeling that he was fighting a losing battle, Major Riddle asked desperately:

'You can't help us at all as to *why* your husband should have taken his life?'

She shrugged her thin shoulders.

'Forces move us – they move us . . . You cannot understand. You move only on the material plane.'

Poirot coughed.

'Talking of the material plane, have you any idea, madame, as to how your husband has left his money?'

'Money?' she stared at him. 'I never think of money.'

Her tone was disdainful.

Poirot switched to another point.

'At what time did you come downstairs to dinner tonight?'

'Time? What is Time? Infinite, that is the answer. Time is infinite.'

Poirot murmured:

'But your husband, madame, was rather particular about time – especially, so I have been told, as regards the dinner hour.'

'Dear Gervase,' she smiled indulgently. 'He was very foolish about that. But it made him happy. So we were never late.'

'Were you in the drawing-room, madame, when the first gong went?'

'No, I was in my room then.'

'Do you remember who was in the drawing-room when you did come down?'

'Nearly everybody, I think,' said Lady Chevenix-Gore vaguely. 'Does it matter?'

'Possibly not,' admitted Poirot. 'Then there is something else. Did your husband ever tell you that he suspected he was being robbed?'

Lady Chevenix-Gore did not seem much interested in the question.

'Robbed? No, I don't think so.'

'Robbed, swindled – victimized in some way –?'

'No – no – I don't think so . . . Gervase would have been very angry if anybody had dared to do anything like that.'

'At any rate he said nothing about it to you?'

'No – no.' Lady Chevenix-Gore shook her head, still without much real interest. 'I should have remembered . . .'

'When did you last see your husband alive?'

'He looked in, as usual, on his way downstairs before dinner. My maid was there. He just said he was going down.'

'What has he talked about most in the last few weeks?'

'Oh, the family history. He was getting on so well with it. He found that funny old thing, Miss Lingard, quite invaluable. She looked up things for him in the British Museum – all that sort of thing. She worked with Lord Mulcaster on his book, you know. And she was tactful – I mean, she didn't look up the wrong things. After all, there are ancestors one doesn't want raked up. Gervase was very sensitive. She helped me, too. She got a lot of information for me about Hatshepsut. I am a reincarnation of Hatshepsut, you know.'

Lady Chevenix-Gore made this announcement in a calm voice.

'Before that,' she went on, 'I was a Priestess in Atlantis.'
Major Riddle shifted a little in his chair.

'Er – er – very interesting,' he said. 'Well, really, Lady Chevenix-Gore, I think that will be all. Very kind of you.'

Lady Chevenix-Gore rose, clasping her oriental robes about her.

'Goodnight,' she said. And then, her eyes shifting to a point behind Major Riddle. 'Goodnight, Gervase dear. I wish you could come, but I know you have to stay here.' She added in an explanatory fashion, 'You have to stay in the place where you've passed over for at least twenty-four hours. It's some time before you can move about freely and communicate.'

She trailed out of the room.

Major Riddle wiped his brow.

'Phew,' he murmured. 'She's a great deal madder than I ever thought. Does she really believe all that nonsense?'

Poirot shook his head thoughtfully.

'It is possible that she finds it helpful,' he said. 'She needs, at this moment, to create for herself a world of illusion so that she can escape the stark reality of her husband's death.'

'She seems almost certifiable to me,' said Major Riddle. 'A long farrago of nonsense without one word of sense in it.'

'No, no, my friend. The interesting thing is, as Mr Hugo Trent casually remarked to me, that amidst all the vapouring there is an occasional shrewd thrust. She showed it by her remark about Miss Lingard's tact in not stressing undesirable ancestors. Believe me, Lady Chevenix-Gore is no fool.'

He got up and paced up and down the room.

'There are things in this affair that I do not like. No, I do not like them at all.'

Riddle looked at him curiously.

'You mean the motive for his suicide?'

'Suicide – suicide! It is all wrong, I tell you. *It is wrong psychologically.* How did Chevenix-Gore think of himself? As a Colossus, as an immensely important person, as the centre of the universe! Does such a man destroy himself? Surely not. He is far more likely to destroy someone else – some miserable crawling ant of a human being who had dared to cause him annoyance . . . Such an act he might regard as necessary – as sanctified! But self-destruction? The destruction of such a Self?'

'It's all very well, Poirot. But the evidence is clear enough. Door locked, key in his own pocket. Window closed and fastened. I know these things happen in books – but I've never come across them in real life. Anything else?'

'But yes, there is something else.' Poirot sat down in the chair. 'Here I am. I am Chevenix-Gore. I am sitting at my desk. I am determined to kill myself – because, let us say, I have made a discovery concerning some terrific dishonour to the family name. It is not very convincing, that, but it must suffice.

'*Eh bien*, what do I do? I scrawl on a piece of paper the word SORRY. Yes, that is quite possible. Then I open a drawer of the desk, take out the pistol which I keep there, load it, if it is not loaded, and then – do I proceed to shoot myself? No, I first turn my chair round – so, and I lean over a little to the right – so – and then I put the pistol to my temple and fire!'

Poirot sprang up from his chair, and wheeling round, demanded:

'I ask you, does that make sense? *Why* turn the chair round? If, for instance, there had been a picture on the wall there, then, yes, there might be an explanation. Some portrait which a dying man might wish to be the last thing on earth his eyes would see, but a window-curtain – *ah non*, that does not make sense.'

'He might have wished to look out of the window. Last view out over the estate.'

'My dear friend, you do not suggest that with any conviction. In fact, you know it is nonsense. At eight minutes past eight it was dark, and in any case the curtains are drawn. No, there must be some other explanation . . .'

'There's only one as far as I can see. Gervase Chevenix-Gore was mad.'

Poirot shook his head in a dissatisfied manner.

Major Riddle rose.

'Come,' he said. 'Let us go and interview the rest of the party. We may get at something that way.'

Chapter 6

After the difficulties of getting a direct statement from Lady Chevenix-Gore, Major Riddle found considerable relief in dealing with a shrewd lawyer like Forbes.

Mr Forbes was extremely guarded and cautious in his statements, but his replies were all directly to the point.

He admitted that Sir Gervase's suicide had been a great shock to him. He should never have considered Sir Gervase the kind of man who would take his own life. He knew nothing of any cause for such an act.

'Sir Gervase was not only my client, but was a very old friend. I have known him since boyhood. I should say that he had always enjoyed life.'

'In the circumstances, Mr Forbes, I must ask you to speak quite candidly. You did not know of any secret anxiety or sorrow in Sir Gervase's life?'

'No. He had minor worries, like most men, but there was nothing of a serious nature.'

'No illness? No trouble between him and his wife?'

'No. Sir Gervase and Lady Chevenix-Gore were devoted to each other.'

Major Riddle said cautiously:

'Lady Chevenix-Gore appears to hold somewhat curious views.'

Mr Forbes smiled – an indulgent, manly smile.

'Ladies,' he said, 'must be allowed their fancies.'

The chief constable went on:

'You managed all Sir Gervase's legal affairs?'

'Yes, my firm, Forbes, Ogilvie and Spence, have acted for the Chevenix-Gore family for well over a hundred years.'

'Were there any – scandals in the Chevenix-Gore family?'

Mr Forbes's eyebrows rose.

'Really, I fail to understand you?'

'M. Poirot, will you show Mr Forbes the letter you showed me?'

In silence Poirot rose and handed the letter to Mr Forbes with a little bow.

Mr Forbes read it and his eyebrows rose still more.

'A most remarkable letter,' he said. 'I appreciate your question now. No, so far as my knowledge went, there was nothing to justify the writing of such a letter.'

'Sir Gervase said nothing of this matter to you?'

'Nothing at all. I must say I find it very curious that he should not have done so.'

'He was accustomed to confide in you?'

'I think he relied on my judgment.'

'And you have no idea as to what this letter refers?'

'I should not like to make any rash speculations.'

Major Riddle appreciated the subtlety of this reply.

'Now, Mr Forbes, perhaps you can tell us how Sir Gervase has left his property.'

'Certainly. I see no objection to such a course. To his wife, Sir Gervase left an annual income of six thousand pounds chargeable on the estate, and the choice of the Dower House or the town house in Lowndes Square, whichever she should prefer. There were, of course, several legacies and bequests, but nothing of an outstanding nature. The residue of his property was left to his adopted daughter, Ruth, on condition that, if she married, her husband should take the name of Chevenix-Gore.'

'Was nothing left to his nephew, Mr Hugo Trent?'

'Yes. A legacy of five thousand pounds.'

'And I take it that Sir Gervase was a rich man?'

'He was extremely wealthy. He had a vast private fortune apart from the estate. Of course, he was not quite so well-off as in the past. Practically all invested incomes have felt the strain. Also, Sir Gervase had dropped a good deal of money over a certain company – the Paragon Synthetic Rubber Substitute in which Colonel Bury persuaded him to invest a good deal of money.'

'Not very wise advice?'

Mr Forbes sighed.

'Retired soldiers are the worst sufferers when they engage in financial operations. I have found that their credulity far exceeds that of widows – and that is saying a good deal.'

'But these unfortunate investments did not seriously affect Sir Gervase's income?'

'Oh, no, not seriously. He was still an extremely rich man.'

'When was this will made?'

'Two years ago.'

Poirot murmured:

'This arrangement, was it not possibly a little unfair to Mr Hugo Trent, Sir Gervase's nephew? He is, after all, Sir Gervase's nearest blood relation.'

Mr Forbes shrugged his shoulders.

'One has to take a certain amount of family history into account.'

'Such as –?'

Mr Forbes seemed slightly unwilling to proceed.

Major Riddle said:

'You mustn't think we're unduly concerned with raking up old scandals or anything of that sort. But this letter of Sir Gervase's to M. Poirot has got to be explained.'

'There is certainly nothing scandalous in the explanation of Sir Gervase's attitude to his nephew,' said Mr Forbes quickly. 'It was simply that Sir Gervase always took his position as head of the family very seriously. He had a younger brother and sister. The brother, Anthony Chevenix-Gore, was killed in the war. The sister, Pamela, married, and Sir Gervase disapproved of the marriage. That is to say, he considered that she ought to obtain his consent and approval before marrying. He thought that Captain Trent's family was not of sufficient prominence to be allied with a Chevenix-Gore. His sister was merely amused by his attitude. As a result, Sir Gervase has always been inclined to dislike his nephew. I think that dislike may have influenced him in deciding to adopt a child.'

'There was no hope of his having children of his own?'

'No. There was a still-born child about a year after his marriage. The doctors told Lady Chevenix-Gore that she would never be able to have another child. About two years later he adopted Ruth.'

'And who *was* Mademoiselle Ruth? How did they come to settle upon her?'

'She was, I believe, the child of a distant connection.'

'That I had guessed,' said Poirot. He looked up at the wall which was hung with family portraits. 'One can see that she was of the same blood – the nose, the line of the chin. It repeats itself on these walls many times.'

'She inherits the temper too,' said Mr Forbes dryly.

'So I should imagine. How did she and her adopted father get on?'

'Much as you might imagine. There was a fierce clash of wills more than once. But in spite of these quarrels I believe there was also an underlying harmony.'

'Nevertheless, she caused him a good deal of anxiety?'

'Incessant anxiety. But I can assure you not to the point of causing him to take his own life.'

'Ah, that, no,' agreed Poirot. 'One does not blow one's brains out because one has a headstrong daughter! And so mademoiselle inherits! Sir Gervase, he never thought of altering his will?'

'Ahem!' Mr Forbes coughed to hide a little discomposure. 'As a matter of fact, I took instructions from Sir Gervase on my arrival here (two days ago, that is to say) as to the drafting of a new will.'

'What's this?' Major Riddle hitched his chair a little closer. 'You didn't tell us this.'

Mr Forbes said quickly:

'You merely asked me what the terms of Sir Gervase's will were. I gave you the information for which you asked. The new will was not even properly drawn up – much less signed.'

'What were its provisions? They may be some guide to Sir Gervase's state of mind.'

'In the main, they were the same as before, but Miss Chevenix-Gore was only to inherit on condition that she married Mr Hugo Trent.'

'Aha,' said Poirot. 'But there is a very decided difference there.'

'I did not approve of the clause,' said Mr Forbes. 'And I felt bound to point out that it was quite possible it might be contested successfully. The Court does not look upon such conditional bequests with approval. Sir Gervase, however, was quite decided.'

'And if Miss Chevenix-Gore (or, incidentally, Mr Trent) refused to comply?'

'If Mr Trent was not willing to marry Miss Chevenix-Gore, then the money went to her unconditionally. But if *he* was willing and *she* refused, then the money went to him instead.'

'Odd business,' said Major Riddle.

Poirot leaned forward. He tapped the lawyer on the knee.

'But what is behind it? What was in the mind of Sir Gervase when he made that stipulation? There must have been something very definite . . . There must, I think, have been the image of another man . . . a man of whom he disapproved. I think, Mr Forbes, that *you* must know who that man was?'

'Really, M. Poirot, I have no information.'

'But you could make a guess.'

'I never guess,' said Mr Forbes, and his tone was scandalized.

Removing his pince-nez, he wiped them with a silk handkerchief and inquired:

'Is there anything else that you desire to know?'

'At the moment, no,' said Poirot. 'Not, that is, as far as I am concerned.'

Mr Forbes looked as though, in his opinion, that was not very far, and bent his attention on the chief constable.

'Thank you, Mr Forbes. I think that's all. I should like, if I may, to speak to Miss Chevenix-Gore.'

'Certainly. I think she is upstairs with Lady Chevenix-Gore.'

'Oh, well, perhaps I'll have a word with – what's his name? – Burrows, first, and the family-history woman.'

'They're both in the library. I will tell them.'

Chapter 7

'Hard work, that,' said Major Riddle, as the lawyer left the room. 'Extracting information from these old-fashioned legal wallahs takes a bit of doing. The whole business seems to me to centre about the girl.'

'It would seem so – yes.'

'Ah, here comes Burrows.'

Godfrey Burrows came in with a pleasant eagerness to be of use. His smile was discreetly tempered with gloom and showed only a fraction too much teeth. It seemed more mechanical than spontaneous.

'Now, Mr Burrows, we want to ask you a few questions.'

'Certainly, Major Riddle. Anything you like.'

'Well, first and foremost, to put it quite simply, have you any ideas of your own about Sir Gervase's suicide?'

'Absolutely none. It was the greatest shock to me.'

'You heard the shot?'

'No; I must have been in the library at the time, as far as I can make out. I came down rather early and went to the library to look up a reference I wanted. The library's right the other side of the house from the study, so I shouldn't hear anything.'

'Was anyone with you in the library?' asked Poirot.

'No one at all.'

'You've no idea where the other members of the household were at that time?'

'Mostly upstairs dressing, I should imagine.'

'When did you come to the drawing-room?'

'Just before M. Poirot arrived. Everybody was there then – except Sir Gervase, of course.'

'Did it strike you as strange that he wasn't there?'

'Yes, it did, as a matter of fact. As a rule he was always in the drawing-room before the first gong sounded.'

'Have you noticed any difference in Sir Gervase's manner lately? Has he been worried? Or anxious? Depressed?'

Godfrey Burrows considered.

'No – I don't think so. A little – well, preoccupied, perhaps.'

'But he did not appear to be worried about any one definite matter?'

'Oh, no.'

'No – financial worries of any kind?'

'He was rather perturbed about the affairs of one particular company – the Paragon Synthetic Rubber Company to be exact.'

'What did he actually say about it?'

Again Godfrey Burrows's mechanical smile flashed out, and again it seemed slightly unreal.

'Well – as a matter of fact – what he said was, "Old Bury's either a fool or a knave. A fool, I suppose. I must go easy with him for Vanda's sake." '

'And why did he say that – *for Vanda's sake?*' inquired Poirot.

'Well, you see, Lady Chevenix-Gore was very fond of Colonel Bury, and he worshipped her. Followed her about like a dog.'

'Sir Gervase was not – jealous at all?'

'Jealous?' Burrows stared and then laughed. 'Sir Gervase jealous? He wouldn't know how to set about it. Why, it would never have entered his head that anyone could ever prefer another man to him. Such a thing couldn't be, you understand.'

Poirot said gently:

'You did not, I think, like Sir Gervase Chevenix-Gore very much?'

Burrows flushed.

'Oh, yes, I did. At least – well, all that sort of thing strikes one as rather ridiculous nowadays.'

'All what sort of thing?' asked Poirot.

'Well, the feudal motif, if you like. This worship of ancestry and personal arrogance. Sir Gervase was a very able man in many ways, and had led an interesting life, but he would have been more interesting if he hadn't been so entirely wrapped up in himself and his own egoism.'

'Did his daughter agree with you there?'

Burrows flushed again – this time a deep purple.

He said:

'I should imagine Miss Chevenix-Gore is quite one of the moderns! Naturally, I shouldn't discuss her father with her.'

'But the moderns *do* discuss their fathers a good deal!' said Poirot. 'It is entirely in the modern spirit to criticize your parents!'

Burrows shrugged his shoulders.

Major Riddle asked:

'And there was nothing else – no other financial anxiety? Sir Gervase never spoke of having been *victimized?*'

'Victimized?' Burrows sounded very astonished. 'Oh, no.'

'And you yourself were on quite good terms with him?'

'Certainly I was. Why not?'

'I am asking you, Mr Burrows.'

The young man looked sulky.

'We were on the best of terms.'

'Did you know that Sir Gervase had written to M. Poirot asking him to come down here?'

'No.'

'Did Sir Gervase usually write his own letters?'

'No, he nearly always dictated them to me.'

'But he did not do so in this case?'

'No.'

'Why was that, do you think?'

'I can't imagine.'

'You can suggest no reason why he should have written this particular letter himself?'

'No, I can't.'

'Ah!' said Major Riddle, adding smoothly, 'Rather curious. When did you last see Sir Gervase?'

'Just before I went to dress for dinner. I took him some letters to sign.'

'What was his manner then?'

'Quite normal. In fact I should say he was feeling rather pleased with himself about something.'

Poirot stirred a little in his chair.

'Ah?' he said. 'So that was your impression, was it? That he was pleased about something. And yet, not so very long afterwards, he shoots himself. It is odd, that!'

Godfrey Burrows shrugged his shoulders.

'I'm only telling you my impressions.'

'Yes, yes, they are very valuable. After all, you are probably one of the last people who saw Sir Gervase alive.'

'Snell was the last person to see him.'

'To see him, yes, but not to speak to him.'

Burrows did not reply.

Major Riddle said:

'What time was it when you went up to dress for dinner?'

'About five minutes past seven.'

'What did Sir Gervase do?'

'I left him in the study.'

'How long did he usually take to change?'

'He usually gave himself a full three-quarters of an hour.'

'Then, if dinner was at a quarter-past eight, he would probably have gone up at half-past seven at the latest?'

'Very likely.'

'You yourself went to change early?'

'Yes, I thought I would change and then go to the library and look up the references I wanted.'

Poirot nodded thoughtfully. Major Riddle said:

'Well, I think that's all for the moment. Will you send Miss What's-her-name along?'

Little Miss Lingard tripped in almost immediately. She was wearing several chains which tinkled a little as she sat down and looked inquiringly from one to the other of the two men.

'This is all very – er – sad, Miss Lingard,' began Major Riddle.

'Very sad indeed,' said Miss Lingard decorously.

'You came to this house – when?'

'About two months ago. Sir Gervase wrote to a friend of his in the Museum – Colonel Fotheringay it was – and Colonel Fotheringay recommended me. I have done a good deal of historical research work.'

'Did you find Sir Gervase difficult to work for?'

'Oh, not really. One had to humour him a little, of course. But then I always find one has to do that with men.'

With an uneasy feeling that Miss Lingard was probably humouring him at this moment, Major Riddle went on:

'Your work here was to help Sir Gervase with the book he was writing?'

'Yes.'

'What did it involve?'

For a moment, Miss Lingard looked quite human. Her eyes twinkled as she replied:

'Well, actually, you know, it involved writing the book! I looked up all the information and made notes, and arranged the material. And then, later, I revised what Sir Gervase had written.'

'You must have had to exercise a good deal of tact, mademoiselle,' said Poirot.

'Tact and firmness. One needs them both,' said Miss Lingard.

'Sir Gervase did not resent your – er – firmness?'

'Oh not at all. Of course I put it to him that he mustn't be bothered with all the petty detail.'

'Oh, yes, I see.'

'It was quite simple, really,' said Miss Lingard. 'Sir Gervase was perfectly easy to manage if one took him the right way.'

'Now, Miss Lingard, I wonder if you know anything that can throw light on this tragedy?'

Miss Lingard shook her head.

'I'm afraid I don't. You see, naturally he wouldn't

confide in me at all. I was practically a stranger. In any case I think he was far too proud to speak to anyone of family troubles.'

'But you think it *was* family troubles that caused him to take his life?'

Miss Lingard looked rather surprised.

'But of course! Is there any other suggestion?'

'You feel sure that there were family troubles worrying him?'

'I know that he was in great distress of mind.'

'Oh, you know that?'

'Why, of course.'

'Tell me, mademoiselle, did he speak to you of the matter?'

'Not explicitly.'

'What did he say?'

'Let me see. I found that he didn't seem to be taking in what I was saying –'

'One moment. *Pardon.* When was this?'

'This afternoon. We usually worked from three to five.'

'Pray go on.'

'As I say, Sir Gervase seemed to be finding it hard to concentrate – in fact, he said as much, adding that he had several grave matters preying on his mind. And he said – let me see – something like this – (of course, I can't be sure of the exact words): "*It's a terrible thing, Miss Lingard, when a family has been one of the proudest in the land, that dishonour should be brought on it.*" '

'And what did you say to that?'

'Oh, just something soothing. I think I said that every generation had its weaklings – that that was one of the penalties of greatness – but that their failings were seldom remembered by posterity.'

'And did that have the soothing effect you hoped?'

'More or less. We got back to Sir Roger Chevenix-Gore. I had found a most interesting mention of him in a

contemporary manuscript. But Sir Gervase's attention
wandered again. In the end he said he would not do any
more work that afternoon. He said he had had a shock.'

'A shock?'

'That is what he said. Of course, I didn't ask any
questions. I just said, "I am sorry to hear it, Sir Gervase."
And then he asked me to tell Snell that M. Poirot would
be arriving and to put off dinner until eight-fifteen, and
send the car to meet the seven-fifty train.'

'Did he usually ask you to make these arrangements?'

'Well – no – that was really Mr Burrows's business.
I did nothing but my own literary work. I wasn't a
secretary in any sense of the word.'

Poirot asked:

'Do you think Sir Gervase had a definite reason for
asking you to make these arrangements, instead of asking
Mr Burrows to do so?'

Miss Lingard considered.

'Well, he may have had . . . I did not think of it at the
time. I thought it was just a matter of convenience. Still,
it's true now I come to think of it, that he *did* ask me not
to tell anyone that M. Poirot was coming. It was to be a
surprise, he said.'

'Ah! he said that, did he? Very curious, very interesting.
And *did* you tell anyone?'

'Certainly not, M. Poirot. I told Snell about dinner and
to send the chauffeur to meet the seven-fifty as a gentleman
was arriving by it.'

'Did Sir Gervase say anything else that may have had
a bearing on the situation?'

Miss Lingard thought.

'No – I don't think so – he was very much strung-up
– I do remember that just as I was leaving the room, he
said, "*Not that it's any good his coming now. It's too late.*" '

'And you have no idea at all what he meant by that?'

'N – no.'

Just the faintest suspicion of indecision about the simple negative. Poirot repeated with a frown:

' "*Too late.*" That is what he said, is it? "*Too late.*" '

Major Riddle said:

'You can give us no idea, Miss Lingard, as to the nature of the circumstance that so distressed Sir Gervase?'

Miss Lingard said slowly:

'I have an idea that it was in some way connected with Mr Hugo Trent.'

'With Hugo Trent? Why do you think that?'

'Well, it was nothing definite, but yesterday afternoon we were just touching on Sir Hugo de Chevenix (who, I'm afraid, didn't bear too good a character in the Wars of the Roses, and Sir Gervase said, "My sister *would* choose the family name of Hugo for her son! It's always been an unsatisfactory name in our family. She might have known no Hugo would turn out well." '

'What you tell us there is suggestive,' said Poirot. 'Yes, it suggests a new idea to me.'

'Sir Gervase said nothing more definite than that?' asked Major Riddle.

Miss Lingard shook her head.

'No, and of course it wouldn't have done for me to say anything. Sir Gervase was really just talking to himself. He wasn't really speaking to me.'

'Quite so.'

Poirot said:

'Mademoiselle, you, a stranger, have been here for two months. It would be, I think, very valuable if you were to tell us quite frankly your impressions of the family and household.'

Miss Lingard took off her pince-nez and blinked reflectively.

'Well, at first, quite frankly, I felt as though I'd walked straight into a madhouse! What with Lady Chevenix-Gore continually seeing things that weren't there, and Sir

Gervase behaving like – like a king – and dramatizing himself in the most extraordinary way – well, I really did think they were the queerest people I had ever come across. Of course, Miss Chevenix-Gore was perfectly normal, and I soon found that Lady Chevenix-Gore was really an extremely kind, nice woman. Nobody could be kinder and nicer to me than she has been. Sir Gervase – well, I really think he *was* mad. His egomania – isn't that what you call it? – was getting worse and worse every day.'

'And the others?'

'Mr Burrows had rather a difficult time with Sir Gervase, I should imagine. I think he was glad that our work on the book gave him a little more breathing space. Colonel Bury was always charming. He was devoted to Lady Chevenix-Gore and he managed Sir Gervase quite well. Mr Trent, Mr Forbes and Miss Cardwell have only been here a few days, so of course I don't know much about them.'

'Thank you, mademoiselle. And what about Captain Lake, the agent?'

'Oh, he's very nice. Everybody likes him.'

'Including Sir Gervase?'

'Oh, yes. I've heard him say Lake was much the best agent he'd had. Of course, Captain Lake had his difficulties with Sir Gervase, too – but he managed pretty well on the whole. It wasn't easy.'

Poirot nodded thoughtfully. He murmured, 'There was something – something – that I had in mind to ask you – some little thing . . . What was it now?'

Miss Lingard turned a patient face towards him.

Poirot shook his head vexedly.

'Tchah! It is on the tip of my tongue.'

Major Riddle waited a minute or two, then as Poirot continued to frown perplexedly, he took up the interrogation once more.

'When was the last time you saw Sir Gervase?'

'At tea-time, in this room.'

'What was his manner then? Normal?'

'As normal as it ever was.'

'Was there any sense of strain among the party?'

'No, I think everybody seemed quite ordinary.'

'Where did Sir Gervase go after tea?'

'He took Mr Burrows with him into the study, as usual.'

'That was the last time you saw him?'

'Yes. I went to the small morning-room where I worked, and typed a chapter of the book from the notes I had gone over with Sir Gervase, until seven o'clock, when I went upstairs to rest and dress for dinner.'

'You actually heard the shot, I understand?'

'Yes, I was in this room. I heard what sounded like a shot and I went out into the hall. Mr Trent was there, and Miss Cardwell. Mr Trent asked Snell if there was champagne for dinner, and made rather a joke of it. It never entered our heads to take the matter seriously, I'm afraid. We felt sure it must have been a car back-firing.'

Poirot said:

'Did you hear Mr Trent say, "*There's always murder*"?'

'I believe he did say something like that – joking, of course.'

'What happened next?'

'We all came in here.'

'Can you remember the order in which the others came down to dinner?'

'Miss Chevenix-Gore was the first, I think, and then Mr Forbes. Then Colonel Bury and Lady Chevenix-Gore together, and Mr Burrows immediately after them. I think that was the order, but I can't be quite sure because they more or less came in all together.'

'Gathered by the sound of the first gong?'

'Yes. Everyone always hustled when they heard that

gong. Sir Gervase was a terrible stickler for punctuality in the evening.'

'What time did he himself usually come down?'

'He was nearly always in the room before the first gong went.'

'Did it surprise you that he was not down on this occasion?'

'Very much.'

'Ah, I have it!' cried Poirot.

As the other two looked inquiringly at him he went on:

'I have remembered what I wanted to ask. This evening, mademoiselle, as we all went along to the study on Snell's reporting it to be locked, you stooped and picked something up.'

'I did?' Miss Lingard seemed very surprised.

'Yes, just as we turned into the straight passage to the study. Something small and bright.'

'How extraordinary – I don't remember. Wait a minute – yes, I do. Only I wasn't thinking. Let me see – it must be in here.'

Opening her black satin bag, she poured the contents on a table.

Poirot and Major Riddle surveyed the collection with interest. There were two handkerchiefs, a powder-compact, a small bunch of keys, a spectacle-case and one other object on which Poirot pounced eagerly.

'A bullet, by jove!' said Major Riddle.

The thing was indeed shaped like a bullet, but it proved to be a small pencil.

'That's what I picked up,' said Miss Lingard. 'I'd forgotten all about it.'

'Do you know who this belongs to, Miss Lingard?'

'Oh, yes, it's Colonel Bury's. He had it made out of a bullet that hit him – or rather, didn't hit him, if you know what I mean – in the South African War.'

'Do you know when he had it last?'

'Well, he had it this afternoon when they were playing bridge, because I noticed him writing with it on the score when I came in to tea.'

'Who was playing bridge?'

'Colonel Bury, Lady Chevenix-Gore, Mr Trent and Miss Cardwell.'

'I think,' said Poirot gently, 'we will keep this and return it to the colonel ourselves.'

'Oh, please do. I am so forgetful, I might not remember to do so.'

'Perhaps, mademoiselle, you would be so good as to ask Colonel Bury to come here now?'

'Certainly. I will go and find him at once.'

She hurried away. Poirot got up and began walking aimlessly round the room.

'We begin,' he said, 'to reconstruct the afternoon. It is interesting. At half-past two Sir Gervase goes over accounts with Captain Lake. *He is slightly preoccupied*. At three, he discusses the book he is writing with Miss Lingard. *He is in great distress of mind*. Miss Lingard associates that distress of mind with Hugo Trent on the strength of a chance remark. At teatime *his behaviour is normal*. After tea, Godfrey Burrows tells us *he was in good spirits over something*. At five minutes to eight he comes downstairs, goes to his study, scrawls "*Sorry*" on a sheet of paper, and shoots himself!'

Riddle said slowly:

'I see what you mean. It isn't consistent.'

'Strange alteration of moods in Sir Gervase Chevenix-Gore! He is preoccupied – he is seriously upset – he is normal – he is in high spirits! There is something very curious here! And then that phrase he used, "*Too late*." That I should get here "Too late." Well, it is true that I *did* get here too late – *to see him alive*.'

'I see. You really think –?'

'I shall never know now why Sir Gervase sent for me! That is certain!'

Poirot was still wandering round the room. He straightened one or two objects on the mantelpiece; he examined a card-table that stood against a wall, he opened the drawer of it and took out the bridge-markers. Then he wandered over to the writing-table and peered into the wastepaper basket. There was nothing in it but a paper bag. Poirot took it out, smelt it, murmured 'Oranges' and flattened it out, reading the name on it. 'Carpenter and Sons, Fruiterers, Hamborough St Mary.' He was just folding it neatly into squares when Colonel Bury entered the room.

Chapter 8

The Colonel dropped into a chair, shook his head, sighed and said:

'Terrible business, this, Riddle. Lady Chevenix-Gore is being wonderful — wonderful. Grand woman! Full of courage!'

Coming softly back to his chair, Poirot said:

'You have known her very many years, I think?'

'Yes, indeed, I was at her coming-out dance. Wore rosebuds in her hair, I remember. And a white, fluffy dress . . . Wasn't anyone to touch her in the room!'

His voice was full of enthusiasm. Poirot held out the pencil to him.

'This is yours, I think?'

'Eh? What? Oh, thank you, had it this afternoon when we were playing bridge. Amazing, you know, I held a hundred honours in spaces three times running. Never done such a thing before.'

'You were playing bridge before tea, I understand?' said Poirot. 'What was Sir Gervase's frame of mind when he came in to tea?'

'Usual — quite usual. Never dreamed he was thinking

155

of making away with himself. Perhaps he was a little more excitable than usual, now I come to think of it.'

'When was the last time you saw him?'

'Why, then! Tea-time. Never saw the poor chap alive again.'

'You didn't go to the study at all after tea?'

'No, never saw him again.'

'What time did you come down to dinner?'

'After the first gong went.'

'You and Lady Chevenix-Gore came down together?'

'No, we – er – met in the hall. 'I think she'd been into the dining-room to see to the flowers – something like that.'

Major Riddle said:

'I hope you won't mind, Colonel Bury, if I ask you a somewhat personal question. Was there any trouble between you and Sir Gervase over the question of the Paragon Synthetic Rubber Company?'

Colonel Bury's face became suddenly purple. He spluttered a little.

'Not at all. Not at all. Old Gervase was an unreasonable sort of fellow. You've got to remember that. He always expected everything he touched to turn out trumps! Didn't seem to realize that the whole world was going through a period of crisis. All stocks and shares bound to be affected.'

'So there *was* a certain amount of trouble between you?'

'No trouble. Just damned unreasonable of Gervase!'

'He blamed you for certain losses he had sustained?'

'Gervase wasn't normal! Vanda knew that. But she could always handle him. I was content to leave it all in her hands.'

Poirot coughed and Major Riddle, after glancing at him, changed the subject.

'You are a very old friend of the family, I know, Colonel

Bury. Had you any knowledge as to how Sir Gervase had left his money?'

'Well, I should imagine the bulk of it would go to Ruth. That's what I gathered from what Gervase let fall.'

'You don't think that was at all unfair on Hugo Trent?'

'Gervase didn't like Hugo. Never could stick him.'

'But he had a great sense of family. Miss Chevenix-Gore was, after all, only his adopted daughter.'

Colonel Bury hesitated, then after humming and hawing a moment, he said:

'Look here, I think I'd better tell you something. Strict confidence, and all that.'

'Of course – of course.'

'Ruth's illegitimate, but she's a Chevenix-Gore all right. Daughter of Gervase's brother, Anthony, who was killed in the war. Seemed he'd had an affair with a typist. When he was killed, the girl wrote to Vanda. Vanda went to see her – girl was expecting a baby. Vanda took it up with Gervase, she'd just been told that she herself could never have another child. Result was they took over the child when it was born, adopted it legally. The mother renounced all rights in it. They've brought Ruth up as their own daughter and to all intents and purposes, she *is* their own daughter, and you've only got to look at her to realize she's a Chevenix-Gore all right!'

'Aha,' said Poirot. 'I see. That makes Sir Gervase's attitude very much clearer. But if he did not like Mr Hugo Trent, why was he so anxious to arrange a marriage between him and Mademoiselle Ruth?'

'To regularize the family position. It pleased his sense of fitness.'

'Even though he did not like or trust the young man?'

Colonel Bury snorted.

'You don't understand old Gervase. He couldn't regard people as human beings. He arranged alliances as though the parties were royal personages! He considered it fitting that Ruth and Hugo should marry, Hugo taking the name of Chevenix-Gore. What Hugo and Ruth thought about it didn't matter.'

'And was Mademoiselle Ruth willing to fall in with this arrangement?'

Colonel Bury chuckled.

'Not she! She's a tartar!'

'Did you know that shortly before his death Sir Gervase was drafting a new will by which Miss Chevenix-Gore would inherit only on condition that she should marry Mr Trent?'

Colonel Bury whistled.

'Then he really *had* got the wind-up about her and Burrows –'

As soon as he had spoken, he bit the words off, but it was too late. Poirot had pounced upon the admission.

'There was something between Mademoiselle Ruth and young Monsieur Burrows?'

'Probably nothing in it – nothing in it at all.'

Major Riddle coughed and said:

'I think, Colonel Bury, that you must tell us all you know. It might have a direct bearing on Sir Gervase's state of mind.'

'I suppose it might,' said Colonel Bury, doubtfully. 'Well, the truth of it is, young Burrows is not a bad-looking chap – at least, women seem to think so. He and Ruth seem to have got as thick as thieves just lately, and Gervase didn't like it – didn't like it at all. Didn't like to sack Burrows for fear of precipitating matters. He knows what Ruth's like. She won't be dictated to in any way. So I suppose he hit on this scheme. Ruth's not the sort of girl to sacrifice everything for love. She's fond of the fleshpots and she likes money.'

'Do you yourself approve of Mr Burrows?'

The colonel delivered himself of the opinion that Godfrey Burrows was slightly hairy at the heel, a pronouncement which baffled Poirot completely, but made Major Riddle smile into his moustache.

A few more questions were asked and answered, and then Colonel Bury departed.

Riddle glanced over at Poirot who was sitting absorbed in thought.

'What do you make of it all, M. Poirot?'

The little man raised his hands.

'I seem to see a pattern – a purposeful design.'

Riddle said, 'It's difficult.'

'Yes, it is difficult. But more and more one phrase, lightly uttered, strikes me as significant.'

'What was that?'

'That laughing sentence spoken by Hugo Trent: *"There's always murder"* . . .'

Riddle said sharply:

'Yes, I can see that you've been leaning that way all along.'

'Do you not agree, my friend, that the more we learn, the less and less motive we find for suicide? But for murder, we begin to have a surprising collection of motives!'

'Still, you've got to remember the facts – door locked, key in dead man's pocket. Oh, I know there are ways and means. Bent pins, strings – all sorts of devices. It would, I suppose, be *possible* . . . But do those things really work? That's what I very much doubt.'

'At all events, let us examine the position from the point of view of murder, not of suicide.'

'Oh, all right. As *you* are on the scene, it probably *would* be murder!'

For a moment Poirot smiled.

'I hardly like that remark.'

Then he became grave once more.

'Yes, let us examine the case from the standpoint of murder. The shot is heard, four people are in the hall,

Miss Lingard, Hugo Trent, Miss Cardwell and Snell. Where are all the others?'

'Burrows was in the library, according to his own story. No one to check that statement. The others were presumably in their rooms, but who is to know if they were really there? Everybody seems to have come down separately. Even Lady Chevenix-Gore and Bury only met in the hall. Lady Chevenix-Gore came from the dining-room. Where did Bury come from? Isn't it possible that he came, not from upstairs, but *from the study*? There's that pencil.'

'Yes, the pencil is interesting. He showed no emotion when I produced it, but that might be because he did not know where I found it and was unaware himself of having dropped it. Let us see, who else was playing bridge when the pencil was in use? Hugo Trent and Miss Cardwell. They're out of it. Miss Lingard and the butler can vouch for their alibis. The fourth was Lady Chevenix-Gore.'

'You can't seriously suspect her.'

'Why not, my friend? I tell you, me, I can suspect everybody! Supposing that, in spite of her apparent devotion to her husband, it is the faithful Bury she really loves?'

'H'm,' said Riddle. 'In a way it has been a kind of *ménage à trois* for years.'

'And there is some trouble about this company between Sir Gervase and Colonel Bury.'

'It's true that Sir Gervase might have been meaning to turn really nasty. We don't know the ins-and-outs of it. It might fit in with that summons to you. Say Sir Gervase suspects that Bury has deliberately fleeced him, but he doesn't want publicity because of a suspicion that his wife may be mixed up in it. Yes, that's possible. That gives either of those two a possible motive. And it *is* a bit odd really that Lady Chevenix-Gore should take her husband's death so calmly. All this spirit business may be acting!'

'Then there is the other complication,' said Poirot. 'Miss Chevenix-Gore and Burrows. It is very much to their interest that Sir Gervase should not sign the new will. As it is, she gets everything on condition that her husband takes the family name –'

'Yes, and Burrows's account of Sir Gervase's attitude this evening is a bit fishy. High spirits, pleased about something! That doesn't fit with anything else we've been told.'

'There is, too, Mr Forbes. Most correct, most severe, of an old and well-established firm. But lawyers, even the most respectable, have been known to embezzle their client's money when they themselves are in a hole.'

'You're getting a bit too sensational, I think, Poirot.'

'You think what I suggest is too like the pictures? But life, Major Riddle, is often amazingly like the pictures.'

'It has been, so far, in Westshire,' said the chief constable. 'We'd better finish interviewing the rest of them, don't you think? It's getting late. We haven't seen Ruth Chevenix-Gore yet, and she's probably the most important of the lot.'

'I agree. There is Miss Cardwell, too. Perhaps we might see her first, since that will not take long, and interview Miss Chevenix-Gore last.'

'Quite a good idea.'

Chapter 9

That evening Poirot had only given Susan Cardwell a fleeting glance. He examined her now more attentively. An intelligent face, he thought, not strictly good-looking, but possessing an attraction that a merely pretty girl might envy. Her hair was magnificent, her face skilfully made-up. Her eyes, he thought, were watchful.

After a few preliminary questions, Major Riddle said:

'I don't know how close a friend you are of the family, Miss Cardwell?'

'I don't know them at all. Hugo arranged that I should be asked down here.'

'You are, then, a friend of Hugo Trent's?'

'Yes, that's my position. Hugo's girl-friend.' Susan Cardwell smiled as she drawled out the words.

'You have known him a long time?'

'Oh, no, just a month or so.'

She paused and then added:

'I'm by way of being engaged to him.'

'And he brought you down here to introduce you to his people?'

'Oh, dear no, nothing like that. We were keeping it very hush-hush. I just came down to spy out the land. Hugo told me the place was just like a madhouse. I thought I'd better come and see for myself. Hugo, poor sweet, is a perfect pet, but he's got absolutely no brains. The position, you see, was rather critical. Neither Hugo nor I have any money, and old Sir Gervase, who was Hugo's main hope, had set his heart on Hugo making a match of it with Ruth. Hugo's a bit weak, you know. He might agree to this marriage and count on being able to get out of it later.'

'That idea did not commend itself to you, mademoiselle?' inquired Poirot gently.

'Definitely not. Ruth might have gone all peculiar and refused to divorce him or something. I put my foot down. No trotting off to St Paul's, Knightsbridge, until I could be there dithering with a sheaf of lilies.'

'So you came down to study the situation for yourself?'

'Yes.'

'*Eh bien!*' said Poirot.

'Well, of course, Hugo was right! The whole family were bughouse! Except Ruth, who seems perfectly sensible. She'd got her own boy-friend and wasn't any keener on the marriage idea than I was.'

'You refer to M. Burrows?'

'Burrows? Of course not. Ruth wouldn't fall for a bogus person like that.'

'Then who was the object of her affection?'

Susan Cardwell paused, stretched for a cigarette, lit it, and remarked:

'You'd better ask her that. After all, it isn't my business.'

Major Riddle asked:

'When was the last time you saw Sir Gervase?'

'At tea.'

'Did his manner strike you as peculiar in any way?'

The girl shrugged her shoulders.

'Not more than usual.'

'What did you do after tea?'

'Played billiards with Hugo.'

'You didn't see Sir Gervase again?'

'No.'

'What about the shot?'

'That was rather odd. You see, I thought the first gong had gone, so I hurried up with my dressing, came dashing out of my room, heard, as I thought, the second gong and fairly raced down the stairs. I'd been one minute late for dinner the first night I was here and Hugo told me it had wrecked our chances with the old man, so I fairly hared down. Hugo was just ahead of me and then there was a queer kind of pop-bang and Hugo said it was a champagne cork, but Snell said "No" to that and, anyway, I didn't think it had come from the dining-room. Miss Lingard thought it came from upstairs, but anyway we agreed it was a back-fire and we trooped into the drawing-room and forgot about it.'

'It did not occur to you for one moment that Sir Gervase might have shot himself?' asked Poirot.

'I ask you, should I be likely to think of such a thing? The Old Man seemed to enjoy himself throwing his weight about. I never imagined he'd do such a thing. I can't think why he did it. I suppose just because he was nuts.'

'An unfortunate occurrence.'

'Very – for Hugo and me. I gather he's left Hugo nothing at all, or practically nothing.'

'Who told you that?'

'Hugo got it out of old Forbes.'

'Well, Miss Cardwell –' Major Riddle paused a moment, 'I think that's all. Do you think Miss Chevenix-Gore is feeling well enough to come down and talk to us?'

'Oh, I should think so. I'll tell her.'

Poirot intervened.

'A little moment, mademoiselle. Have you seen this before?'

He held out the bullet pencil.

'Oh, yes, we had it at bridge this afternoon. Belongs to old Colonel Bury, I think.'

'Did he take it when the rubber was over?'

'I haven't the faintest idea.'

'Thank you, mademoiselle. That is all.'

'Right, I'll tell Ruth.'

Ruth Chevenix-Gore came into the room like a queen. Her colour was vivid, her head held high. But her eyes, like the eyes of Susan Cardwell, were watchful. She wore the same frock she had had on when Poirot arrived. It was a pale shade of apricot. On her shoulder was pinned a deep, salmon-pink rose. It had been fresh and blooming an hour earlier, now it drooped.

'Well?' said Ruth.

'I'm extremely sorry to bother you,' began Major Riddle.

She interrupted him.

'Of course you have to bother me. You have to bother everyone. I can save you time, though. I haven't the faintest idea why the Old Man killed himself. All I can tell you is that it wasn't a bit like him.'

'Did you notice anything amiss in his manner today? Was he depressed, or unduly excited – was there anything at all abnormal?'

'I don't think so. I wasn't noticing –'

'When did you see him last?'

'Tea-time.'

Poirot spoke:

'You did not go to the study – later?'

'No. The last I saw of him was in this room. Sitting there.' She indicated a chair.

'I see. Do you know this pencil, mademoiselle?'

'It's Colonel Bury's.'

'Have you seen it lately?'

'I don't really remember.'

'Do you know anything of a – disagreement between Sir Gervase and Colonel Bury?'

'Over the Paragon Rubber Company, you mean?'

'Yes.'

'I should think so. The Old Man was rabid about it!'

'He considered, perhaps, that he had been swindled?'

Ruth shrugged her shoulders.

'He didn't understand the first thing about finance.'

Poirot said:

'May I ask you a question, mademoiselle – a somewhat impertinent question?'

'Certainly, if you like.'

'It is this – are you sorry that your – father is dead?'

She stared at him.

'Of course I'm sorry. I don't indulge in sob-stuff. But I shall miss him . . . I was fond of the Old Man. That's what we called him, Hugo and I, always. The "Old Man" – you know – something of the primitive – anthropoid-ape-original-Patriarch-of-the-tribe business. It sounds disrespectful, but there's really a lot of affection behind it. Of course, he was really the most complete, muddle-headed old ass that ever lived!'

165

'You interest me, mademoiselle.'

'The Old Man had the brains of a louse! Sorry to have to say it, but it's true. He was incapable of any kind of headwork. Mind you, he was a character. Fantastically brave and all that! Could go careering off to the Pole, or fighting duels. I always think that he blustered such a lot because he really knew that his brains weren't up to much. Anyone could have got the better of him.'

Poirot took the letter from his pocket.

'Read this, mademoiselle.'

She read it through and handed it back to him.

'So that's what brought you here!'

'Does it suggest anything to you, that letter?'

She shook her head.

'No. It's probably quite true. Anyone could have robbed the poor old pet. John says the last agent before him swindled him right and left. You see, the Old Man was so grand and so pompous that he never really condescended to look into details! He was an invitation to crooks.'

'You paint a different picture of him, mademoiselle, from the accepted one.'

'Oh, well – he put up a pretty good camouflage. Vanda (my mother) backed him for all she was worth. He was so happy stalking round pretending he was God Almighty. That's why, in a way, I'm glad he's dead. It's the best thing for him.'

'I do not quite follow you, mademoiselle.'

Ruth said broodingly:

'It was growing on him. One of these days he would have had to be locked up . . . People were beginning to talk as it was.'

'Did you know, mademoiselle, that he was contemplating a will whereby you could only inherit his money if you married Mr Trent?'

She cried:

'How absurd! Anyway, I'm sure that could be set aside by law . . . I'm sure you can't dictate to people about whom they shall marry.'

'If he had actually signed such a will, would you have complied with its provisions, mademoiselle?'

She stared.

'I – I –'

She broke off. For two or three minutes she sat irresolute, looking down at her dangling slipper. A little piece of earth detached itself from the heel and fell on the carpet.

Suddenly Ruth Chevenix-Gore said:

'Wait!'

She got up and ran out of the room. She returned almost immediately with Captain Lake by her side.

'It's got to come out,' she said rather breathlessly. 'You might as well know now. John and I were married in London three weeks ago.'

Chapter 10

Of the two of them, Captain Lake looked far the more embarrassed.

'This is a great surprise, Miss Chevenix-Gore – Mrs Lake, I should say,' said Major Riddle. 'Did no one know of this marriage of yours?'

'No, we kept it quite dark. John didn't like that part of it much.'

Lake said, stammering a little:

'I – I know that it seems rather a rotten way to set about things. I ought to have gone straight to Sir Gervase –'

Ruth interrupted:

'And told him you wanted to marry his daughter, and have been kicked out on your head and he'd probably have disinherited me, raised hell generally in the house, and we could have told each other how beautifully we'd behaved! Believe me, my way was better! If a thing's done, it's done. There would still have been a row – but he'd have come round.'

Lake still looked unhappy. Poirot asked:

'When did you intend to break the news to Sir Gervase?'

Ruth answered:

'I was preparing the ground. He'd been rather suspicious about me and John, so I pretended to turn my attentions to Godfrey. Naturally, he was ready to go quite off the deep-end about that. I figured it out that the news I was married to John would come almost as a relief!'

'Did anybody at all know of this marriage?'

'Yes, I told Vanda in the end. I wanted to get her on my side.'

'And you succeeded in doing so?'

'Yes. You see, she wasn't very keen about my marrying Hugo – because he was a cousin, I think. She seemed to think the family was so batty already that we'd probably have completely batty children. That was probably rather absurd, because I'm only adopted, you know. I believe I'm some quite distant cousin's child.'

'You are sure Sir Gervase had no suspicion of the truth?'

'Oh, no.'

Poirot said:

'Is that true, Captain Lake? In your interview with Sir Gervase this afternoon, are you quite sure the matter was not mentioned?'

'No, sir. It was not.'

'Because, you see, Captain Lake, there is certain evidence to show that Sir Gervase was in a highly-excitable condition after the time he spent with you, and that he spoke once or twice of family dishonour.'

'The matter was not mentioned,' Lake repeated. His face had gone very white.

'Was that the last time you saw Sir Gervase?'

'Yes, I have already told you so.'

'Where were you at eight minutes past eight this evening?'

'Where was I? In my house. At the end of the village, about half a mile away.'

'You did not come up to Hamborough Close round about that time?'

'No.'

Poirot turned to the girl.

'Where were you, mademoiselle, when your father shot himself?'

'In the garden.'

'In the garden? You heard the shot?'

'Oh, yes. But I didn't think about it particularly. I thought it was someone out shooting rabbits, although now I remember I did think it sounded quite close at hand.'

'You returned to the house – which way?'

'I came in through this window.'

Ruth indicated with a turn of her head the window behind her.

'Was anyone in here?'

'No. But Hugo and Susan and Miss Lingard came in from the hall almost immediately. They were talking about shooting and murders and things.'

'I see,' said Poirot. 'Yes, I think I see now . . .'

Major Riddle said rather doubtfully:

'Well – er – thank you. I think that's all for the moment.'

Ruth and her husband turned and left the room.

'What the devil –' began Major Riddle, and ended rather hopelessly: 'It gets more and more difficult to keep track of this business.'

Poirot nodded. He had picked up the little piece of earth that had fallen from Ruth's shoe and was holding it thoughtfully in his hand.

'It is like the mirror smashed on the wall,' he said. 'The

dead man's mirror. Every new fact we come across shows us some different angle of the dead man. He is reflected from every conceivable point of view. We shall have soon a complete picture . . .'

He rose and put the little piece of earth tidily in the waste-paper basket.

'I will tell you one thing, my friend. The clue to the whole mystery is the mirror. Go into the study and look for yourself, if you do not believe me.'

Major Riddle said decisively:

'If it's murder, it's up to you to prove it. If you ask me, I say it's definitely suicide. Did you notice what the girl said about a former agent having swindled old Gervase? I bet Lake told that tale for his own purposes. He was probably helping himself a bit, Sir Gervase suspected it, and sent for you because he didn't know how far things had gone between Lake and Ruth. Then this afternoon Lake told him they were married. That broke Gervase up. It was "too late" now for anything to be done. He determined to get out of it all. In fact his brain, never very well balanced at the best of times, gave way. In my opinion that's what happened. What have you got to say against it?'

Poirot stood still in the middle of the room.

'What have I to say? This: I have nothing to say against your theory — but it does not go far enough. There are certain things it does not take into account.'

'Such as?'

'The discrepancies in Sir Gervase's moods today, the finding of Colonel Bury's pencil, the evidence of Miss Cardwell (which is very important), the evidence of Miss Lingard as to the order in which people came down to dinner, the position of Sir Gervase's chair when he was found, the paper bag which had held oranges and, finally, the all-important clue of the broken mirror.'

Major Riddle stared.

'Are you going to tell me that that rigmarole makes *sense*?' he asked.

'Hercule Poirot replied softly:

'I hope to make it do so – by tomorrow.'

Chapter 11

It was just after dawn when Hercule Poirot awoke on the following morning. He had been given a bedroom on the east side of the house.

Getting out of bed, he drew aside the window-blind and satisfied himself that the sun had risen, and that it was a fine morning.

He began to dress with his usual meticulous care. Having finished his toilet, he wrapped himself up in a thick overcoat and wound a muffler round his neck.

Then he tiptoed out of his room and through the silent house down to the drawing-room. He opened the french windows noiselessly and passed out into the garden.

The sun was just showing now. The air was misty, with the mist of a fine morning. Hercule Poirot followed the terraced walk round the side of the house till he came to the windows of Sir Gervase's study. Here he stopped and surveyed the scene.

Immediately outside the windows was a strip of grass that ran parallel with the house. In front of that was a wide herbaceous border. The michaelmas daisies still made a fine show. In front of the border was the flagged walk where Poirot was standing. A strip of grass ran from the grass walk behind the border to the terrace. Poirot examined it carefully, then shook his head. He turned his atention to the border on either side of it.

Very slowly he nodded his head. In the right-hand bed, distinct in the soft mould, there were footprints.

As he stared down at them, frowning, a sound caught his ears and he lifted his head sharply.

Above him a window had been pushed up. He saw a red head of hair. Framed in an aureole of golden red he saw the intelligent face of Susan Cardwell.

'What on earth are you doing at this hour, M. Poirot? A spot of sleuthing?'

Poirot bowed with the utmost correctitude.

'Good morning, mademoiselle. Yes, it is as you say. You now behold a detective – a great detective, I may say – in the act of detecting!'

The remark was a little flamboyant. Susan put her head on one side.

'I must remember this in my memoirs,' she remarked. 'Shall I come down and help?'

'I should be enchanted.'

'I thought you were a burglar at first. Which way did you get out?'

'Through the drawing-room window.'

'Just a minute and I'll be with you.'

She was as good as her word. To all appearances Poirot was exactly in the same position as when she had first seen him.

'You are awake very early, mademoiselle?'

'I haven't been to sleep really properly. I was just getting that desperate feeling that one does get at five in the morning.'

'It's not quite so early as that!'

'It feels like it! Now then, my super-sleuth, what are we looking at?'

'But observe, mademoiselle, footprints.'

'So they are.'

'Four of them,' continued Poirot. 'See, I will point them out to you. Two going towards the window, two coming from it.'

'Whose are they? The gardener's?'

'Mademoiselle, mademoiselle! Those footmarks are made by the small dainty high-heeled shoes of a woman. See, convince yourself. Step, I beg of you, in the earth here beside them.'

Susan hesitated a minute, then placed a foot gingerly on to the mould in the place indicated by Poirot. She was wearing small high-heeled slippers of dark brown leather.

'You see, yours are nearly the same size. Nearly, but not quite. These others are made by a rather longer foot than yours. Perhaps Miss Chevenix-Gore's – or Miss Lingard's – or even Lady Chevenix-Gore's.'

'Not Lady Chevenix-Gore – she's got tiny feet. People did in those days – manage to have small feet, I mean. And Miss Lingard wears queer flat-heeled things.'

'Then they are the marks of Miss Chevenix-Gore. Ah, yes, I remember she mentioned having been out in the garden yesterday evening.'

He led the way back round the house.

'Are we still sleuthing?' asked Susan.

'But certainly. We will go now to Sir Gervase's study.'

He led the way. Susan Cardwell followed him.

The door still hung in a melancholy fashion. Inside, the room was as it had been last night. Poirot pulled the curtains and admitted the daylight.

He stood looking out at the border a minute or two, then he said:

'You have not, I presume, mademoiselle, much acquaintance with burglars?'

Susan Cardwell shook her red head regretfully.

'I'm afraid not, M. Poirot.'

'The chief constable, he, too, has not had the advantages of a friendly relationship with them. His connection with the criminal classes has always been strictly official. With me that is not so. I had a very pleasant chat with a burglar once. He told me an interesting thing about french

windows – a trick that could sometimes be employed if
the fastening was sufficiently loose.'

He turned the handle of the left-hand window as he
spoke, the middle shaft came up out of the hole in the
ground, and Poirot was able to pull the two doors of the
window towards him. Having opened them wide, he closed
them again – closed them without turning the handle, so
as not to send the shaft down into its socket. He let go
of the handle, waited a moment, then struck a quick,
jarring blow high up on the centre of the shaft. The jar
of the blow sent the shaft down into the socket in the
ground – the handle turned of its own accord.

'You see, mademoiselle?'

'I think I do.'

Susan had gone rather pale.

'The window is now closed. It is impossible to *enter* a
room when the window is closed, but it *is* possible to *leave*
a room, pull the doors to from outside, then hit it as I did,
and the bolt goes down into the ground, turning the
handle. The window then is firmly closed, and anyone
looking at it would say it had been closed from the *inside*.'

'Is that' – Susan's voice shook a little – 'is that what
happened last night?'

'I think so, yes, mademoiselle.'

Susan said violently:

'I don't believe a word of it.'

Poirot did not answer. He walked over to the
mantelpiece. He wheeled sharply round.

'Mademoiselle, I have need of you as a witness. I have
already one witness, Mr Trent. He saw me find this tiny
sliver of looking-glass last night. I spoke of it to him. I
left it where it was for the police. I even told the chief
constable that a valuable clue was the broken mirror. But
he did not avail himself of my hint. Now you are a witness
that I place this sliver of looking-glass (to which,
remember, I have already called Mr Trent's attention) into

a little envelope – so.' He suited the action to the word. 'And I write on it – so – and seal it up. You are a witness, mademoiselle?'

'Yes – but – but I don't know what it means.'

Poirot walked over to the other side of the room. He stood in front of the desk and stared at the shattered mirror on the wall in front of him.

'I will tell you what it means, mademoiselle. If you had been standing here last night, looking into this mirror, you could have seen in it *murder being committed . . .*'

Chapter 12

For once in her life Ruth Chevenix-Gore – now Ruth Lake – came down to breakfast in good time. Hercule Poirot was in the hall and drew her aside before she went into the dining-room.

'I have a question to ask you, madame.'

'Yes?'

'You were in the garden last night. Did you at any time step in the flower-bed outside Sir Gervase's study window?'

Ruth stared at him.

'Yes, twice.'

'Ah! *Twice.* How twice?'

'The first time I was picking michaelmas daisies. That was about seven o'clock.'

'Was it not rather an odd time of day to pick flowers?'

'Yes, it was, as a matter of fact. I'd done the flowers yesterday morning, but Vanda said after tea that the flowers on the dinner-table weren't good enough. I had thought they would be all right, so I hadn't done them fresh.'

'But your mother requested you to do them? Is that right?'

'Yes. So I went out just before seven. I took them from that part of the border because hardly anyone goes round there, and so it didn't matter spoiling the effect.'

'Yes, yes, but the *second* time. You went there a *second* time, you said?'

'That was just before dinner. I had dropped a spot of brilliantine on my dress – just by the shoulder. I didn't want to bother to change, and none of my artificial flowers went with the yellow of that dress. I remembered I'd seen a late rose when I was picking the michaelmas daisies, so I hurried out and got it and pinned it on my shoulder.'

Poirot nodded his head slowly.

'Yes, I remember that you wore a rose last night. What time was it, madame, when you picked that rose?'

'I don't really know.'

'But it is *essential*, madame. Consider – reflect.'

Ruth frowned. She looked swiftly at Poirot and then away again.

'I can't say exactly,' she said at last. 'It must have been – oh, of course – it must have been about five minutes past eight. It was when I was on my way back round the house that I heard the gong go, and then that funny bang. I was hurrying because I thought it was the second gong and not the first.'

'Ah, so you thought that – and did you not try the study window when you stood there in the flower-bed?'

'As a matter of fact, I did. I thought it might be open, and it would be quicker to come in that way. But it was fastened.'

'So everything is explained. I congratulate you, madame.'

She stared at him.

'What do you mean?'

'That you have an explanation for everything, for the mould on your shoes, for your footprints in the flower-bed, for your fingerprints on the outside of the window. It is very convenient that.'

Before Ruth could answer, Miss Lingard came hurrying down the stairs. There was a queer purple flush on her cheeks, and she looked a little startled at seeing Poirot and Ruth standing together.

'I beg your pardon,' she said. 'Is anything the matter?'

Ruth said angrily:

'I think M. Poirot has gone mad!'

She swept by them and into the dining-room. Miss Lingard turned an astonished face on Poirot.

He shook his head.

'After breakfast,' he said. 'I will explain. I should like everyone to assemble in Sir Gervase's study at ten o'clock.'

He repeated this request on entering the dining-room.

Susan Cardwell gave him a quick glance, then transferred her gaze to Ruth. When Hugo said:

'Eh? What's the idea?' she gave him a sharp nudge in the side, and he shut up obediently.

When he had finished his breakfast, Poirot rose and walked to the door. He turned and drew out a large old-fashioned watch.

'It is five minutes to ten. In five minutes – in the study.'

Poirot looked round him. A circle of interested faces stared back at him. Everyone was there, he noted, with one exception, and at that very moment the exception swept into the room. Lady Chevenix-Gore came in with a soft, gliding step. She looked haggard and ill.

Poirot drew forward a big chair for her, and she sat down.

She looked up at the broken mirror, shivered, and pulled her chair a little way round.

'Gervase is still here,' she remarked in a matter-of-fact tone. 'Poor Gervase . . . He will soon be free now.'

Poirot cleared his throat and announced:

'I have asked you all to come here so that you may hear the true facts of Sir Gervase's suicide.'

'It was Fate,' said Lady Chevenix-Gore. 'Gervase was strong, but his Fate was stronger.'

Colonel Bury moved forward a little.

'Vanda – my dear.'

She smiled up at him, then put up her hand. He took it in his. She said softly: 'You are such a comfort, Ned.'

Ruth said sharply:

'Are we to understand, M. Poirot, that you have definitely ascertained the cause of my father's suicide?'

Poirot shook his head.

'No, madame.'

'Then what is all this rigmarole about?'

Poirot said quietly:

'I do not know the cause of Sir Gervase Chevenix-Gore's suicide, *because Sir Gervase Chevenix-Gore did not commit suicide*. He did not kill himself. *He was killed . . .*'

'Killed?' Several voices echoed the word. Startled faces were turned in Poirot's direction. Lady Chevenix-Gore looked up, said, 'Killed? Oh, no!' and gently shook her head.

'Killed, did you say?' It was Hugo who spoke now. 'Impossible. There was no one in the room when we broke in. The window was fastened. The door was locked on the inside, and the key was in my uncle's pocket. How could he have been killed?'

'Nevertheless, he was killed.'

'And the murderer escaped through the keyhole, I suppose?' said Colonel Bury sceptically. 'Or flew up the chimney?'

'The murderer,' said Poirot, 'went out through the window. I will show you how.'

He repeated his manoeuvres with the window.

'You see?' he said. 'That was how it was done! From the first I could not consider it likely that Sir Gervase had committed suicide. He had pronounced egomania, and such a man does not kill himself.

'And there were other things! Apparently, just before his death, Sir Gervase had sat down at his desk, scrawled the word *SORRY* on a sheet of note-paper and had then shot himself. But before this last action he had, for some reason or other, altered the position of his chair, turning it so that it was sideways to the desk. Why? There must be some reason. I began to see light when I found, sticking to the base of a heavy bronze statuette, a tiny sliver of looking-glass . . .

'I asked myself, how does a sliver of broken looking-glass come to be there? – and an answer suggested itself to me. The mirror had been broken, not by a bullet, *but by being struck with the heavy bronze figure*. That mirror had been broken *deliberately*.

'But why? I returned to the desk and looked down at the chair. Yes, I saw now. It was all wrong. No suicide would turn his chair round, lean over the edge of it, and then shoot himself. The whole thing was arranged. The suicide was a fake!

'And now I come to something very important. The evidence of Miss Cardwell. Miss Cardwell said that she hurried downstairs last night because she thought that the *second* gong had sounded. That is to say, she thought that she had already heard the *first* gong.

'Now observe, *if* Sir Gervase was sitting at his desk in the normal fashion when he was shot, where would the bullet go? Travelling in a straight line, it would pass through the door, if the door were open, and finally *hit the gong*!

'You see now the importance of Miss Cardwell's statement? No one else heard the first gong, but, then, her room is situated immediately above this one, and she was in the best position for hearing it. It would consist of only one single note, remember.

'There could be no question of Sir Gervase's shooting himself. A dead man cannot get up, shut the door, lock

179

it and arrange himself in a convenient position! Somebody
else was concerned, and therefore it was not suicide, but
murder. Someone whose presence was easily accepted by
Sir Gervase, stood by his side talking to him. Sir Gervase
was busy writing, perhaps. The murderer brings the pistol
up to the right side of his head and fires. The deed is done!
Then quick, to work! The murderer slips on gloves. The
door is locked, the key put in Sir Gervase's pocket. But
supposing that one loud note of the gong has been heard?
Then it will be realized that the door was *open*, not *shut*,
when the shot was fired. So the chair is turned, the body
rearranged, the dead man's fingers pressed on the pistol,
the mirror deliberately smashed. Then the murderer goes
out through the window, jars it shut, steps, not on the
grass, but in the flower-bed where footprints can be
smoothed out afterwards; then round the side of the house
and into the drawing-room.'

He paused and said:

'*There was only one person who was out in the garden when
the shot was fired.* That same person left her footprints in
the flower-bed and her fingerprints on the outside of the
window.'

He came towards Ruth.

'And there was a motive, wasn't there? Your father had
learnt of your secret marriage. He was preparing to
disinherit you.'

'It's a lie!' Ruth's voice came scornful and clear.
'There's not a word of truth in your story. It's a lie from
start to finish!'

'The proofs against you are very strong, madame. A jury
may believe you. It may *not*!'

'She won't have to face a jury.'

The others turned – startled. Miss Lingard was on her
feet. Her face altered. She was trembling all over.

'*I* shot him. I admit it! I had my reason. I – I've been
waiting for some time. M. Poirot is quite right. I followed

him in here. I had taken the pistol out of the drawer earlier.
I stood beside him talking about the book – and I shot
him. That was just after eight. The bullet struck the gong.
I never dreamt it would pass right through his head like
that. There wasn't time to go out and look for it. I locked
the door and put the key in his pocket. Then I swung the
chair round, smashed the mirror, and, after scrawling
'Sorry' on a piece of paper, I went out through the window
and shut it the way M. Poirot showed you. I stepped in
the flower-bed, but I smoothed out the footprints with a
little rake I had put there ready. Then I went round to
the drawing-room. I had left the window open. I didn't
know Ruth had gone out through it. She must have come
round the front of the house while I went round the back.
I had to put the rake away, you see, in a shed. I waited
in the drawing-room till I heard someone coming
downstairs and Snell going to the gong, and then –'

She looked at Poirot.

'You don't know what I did then?'

'Oh yes, I do. I found the bag in the wastepaper basket.
It was very clever, that idea of yours. You did what
children love to do. You blew up the bag and then hit it.
It made a satisfactory big bang. You threw the bag into
the wastepaper basket and rushed out into the hall. You
had established the time of the suicide – and an alibi for
yourself. But there was still one thing that worried you.
You had not had time to pick up the bullet. It must be
somewhere near the gong. It was essential that the bullet
should be found in the study somewhere near the mirror.
I didn't know when you had the idea of taking Colonel
Bury's pencil –'

'It was just then,' said Miss Lingard. 'When we all came
in from the hall. I was surprised to see Ruth in the room.
I realized she must have come from the garden through
the window. Then I noticed Colonel Bury's pencil lying
on the bridge table. I slipped it into my bag. If, later,

anyone saw me pick up the bullet, I could pretend it was the pencil. As a matter of fact, I didn't think anyone saw me pick up the bullet. I dropped it by the mirror while you were looking at the body. When you tackled me on the subject, I was very glad I had thought of the pencil.'

'Yes, that was clever. It confused me completely.'

'I was afraid someone must hear the real shot, but I knew everyone was dressing for dinner, and would be shut away in their rooms. The servants were in their quarters. Miss Cardwell was the only one at all likely to hear it, and she would probably think it was a backfire. What she did hear was the gong. I thought – I thought everything had gone without a hitch . . .'

Mr Forbes said slowly in his precise tones:

'This is a most extraordinary story. There seems no motive –'

Miss Lingard said clearly: 'There *was* a motive . . .'

She added fiercely:

'Go on, ring up the police! What are you waiting for?'

Poirot said gently:

'Will you all please leave the room? Mr Forbes, ring up Major Riddle. I will stay here till he comes.'

Slowly, one by one, the family filed out of the room. Puzzled, uncomprehending, shocked, they cast abashed glances at the trim, upright figure with its neatly-parted grey hair.

Ruth was the last to go. She stood, hesitating in the doorway.

'I don't understand.' She spoke angrily, defiantly, accusing Poirot. 'Just now, you thought *I* had done it.'

'No, no,' Poirot shook his head. 'No, I never thought that.'

Ruth went out slowly.

Poirot was left with the little middle-aged prim woman who had just confessed to a cleverly-planned and cold-blooded murder.

'No,' said Miss Lingard. 'You didn't think she had done it. You accused *her* to make *me* speak. That's right, isn't it?'

Poirot bowed his head.

'While we're waiting,' said Miss Lingard in a conversational tone, 'you might tell me what made you suspect *me*.'

'Several things. To begin with, your account of Sir Gervase. A proud man like Sir Gervase would never speak disparagingly of his nephew to an outsider, especially someone in your position. You wanted to strengthen the theory of suicide. You also went out of your way to suggest that the cause of the suicide was some dishonourable trouble connected with Hugo Trent. That, again, was a thing Sir Gervase would never have admitted to a stranger. Then there was the object you picked up in the hall, and the very significant fact that you did not mention that Ruth, when she entered the drawing-room, did so *from the garden*. And then I found the paper bag – a most unlikely object to find in the wastepaper basket in the drawing-room of a house like Hamborough Close! You were the only person who had been in the drawing-room when the ''shot'' was heard. The paper bag trick was one that would suggest itself to a woman – an ingenious home-made device. So everything fitted in. The endeavour to throw suspicion on Hugo, and to keep it away from Ruth. The mechanism of crime – and its motive.'

The little grey-haired woman stirred.

'You know the motive?'

'I think so. Ruth's happiness – that was the motive! I fancy that you had seen her with John Lake – you knew how it was with them. And then with your easy access to Sir Gervase's papers, you came across the draft of his new will – Ruth disinherited unless she married Hugo Trent. That decided you to take the law into your own hands, using the fact that Sir Gervase had previously written to me. You probably saw a copy of that letter. What muddled feeling of suspicion and fear had caused him to write originally, I do not know. He must have suspected either Burrows or Lake of systematically robbing him. His uncertainty regarding Ruth's feelings made him seek a private investigation. You used that fact and deliberately set the stage for suicide, backing it up by your account of his being very distressed over something connected with Hugo Trent. You sent a telegram to me and reported Sir Gervase as having said I should arrive "too late." '

Miss Lingard said fiercely:

'Gervase Chevenix-Gore was a bully, a snob and a windbag! I wasn't going to have him ruin Ruth's happiness.'

Poirot said gently:

'Ruth is your daughter?'

'Yes – she is my daughter – I've often – thought about her. When I heard Sir Gervase Chevenix-Gore wanted someone to help him with a family history, I jumped at the chance. I was curious to see my – my girl. I knew Lady Chevenix-Gore wouldn't recognize me. It was years ago – I was young and pretty then, and I changed my name after that time. Besides Lady Chevenix-Gore is too vague to know anything definitely. I liked her, but I hated the Chevenix-Gore family. They treated me like dirt. And here was Gervase going to ruin Ruth's life with pride and snobbery. But I determined that she should be happy. And she *will* be happy – *if she never knows about me*!'

It was a plea – not a question.

Poirot bent his head gently.

'No one shall know from me.'

Miss Lingard said quietly:

'Thank you.'

Later, when the police had come and gone, Poirot found Ruth Lake with her husband in the garden.

She said challengingly:

'Did you really think that I had done it, M. Poirot?'

'I knew, madame, that you could *not* have done it – because of the michaelmas daisies.'

'The michaelmas daisies? I don't understand.'

'Madame, there were four footprints and four footprints *only* in the border. But if you had been picking flowers there would have been many more. That meant that between your first visit and your second, *someone had smoothed all those footsteps away.* That could only have been done by the guilty person, and since your footprints had *not* been removed, you were *not* the guilty person. You were automatically cleared.'

Ruth's face lightened.

'Oh, I see. You know – I suppose it's dreadful, but I feel rather sorry for that poor woman. After all, she did confess rather than let me be arrested – or at any rate, that is what she thought. That was – rather noble in a way. I hate to think of her going through a trial for murder.'

Poirot said gently:

'Do not distress yourself. It will not come to that. The doctor, he tells me that she has serious heart trouble. She will not live many weeks.'

'I'm glad of that.' Ruth picked an autumn crocus and pressed it idly against her cheek.

'Poor woman. I wonder why she did it . . .'

THE UNDER DOG

Lily Margrave smoothed her gloves out on her knee with a nervous gesture, and darted a glance at the occupant of the big chair opposite her.

She had heard of M. Hercule Poirot, the well-known investigator, but this was the first time she had seen him in the flesh.

The comic, almost ridiculous, aspect that he presented disturbed her conception of him. Could this funny little man, with the egg-shaped head and the enormous moustaches, really do the wonderful things that were claimed for him? His occupation at the moment struck her as particularly childish. He was piling small blocks of coloured wood one upon the other, and seemed far more interested in the result than in the story she was telling.

At her sudden silence, however, he looked sharply across at her.

'Mademoiselle, continue, I pray of you. It is not that I do not attend; I attend very carefully, I assure you.'

He began once more to pile the little blocks of wood one upon the other, while the girl's voice took up the tale again. It was a gruesome tale, a tale of violence and tragedy, but the voice was so calm and unemotional, the recital was so concise that something of the savour of humanity seemed to have been left out of it.

She stopped at last.

'I hope,' she said anxiously, 'that I have made everything clear.'

Poirot nodded his head several times in emphatic assent.

Then he swept his hand across the wooden blocks, scattering them over the table, and, leaning back in his chair, his fingertips pressed together and his eyes on the ceiling, he began to recapitulate.

'Sir Reuben Astwell was murdered ten days ago. On Wednesday, the day before yesterday, his nephew, Charles Leverson, was arrested by the police. The facts against him as far as you know are: – you will correct me if I am wrong, Mademoiselle – Sir Reuben was sitting up late writing in his own special sanctum, the Tower room. Mr Leverson came in late, letting himself in with a latch-key. He was overheard quarrelling with his uncle by the butler, whose room is directly below the Tower room. The quarrel ended with a sudden thud as of a chair being thrown over and a half-smothered cry.

'The butler was alarmed, and thought of getting up to see what was the matter, but as a few seconds later he heard Mr Leverson leave the room gaily whistling a tune, he thought nothing more of it. On the following morning, however, a housemaid discovered Sir Reuben dead by his desk. He had been struck down by some heavy instrument. The butler, I gather, did not at once tell his story to the police. That was natural, I think, eh, Mademoiselle?'

The sudden question made Lily Margrave start.

'I beg your pardon?' she said.

'One looks for humanity in these matters, does one not?' said the little man. 'As you recited the story to me – so admirably, so concisely – you made of the actors in the drama machines – puppets. But me, I look always for human nature. I say to myself, this butler, this – what did you say his name was?'

'His name is Parsons.'

'This Parsons, then, he will have the characteristics of his class, he will object very strongly to the police, he will tell them as little as possible. Above all, he will say nothing that might seem to incriminate a member of the household. A house-breaker, a burglar, he will cling to that idea with all the strength of extreme obstinacy. Yes, the loyalties of the servant class are an interesting study.'

He leaned back beaming.

'In the meantime,' he went on, 'everyone in the household has told his or her tale, Mr Leverson among the rest, and his tale was that he had come in late and gone up to bed without seeing his uncle.'

'That is what he said.'

'And no one saw reason to doubt that tale,' mused Poirot, 'except, of course, Parsons. Then there comes down an inspector from Scotland Yard, Inspector Miller you said, did you not? I know him, I have come across him once or twice in the past. He is what they call the sharp man, the ferret, the weasel.

'Yes, I know him! And the sharp Inspector Miller, he sees what the local inspector has not seen, that Parsons is ill at ease and uncomfortable, and knows something that he has not told. *Eh bien*, he makes short work of Parsons. By now it has been clearly proved that no one broke into the house that night, that the murderer must be looked for inside the house and not outside. And Parsons is unhappy and frightened, and feels very relieved to have his secret knowledge drawn out of him.

'He has done his best to avoid scandal, but there are limits; and so Inspector Miller listens to Parsons's story, and asks a question or two, and then makes some private investigations of his own. The case he builds up is very strong – very strong.

'Blood-stained fingers rested on the corner of the chest in the Tower room, and the fingerprints were those of Charles Leverson. The housemaid told him she emptied a basin of blood-stained water in Mr Leverson's room the morning after the crime. He explained to her that he had cut his finger, and he *had* a little cut there, oh yes, but such a very little cut! The cuff of his evening shirt had been washed, but they found blood-stains in the sleeve of his coat. He was hard pressed for money, and he inherited money at Sir Reuben's death. Oh, yes, a very strong case, Mademoiselle.' He paused.

'And yet you come to me today.'

Lily Margrave shrugged her slender shoulders.

'As I told you, M. Poirot, Lady Astwell sent me.'

'You would not have come of your own accord, eh?'

The little man glanced at her shrewdly. The girl did not answer.

'You do not reply to my question.'

Lily Margrave began smoothing her gloves again.

'It is rather difficult for me, M. Poirot. I have my loyalty to Lady Astwell to consider. Strictly speaking, I am only her paid companion, but she has treated me more as though I were a daughter or a niece. She has been extraordinarily kind and, whatever her faults, I should not like to appear to criticize her actions, or – well, to prejudice you against taking up the case.'

'Impossible to prejudice Hercule Poirot, *cela ne ce fait pas*,' declared the little man cheerily. 'I perceive that you think Lady Astwell has in her bonnet the buzzing bee. Come now, is it not so?'

'If I must say – '

'Speak, Mademoiselle.'

'I think the whole thing is simply silly.'

'It strikes you like that, eh?'

'I don't want to say anything against Lady Astwell – '

'I comprehend,' murmured Poirot gently. 'I comprehend perfectly.' His eyes invited her to go on.

'She really is a very good sort, and frightfully kind, but she isn't – how can I put it? She isn't an educated woman. You know she was an actress when Sir Reuben married her, and she has all sorts of prejudices and superstitions. If she says a thing, it must be so, and she simply won't

189

listen to reason. The inspector was not very tactful with her, and it put her back up. She says it is nonsense to suspect Mr Leverson and just the sort of stupid, pig-headed mistake the police would make, and that, of course, dear Charles did not do it.'

'But she has no reasons, eh?'

'None whatever.'

'Ha! Is that so? Really, now.'

'I told her,' said Lily, 'that it would be no good coming to you with a mere statement like that and nothing to go on.'

'You told her that,' said Poirot, 'did you really? That is interesting.'

His eyes swept over Lily Margrave in a quick comprehensive survey, taking in the details of her neat black suit, the touch of white at her throat and the smart little black hat. He saw the elegance of her, the pretty face with its slightly pointed chin, and the dark-blue, long-lashed eyes. Insensibly his attitude changed; he was interested now, not so much in the case as in the girl sitting opposite him.

'Lady Astwell is, I should imagine, Mademoiselle, just a trifle inclined to be unbalanced and hysterical?'

Lily Margrave nodded eagerly.

'That describes her exactly. She is, as I told you, very kind, but it is impossible to argue with her or to make her see things logically.'

'Possibly she suspects someone on her own account,' suggested Poirot, 'someone quite absurd.'

'That is exactly what she does do,' cried Lily. 'She has taken a great dislike to Sir Reuben's secretary, poor man. She says she *knows* he did it, and yet it has been proved quite conclusively that poor Owen Trefusis cannot possibly have done it.'

'And she has no reasons?'

'Of course not; it is all intuition with her.'

Lily Margrave's voice was very scornful.

'I perceive, Mademoiselle,' said Poirot, smiling, 'that you do not believe in intuition?'

'I think it is nonsense,' replied Lily.

Poirot leaned back in his chair.

'*Les femmes*,' he murmured, 'they like to think that it is a special weapon the the good God has given them, and for every once that it shows them the truth, at least nine times it leads them astray.'

'I know,' said Lily, 'but I have told you what Lady Astwell is like. You simply cannot argue with her.'

'So you, Mademoiselle, being wise and discreet, came along to me as you were bidden, and have managed to put me *au courant* of the situation.'

Something in the tone of his voice made the girl look up sharply.

'Of course, I know,' said Lily apologetically, 'how very valuable your time is.'

'You are too flattering, Mademoiselle,' said Poirot, 'but indeed – yes, it is true, at this present time I have many cases of moment on hand.'

'I was afraid that might be so,' said Lily, rising. 'I will tell Lady Astwell – '

But Poirot did not rise also. Instead he lay back in his chair and looked steadily up at the girl.

'You are in haste to be gone, Mademoiselle? Sit down one more little moment, I pray of you.'

He saw the colour flood into her face and ebb out again. She sat down once more slowly and unwillingly.

'Mademoiselle is quick and decisive,' said Poirot. 'She must make allowances for an old man like myself, who comes to his decisions slowly. You mistook me, Mademoiselle. I did not say that I would not go down to Lady Astwell.'

'You will come, then?'

The girl's tone was flat. She did not look at Poirot, but

191

down at the ground, and so was unaware of the keen scrutiny with which he regarded her.

'Tell Lady Astwell, Mademoiselle, that I am entirely at her service. I will be at – Mon Repos, is it not? – this afternoon.'

He rose. The girl followed suit.

'I – I will tell her. It is very good of you to come, M. Poirot. I am afraid, though, you will find you have been brought on a wild goose chase.'

'Very likely, but – who knows?'

He saw her out with punctilious courtesy to the door. Then he returned to the sitting-room, frowning, deep in thought. Once or twice he nodded his head, then he opened the door and called to his valet.

'My good George, prepare me, I pray of you, a little valise. I go down to the country this afternoon.'

'Very good, sir,' said George.

He was an extremely English-looking person. Tall, cadaverous and unemotional.

'A young girl is a very interesting phenomenon, George,' said Poirot, as he dropped once more into his arm-chair and lighted a tiny cigarette. 'Especially, you understand, when she has brains. To ask someone to do a thing and at the same time to put them against doing it, that is a delicate operation. It requires finesse. She was very adroit – oh, very adroit – but Hercule Poirot, my good George, is of a cleverness quite exceptional.'

'I have heard you say so, sir.'

'It is not the secretary she has in mind,' mused Poirot. 'Lady Astwell's accusation of him she treats with contempt. Just the same she is anxious that no one should disturb the sleeping dogs. I, my good George, I go to disturb them, I go to make the dog fight! There is a drama there, at Mon Repos. A human drama, and it excites me. She was adroit, the little one, but not adroit enough. I wonder – I wonder what I shall find there?'

Into the dramatic pause which succeeded these words George's voice broke apologetically:

'Shall I pack dress clothes, sir?'

Poirot looked at him sadly.

'Always the concentration, the attention to your own job. You are very good for me, George.'

When the 4.55 drew up at Abbots Cross station, there descended from it M. Hercule Poirot, very neatly and foppishly attired, his moustaches waxed to a stiff point. He gave up his ticket, passed through the barrier, and was accosted by a tall chauffeur.

'M. Poirot?'

The little man beamed upon him.

'That is my name.'

'This way, sir, if you please.'

He held open the door of the big Rolls-Royce.

The house was a bare three minutes from the station. The chauffeur descended once more and opened the door of the car, and Poirot stepped out. The butler was already holding the front door open.

Poirot gave the outside of the house a swift appraising glance before passing through the open door. It was a big, solidly built red-brick mansion, with no pretensions to beauty, but with an air of solid comfort.

Poirot stepped into the hall. The butler relieved him deftly of his hat and overcoat, then murmured with that deferential undertone only to be achieved by the best servants:

'Her ladyship is expecting you, sir.'

Poirot followed the butler up the soft-carpeted stairs. This, without doubt, was Parsons, a very well-trained servant, with a manner suitably devoid of emotion. At the top of the staircase he turned to the right along a corridor. He passed through a door into a little ante-room, from which two more doors led. He threw open the left-hand one of these, and announced:

'M. Poirot, m'lady.'

The room was not a very large one, and it was crowded with furniture and knick-knacks. A woman, dressed in black, got up from a sofa and came quickly towards Poirot.

'M. Poirot,' she said with outstretched hand. Her eye ran rapidly over the dandified figure. She paused a minute, ignoring the little man's bow over her hand, and his murmured 'Madame,' and then, releasing his hand after a sudden vigorous pressure, she exclaimed:

'I believe in small men! They are the clever ones.'

'Inspector Miller,' murmured Poirot, 'is, I think, a tall man?'

'He is a bumptious idiot,' said Lady Astwell. 'Sit down here by me, will you, M. Poirot?'

She indicated the sofa and went on:

'Lily did her best to put me off sending for you, but I have not come to my time of life without knowing my own mind.'

'A rare accomplishment,' said Poirot, as he followed her to the settee.

Lady Astwell settled herself comfortably among the cushions and turned so as to face him.

'Lily is a dear girl,' said Lady Astwell, 'but she thinks she knows everything, and as often as not in my experience those sort of people are wrong. I am not clever, M. Poirot, I never have been, but I am right where many a less stupid person is wrong. I believe in *guidance*. Now do you want me to tell you who is the murderer, or do you not? A woman knows, M. Poirot.'

'Does Miss Margrave know?'

'What did she tell you?' asked Lady Astwell sharply.

'She gave me the facts of the case.'

'The facts? Oh, of course they are dead against Charles, but I tell you, M. Poirot, he didn't do it. I *know* he didn't!' She bent upon him an earnestness that was almost disconcerting.

'You are very positive, Lady Astwell?'

'Trefusis killed my husband, M. Poirot. I am sure of it.'

'Why?'

'Why should he kill him, do you mean, or why am I sure? I tell you I *know* it! I am funny about those things. I make up my mind at once, and I stick to it.'

'Did Mr Trefusis benefit in any way by Sir Reuben's death?'

'Never left him a penny,' returned Lady Astwell promptly. 'Now that shows you dear Reuben couldn't have liked or trusted him.'

'Had he been with Sir Reuben long, then?'

'Close on nine years.'

'That is a long time,' said Poirot softly, 'a very long time to remain in the employment of one man. Yes, Mr Trefusis, he must have known his employer well.'

Lady Astwell stared at him.

'What are you driving at? I don't see what that has to do with it.'

'I was following out a little idea of my own,' said Poirot. 'A little idea, not interesting, perhaps, but original, on the effects of service.'

Lady Astwell still stared.

'You *are* very clever, aren't you?' she said in rather a doubtful tone. 'Everybody says so.'

Hercule Poirot laughed.

'Perhaps you shall pay me that compliment, too, Madame, one of these days. But let us return to the motive. Tell me now of your household, of the people who were here in the house on the day of the tragedy.'

'There was Charles, of course.'

'He was your husband's nephew, I understand, not yours.'

'Yes, Charles was the only son of Reuben's sister. She married a comparatively rich man, but one of those crashes came – they do, in the city – and he died, and his wife,

195

too, and Charles came to live with us. He was twenty-three at the time, and going to be a barrister. But when the trouble came, Reuben took him into his office.'

'He was industrious, M. Charles?'

'I like a man who is quick on the uptake,' said Lady Astwell with a nod of approval. 'No, that's just the trouble, Charles was *not* industrious. He was always having rows with his uncle over some muddle or other that he had made. Not that poor Reuben was an easy man to get on with. Many's the time I've told him he had forgotten what it was to be young himself. He was very different in those days, M. Poirot.'

Lady Astwell heaved a sigh of reminiscence.

'Changes must come, Madame,' said Poirot. 'It is the law.'

'Still,' said Lady Astwell, 'he was never really rude to *me*. At least if he was, he was always sorry afterwards – poor dear Reuben.'

'He was difficult, eh?' said Poirot.

'I could always manage him,' said Lady Astwell with the air of a successful lion tamer. 'But it was rather awkward sometimes when he would lose his temper with the servants. There are ways of doing that, and Reuben's was not the right way.'

'How exactly did Sir Reuben leave his money, Lady Astwell?'

'Half to me and half to Charles,' replied Lady Astwell promptly. 'The lawyers don't put it simply like that, but that's what it amounts to.'

Poirot nodded his head.

'I see – I see,' he murmured. 'Now, Lady Astwell, I will demand of you that you will describe to me the household. There was yourself, and Sir Reuben's nephew, Mr Charles Leverson, and the secretary, Mr Owen Trefusis, and there was Miss Lily Margrave. Perhaps you will tell me something of that young lady.'

'You want to know about Lily?'

'Yes, she had been with you long?'

'About a year. I have had a lot of secretary-companions you know, but somehow or other they all got on my nerves. Lily was different. She was tactful and full of common sense and besides she looks so nice. I do like to have a pretty face about me, M. Poirot. I am a funny kind of person; I take likes and dislikes straight away. As soon as I saw that girl, I said to myself: "She'll do".'

'Did she come to you through friends, Lady Astwell?'

'I think she answered an advertisement. Yes – that was it.'

'You know something of her people, of where she comes from?'

'Her father and mother are out in India, I believe. I don't really know much about them, but you can see at a glance that Lily is a lady, can't you, M. Poirot?'

'Oh, perfectly, perfectly.'

'Of course,' went on Lady Astwell, 'I am not a lady myself. I know it, and the servants know it, but there is nothing mean-spirited about me. I can appreciate the real thing when I see it, and no one could be nicer than Lily has been to me. I look upon that girl almost as a daughter, M. Poirot, indeed I do.'

Poirot's right hand strayed out and straightened one or two of the objects lying on a table near him.

'Did Sir Reuben share this feeling?' he asked.

His eyes were on the knick-knacks, but doubtless he noted the pause before Lady Astwell's answer came.

'With a man it's different. Of course they – they got on very well.'

'Thank you, Madame,' said Poirot. He was smiling to himself.

'And these were the only people in the house that night?' he asked. 'Excepting, of course, the servants.'

'Oh, there was Victor.'

'Victor?'

'Yes, my husband's brother, you know, and his partner.'

'He lived with you?'

'No, he had just arrived on a visit. He has been out in West Africa for the past few years.'

'West Africa,' murmured Poirot.

He had learned that Lady Aswell could be trusted to develop a subject herself if sufficient time was given her.

'They say it's a wonderful country, but I think it's the kind of place that has a very bad effect upon a man. They drink too much, and they get uncontrolled. None of the Astwells has a good temper, and Victor's, since he came back from Africa, has been simply too shocking. He has frightened *me* once or twice.'

'Did he frighten Miss Margrave, I wonder?' murmured Poirot gently.

'Lily? Oh, I don't think he has seen much of Lily.'

Poirot made a note or two in a diminutive note-book; then he put the pencil back in its loop and returned the note-book to his pocket.

'I thank you, Lady Astwell. I will now, if I may, interview Parsons.'

'Will you have him up here?'

Lady Astwell's hand moved towards the bell. Poirot arrested the gesture quickly.

'No, no, a thousand times no. I will descend to him.'

'If you think it is better – '

Lady Astwell was clearly disappointed at not being able to participate in the forthcoming scene. Poirot adopted an air of secrecy.

'It is essential,' he said mysteriously, and left Lady Astwell duly impressed.

He found Parsons in the butler's pantry, polishing silver. Poirot opened the proceedings with one of his funny little bows.

'I must explain myself,' he said. 'I am a detective agent.'

'Yes, sir,' said Parsons, 'we gathered as much.'

His tone was respectful but aloof.

'Lady Astwell sent for me,' continued Poirot. 'She is not satisfied; no, she is not satisfied at all.'

'I have heard her ladyship say so on several occasions,' said Parsons.

'In fact,' said Poirot, 'I recount to you the things you already know? Eh? Let us then not waste time on these bagatelles. Take me, if you will be so good, to your bedroom and tell me exactly what it was you heard there on the night of the murder.'

The butler's room was on the ground floor, adjoining the servants' hall. It had barred windows, and the strong-room was in one corner of it. Parsons indicated the narrow bed.

'I had retired, sir, at eleven o'clock. Miss Margrave had gone to bed, and Lady Astwell was with Sir Reuben in the Tower room.'

'Lady Astwell was with Sir Reuben? Ah, proceed.'

'The Tower room, sir, is directly over this. If people are talking in it one can hear the murmurs of voices, but naturally not anything that is said. I must have fallen asleep about half past eleven. It was just twelve o'clock when I was awakened by the sound of the front door being slammed to and knew Mr Leverson had returned. Presently I heard footsteps overhead, and a minute or two later Mr Leverson's voice talking to Sir Reuben.

'It was my fancy at the time, sir, that Mr Leverson was – I should not exactly like to say drunk, but inclined to be a little indiscreet and noisy. He was shouting at his uncle at the top of his voice. I caught a word or two here or there, but not enough to understand what it was all about, and then there was a sharp cry and a heavy thud.'

There was a pause, and Parsons repeated the last words.

'A heavy thud,' he said impressively.

'If I mistake not, it is a *dull* thud in most works of romance,' murmured Poirot.

'Maybe, sir,' said Parsons severely, 'It was a *heavy* thud I heard.'

'A thousand pardons,' said Poirot.

'Do not mention it, sir. After the thud, in the silence, I heard Mr Leverson's voice as plain as plain can be, raised high. "My God," he said, "my God," just like that, sir.'

Parsons, from his first reluctance to tell the tale, had now progressed to a thorough enjoyment of it. He fancied himself mightily as a narrator. Poirot played up to him.

'*Mon Dieu*,' he murmured. 'What emotion you must have experienced!'

'Yes, indeed, sir,' said Parsons, 'as you say, sir. Not that I thought very much of it at the time. But it *did* occur to me to wonder if anything was amiss, and whether I had better go up and see. I went to turn the electric light on, and was unfortunate enough to knock over a chair.

'I opened the door, and went through the servants' hall, and opened the other door which gives on a passage. The back stairs lead up from there, and as I stood at the bottom of them, hesitating, I heard Mr Leverson's voice from up above, speaking hearty and cheery-like. "No harm done, luckily," he says. "Good night," and I heard him move off along the passage to his own room, whistling.

'Of course I went back to bed at once. Just something knocked over, that's all I thought it was. I ask you, sir, was I to think Sir Reuben was murdered, with Mr Leverson saying good night and all?'

'You are sure it was Mr Leverson's voice you heard?'

Parsons looked at the little Belgian pityingly, and Poirot saw clearly enough that, right or wrong, Parsons's mind was made up on this point.

'Is there anything further you would like to ask me, sir?'

'There is one thing,' said Poirot, 'do you like Mr Leverson?'

'I – I beg your pardon, sir?'

'It is a simple question. Do you like Mr Leverson?'

Parsons, from being startled at first, now seemed embarrassed.

'The general opinion in the servants' hall, sir,' he said, and paused.

'By all means,' said Poirot, 'put it that way if it pleases you.'

'The opinion is, sir, that Mr Leverson is an open-handed young gentleman, but not, if I may say so, particularly intelligent, sir.'

'Ah!' said Poirot. 'Do you know, Parsons, that without having seen him, that is also precisely my opinion of Mr Leverson.'

'Indeed, sir.'

'What is your opinion – I beg your pardon – the opinion of the servants' hall of the secretary?'

'He is a very quiet, patient gentleman, sir. Anxious to give no trouble.'

'*Vraiment*,' said Poirot.

The butler coughed.

'Her ladyship, sir,' he murmured, 'is apt to be a little hasty in her judgments.'

'Then in the opinion of the servants' hall, Mr Leverson committed the crime?'

'We none of us wish to think it was Mr Leverson,' said Parsons. 'We – well, plainly, we didn't think he had it in him, sir.'

'But he has a somewhat violent temper, has he not?' asked Poirot.

Parsons came nearer to him.

'If you are asking me who had the most violent temper in the house – '

Poirot held up a hand.

'Ah! But that is not the question I should ask,' he said softly. 'My question would be, who has the best temper?' Parsons stared at him open-mouthed.

Poirot wasted no further time on him. With an amiable little bow – he was always amiable – he left the room and wandered out into the big square hall of Mon Repos. There he stood a minute or two in thought, then, at a slight sound that came to him, cocked his head on one side in the manner of a perky robin, and finally, with noiseless steps, crossed to one of the doors that led out of the hall.

He stood in the doorway, looking into the room; a small room furnished as a library. At a big desk at the farther end of it sat a thin, pale young man busily writing. He had a receding chin, and wore pince-nez.

Poirot watched him for some minutes, and then he broke the silence by giving a completely artificial and theatrical cough.

'Ahem!' coughed M. Hercule Poirot.

The young man at the desk stopped writing and turned his head. He did not appear unduly startled, but an expression of perplexity gathered on his face as he eyed Poirot.

The latter came forward with a little bow.

'I have the honour of speaking to M. Trefusis, yes? Ah! My name is Poirot, Hercule Poirot. You may perhaps have heard of me.'

'Oh – er – yes, certainly,' said the young man.

Poirot eyed him attentively.

Owen Trefusis was about thirty-three years of age, and the detective saw at once why nobody was inclined to treat Lady Astwell's accusation seriously. Mr Owen Trefusis was a prim, proper young man, disarmingly meek, the type of man who can be, and is, systematically bullied. One could feel quite sure that he would never display resentment.

'Lady Astwell sent for you, of course,' said the secretary.

'She mentioned that she was going to do so. Is there any way in which I can help you?'

His manner was polite without being effusive. Poirot accepted a chair, and murmured gently:

'Has Lady Astwell said anything to you of her beliefs and suspicions?'

Owen Trefusis smiled a little.

'As far as that goes,' he said, 'I believe she suspects me. It is absurd, but there it is. She has hardly spoken a civil word to me since Sir Reuben's death, and she shrinks against the wall as I pass by.'

His manner was perfectly natural, and there was more amusement than resentment in his voice. Poirot nodded with an air of engaging frankness.

'Between ourselves,' he explained, 'she said the same thing to me. I did not argue with her – me, I have made it a rule never to argue with very positive ladies. You comprehend, it is a waste of time.'

'Oh, quite.'

'I say, yes, Madame – oh, perfectly, Madame – *précisément*, Madame. They mean nothing, those words, but they soothe all the same. I make my investigations, for though it seems almost impossible that anyone except M. Leverson could have committed the crime, yet – well, the impossible has happened before now.'

'I understand your position perfectly,' said the secretary. 'Please regard me as entirely at your service.'

'*Bon*,' said Poirot. 'We understand one another. Now recount to me the events of that evening. Better start with dinner.'

'Leverson was not at dinner, as you doubtless know,' said the secretary. 'He had a serious disagreement with his uncle, and went off to dine at the golf club. Sir Reuben was in a very bad temper in consequence.'

'Not too amiable, *ce Monsieur*, eh?' hinted Poirot delicately.

Trefusis laughed.

'Oh! He was a Tartar! I haven't worked with him for nine years without knowing most of his little ways. He was an extraordinarily difficult man, M. Poirot. He would get into childish fits of rage and abuse anybody who came near him.

'I was used to it by that time. I got into the habit of paying absolutely no attention to anything he said. He was not bad-hearted really, but he could be most foolish and exasperating in his manner. The great thing was never to answer him back.'

'Were other people as wise as you were in that respect?'

Trefusis shrugged his shoulders.

'Lady Astwell enjoyed a good row,' he said. 'She was not in the least afraid of Sir Reuben, and she always stood up to him and gave him as good as she got. They always made it up afterwards, and Sir Reuben was really devoted to her.'

'Did they quarrel that night?'

The secretary looked at him sideways, hesitated a minute, then he said:

'I believe so; what made you ask?'

'An idea, that is all.'

'I don't know, of course,' explained the secretary, 'but things looked as though they were working up that way.'

Poirot did not pursue the topic.

'Who else was at dinner?'

'Miss Margrave, Mr Victor Astwell, and myself.'

'And afterwards?'

'We went into the drawing-room. Sir Reuben did not accompany us. About ten minutes later he came in and hauled me over the coals for some trifling matter about a letter. I went up with him to the Tower room and set the thing straight; then Mr Victor Astwell came in and said he had something he wished to talk to his brother about, so I went downstairs and joined the two ladies.

'About a quarter of an hour later I heard Sir Reuben's bell ringing violently, and Parsons came to say I was to go up to Sir Reuben at once. As I entered the room, Mr Victor Astwell was coming out. He nearly knocked me over. Something had evidently happened to upset him. He has a very violent temper. I really believe he didn't see me.'

'Did Sir Reuben make any comment on the matter?'

'He said: "Victor is a lunatic; he will do for somebody some day when he is in one of these rages." '

'Ah!' said Poirot. 'Have you any idea what the trouble was about?'

'I couldn't say at all.'

Poirot turned his head very slowly and looked at the secretary. Those last words had been uttered too hastily. He formed the conviction that Trefusis could have said more had he wished to do so. But once again Poirot did not press the question.

'And then? Proceed, I pray of you.'

'I worked with Sir Reuben for about an hour and a half. At eleven o'clock Lady Astwell came in, and Sir Reuben told me I could go to bed.'

'And you went?'

'Yes.'

'Have you any idea how long she stayed with him?'

'None at all. Her room is on the first floor, and mine is on the second, so I would not hear her go to bed.'

'I see.'

Poirot nodded his head once or twice and sprang to his feet.

'And now, Monsieur, take me to the Tower room.'

He followed the secretary up the broad stairs to the first landing. Here Trefusis led him along the corridor, and through a baize door at the end of it, which gave on the servants' staircase and on a short passage that ended in a door. They passed through this door and found themselves on the scene of the crime.

It was a lofty room twice as high as any of the others, and was roughly about thirty feet square. Swords and assagais adorned the walls, and many native curios were arranged about on tables. At the far end, in the embrasure of the window, was a large writing-table. Poirot crossed straight to it.

'It was here Sir Reuben was found?'

Trefusis nodded.

'He was struck from behind, I understand?'

Again the secretary nodded.

'The crime was committed with one of these native clubs,' he explained. 'A tremendously heavy thing. Death must have been practically instantaneous.'

'That strengthens the conviction that the crime was not premeditated. A sharp quarrel, and a weapon snatched up almost unconsciously.'

'Yes, it does not look well for poor Leverson.'

'And the body was found fallen forward on the desk?'

'No, it had slipped sideways to the ground.'

'Ah,' said Poirot, 'that is curious.'

'Why curious?' asked the secretary.

'Because of this.'

Poirot pointed to a round irregular stain on the polished surface of the writing-table.

'That is a blood-stain, *mon ami*.'

'It may have spattered there,' suggested Trefusis, 'or it may have been made later, when they moved the body.'

'Very possibly, very possibly,' said the little man. 'There is only the one door to this room?'

'There is a staircase here.'

Trefusis pulled aside a velvet curtain in the corner of the room nearest the door, where a small spiral staircase led upwards.

'This place was originally built by an astronomer. The stairs led up to the tower where the telescope was fixed. Sir Reuben had the place fitted up as a bedroom, and sometimes slept there if he was working very late.'

Poirot went nimbly up the stairs. The circular room upstairs was plainly furnished, with a camp-bed, a chair and dressing-table. Poirot satisfied himself that there was no other exit, and then came down again to where Trefusis stood waiting for him.

'Did you hear Mr Leverson come in?' he asked.

Trefusis shook his head.

'I was fast asleep by that time.'

Poirot nodded. He looked slowly round the room.

'*Eh bien!*' he said at last. 'I do not think there is anything further here, unless – perhaps you would be so kind as to draw the curtains.'

Obediently Trefusis pulled the heavy black curtains across the window at the far end of the room. Poirot switched on the light – which was masked by a big alabaster bowl hanging from the ceiling.

'There was a desk light?' he asked.

For reply the secretary clicked on a powerful green-shaded hand lamp, which stood on the writing-table. Poirot switched the other light off, then on, then off again.

'*C'est bien!* I have finished here.'

'Dinner is at half past seven,' murmured the secretary.

'I thank you, M. Trefusis, for your many amiabilities.'

'Not at all.'

Poirot went thoughtfully along the corridor to the room appointed for him. The inscrutable George was there laying out his master's things.

'My good George,' he said presently, 'I shall, I hope, meet at dinner a certain gentleman who begins to intrigue me greatly. A man who has come home from the tropics, George. With a tropical temper – so it is said. A man whom Parsons tries to tell me about, and whom Lily Margrave does not mention. The late Sir Reuben had a temper of his own, George. Supposing such a man to come into contact with a man whose temper was worse than his own – how do you say it? The fur would jump about, eh?'

' "Would fly" is the correct expression, sir, and it is not always the case, sir, not by a long way.'

'No?'

'No, sir. There was my Aunt Jemima, sir, a most shrewish tongue she had, bullied a poor sister of hers who lived with her, something shocking she did. Nearly worried the life out of her. But if anyone came along who stood up to her, well, it was a very different thing. It was meekness she couldn't bear.'

'Ha!' said Poirot, 'it is suggestive – that.'

George coughed apologetically.

'Is there anything I can do in any way,' he inquired delicately, 'to – er – assist you, sir?'

'Certainly,' said Poirot promptly. 'You can find out for me what colour evening dress Miss Lily Margrave wore that night, and which housemaid attends her.'

George received these commands with his usual stolidity.

'Very good, sir, I will have the information for you in the morning.'

Poirot rose from his seat and stood gazing into the fire.

'You are very useful to me, George,' he murmured. 'Do you know, I shall not forget your Aunt Jemima?'

Poirot did not, after all, see Victor Astwell that night. A telephone message came from him that he was detained in London.

'He attends to the affairs of your late husband's business, eh?' asked Poirot of Lady Astwell.

'Victor is a partner,' she explained. 'He went out to Africa to look into some mining concessions for the firm. It *was* mining, wasn't it, Lily?'

'Yes, Lady Astwell.'

'Gold mines, I think, or was it copper or tin? You ought to know, Lily, you were always asking Reuben questions about it all. Oh, do be careful, dear, you will have that vase over!'

'It is dreadfully hot in here with the fire,' said the girl. 'Shall I – shall I open the window a little?'

Poirot watched while the girl went across to the window and opened it. She stood there a minute or two breathing in the cool night air. When she returned and sat down in her seat, Poirot said to her politely:

'So Mademoiselle is interested in mines?'

'Oh, not really,' said the girl indifferently. 'I listened to Sir Reuben, but I don't know anything about the subject.'

'You pretended very well, then,' said Lady Astwell. 'Poor Reuben actually thought you had some ulterior motive in asking all those questions.'

The little detective's eyes had not moved from the fire, into which he was steadily staring, but nevertheless, he did not miss the quick flush of vexation on Lily Margrave's face. Tactfully he changed the conversation. When the hour for good nights came, Poirot said to his hostess:

'May I have just two little words with you, Madame?'

Lily Margrave vanished discreetly. Lady Astwell looked inquiringly at the detective.

'You were the last person to see Sir Reuben alive that night?'

She nodded. Tears sprang into her eyes, and she hastily held a black-edged handkerchief to them.

'Ah, do not distress yourself, I beg of you do not distress yourself.'

'It's all very well, M. Poirot, but I can't help it.'

'I am a triple imbecile thus to vex you.'

'No, no, go on. What were you going to say?'

'It was about eleven o'clock, I fancy, when you went into the Tower room, and Sir Reuben dismissed Mr Trefusis. Is that right?'

'It must have been about then.'

'How long were you with him?'

'It was just a quarter to twelve when I got up to my room; I remember glancing at the clock.'

'Lady Astwell, will you tell me what your conversation with your husband was about?'

Lady Astwell sank down on the sofa and broke down completely. Her sobs were vigorous.

'We – qua – qua – quarrelled,' she moaned.

'What about?' Poirot's voice was coaxing, almost tender.

'L-l-lots of things. It b-b-began with L-Lily. Reuben took a dislike to her – for no reason, and said he had caught her interfering with his papers. He wanted to send her away, and I said she was a dear girl, and I would not have it. And then he s-s-started shouting me down, and I wouldn't have that, so I just told him what I thought of him.

'Not that I really meant it, M. Poirot. He said he had taken me out of the gutter to marry me, and I said – ah, but what does it all matter now? I shall never forgive myself. You know how it is, M. Poirot, I always did say a good row clears the air, and how was I to know someone was going to murder him that very night? Poor old Reuben.'

Poirot had listened sympathetically to all this outburst.

'I have caused you suffering,' he said. 'I apologize. Let us now be very business-like – very practical, very exact. You still cling to your idea that Mr Trefusis murdered your husband?'

Lady Astwell drew herself up.

'A woman's instinct, M. Poirot,' she said solemnly, 'never lies.'

'Exactly, exactly,' said Poirot. 'But when did he do it?'

'When? After I left him, of course.'

'You left Sir Reuben at a quarter to twelve. At five minutes to twelve Mr Leverson came in. In that ten minutes you say the secretary came along from his bedroom and murdered him?'

'It is perfectly possible.'

'So many things are possible,' said Poirot. 'It could be done in ten minutes. Oh, yes! But was it?'

'Of course he *says* he was in bed and fast asleep,' said Lady Astwell, 'but who is to know if he was or not?'

'Nobody saw him about,' Poirot reminded her.

'Everybody was in bed and fast asleep,' said Lady Astwell triumphantly. 'Of course nobody saw him.'

'I wonder,' said Poirot to himself.

A short pause.

'*Eh bien*, Lady Astwell, I wish you good night.'

George deposited a tray of early-morning coffee by his master's bedside.

'Miss Margrave, sir, wore a dress of light green chiffon on the night in question.'

'Thank you, George, you are most reliable.'

'The third housemaid looks after Miss Margrave, sir. Her name is Gladys.'

'Thank you, George. You are invaluable.'

'Not at all, sir.'

'It is a fine morning,' said Poirot, looking out of the window, 'and no one is likely to be astir very early. I think, my good George, that we shall have the Tower room to ourselves if we proceed there to make a little experiment.'

'You need me, sir?'

'The experiment,' said Poirot, 'will not be painful.'

The curtains were still drawn in the Tower room when they arrived there. George was about to pull them, when Poirot restrained him.

'We will leave the room as it is. Just turn on the desk lamp.'

The valet obeyed.

'Now, my good George, sit down in that chair. Dispose yourself as though you were writing. *Très bien*. Me, I seize a club, I steal up behind you, so, and I hit you on the back of the head.'

'Yes, sir,' said George.

'Ah!' said Poirot, 'but when I hit you, do not continue to write. You comprehend I cannot be exact. I cannot hit you with the same force with which the assassin hit Sir Reuben. When it comes to that point, we must do the make-believe. I hit you on the head, and you collapse, so. The arms well relaxed, the body limp. Permit me to arrange you. But no, do not flex your muscles.'

He heaved a sigh of exasperation.

'You press admirably the trousers, George,' he said, 'but the imagination you possess it not. Get up and let me take your place.'

Poirot in his turn sat down at the writing-table.

'I write,' he declared, 'I write busily. You steal up behind me, you hit me on the head with the club. Crash! The pen slips from my fingers, I drop forward, but not very far forward, for the chair is low, and the desk is high, and, moreover, my arms support me. Have the goodness, George, to go back to the door, stand there, and tell me what you see.'

'Ahem!'

'Yes, George?' encouragingly.

'I see you, sir, sitting at the desk.'

'*Sitting* at the desk?'

'It is a little difficult to see plainly, sir,' explained George, 'being such a long way away, sir, and the lamp being so heavily shaded. If I might turn on this light, sir?'

His hand reached out to the switch.

'Not at all,' said Poirot sharply. 'We shall do very well as we are. Here am I bending over the desk, there are you standing by the door. Advance now, George, advance, and put your hand on my shoulder.'

George obeyed.

'Lean on me a little, George, to steady yourself on your feet, as it were. Ah! *Voilà*.'

Hercule Poirot's limp body slid artistically sideways.

'I collapse – so!' he observed. 'Yes, it is very well imagined. There is now something most important that must be done.'

'Indeed, sir?' said the valet.

'Yes, it is necessary that I should breakfast well.'

The little man laughed heartily at his own joke.

'The stomach, George; it must not be ignored.'

George maintained a disapproving silence. Poirot went downstairs chuckling happily to himself. He was pleased at the way things were shaping. After breakfast he made the acquaintance of Gladys, the third housemaid. He was very interested in what she could tell him of the crime. She was sympathetic towards Charles, although she had no doubt of his guilt.

'Poor young gentleman, sir, it seems hard, it does, him not being quite himself at the time.'

'He and Miss Margrave should have got on well together,' suggested Poirot, 'as the only two young people in the house.'

Gladys shook her head.

'Very stand-offish Miss Lily was with him. She wouldn't have no carryings-on, and she made it plain.'

'He was fond of her, was he?'

'Oh, only in passing, so to speak; no harm in it, sir. Mr Victor Astwell, now he *is* properly gone on Miss Lily.'

She giggled.

'Ah *vraiment*!'

Gladys giggled again.

'Sweet on her straight away he was. Miss Lily *is* just like a lily, isn't she, sir? So tall and such a lovely shade of gold hair.'

'She should wear a green evening frock,' mused Poirot. 'There is a certain shade of green – '

'She has one, sir,' said Gladys. 'Of course, she can't wear it now, being in mourning, but she had it on the very night Sir Reuben died.'

'It should be a light green, not a dark green,' said Poirot.

'It is a light green, sir. If you wait a minute I'll show it to you. Miss Lily has just gone out with the dogs.'

Poirot nodded. He knew that as well as Gladys did. In fact, it was only after seeing Lily safely off the premises that he had gone in search of the housemaid. Gladys hurried away, and returned a few minutes later with a green evening dress on a hanger.

'*Exquis*!' murmured Poirot, holding up hands of admiration. 'Permit me to take it to the light a minute.'

He took the dress from Gladys, turned his back on her and hurried to the window. He bent over it, then held it out at arm's length.

'It is perfect,' he declared. 'Perfectly ravishing. A thousand thanks for showing it to me.'

'Not at all, sir,' said Gladys. 'We all know that Frenchmen are interested in ladies' dresses.'

'You are too kind,' murmured Poirot.

He watched her hurry away again with the dress. Then he looked down at his two hands and smiled. In the right hand was a tiny pair of nail scissors, in the left was a neatly clipped fragment of green chiffon.

'And now,' he murmured, 'to be heroic.'

He returned to his own apartment and summoned George.

'On the dressing-table, my good George, you will perceive a gold scarf pin.'

'Yes, sir.'

'On the washstand is a solution of carbolic. Immerse, I pray you, the point of the pin in the carbolic.'

George did as he was bid. He had long ago ceased to wonder at the vagaries of his master.

'I have done that, sir.'

'*Très bien*! Now approach. I tender to you my first finger; insert the point of the pin in it.'

'Excuse me, sir, you want me to prick you, sir?'

'But yes, you have guessed correctly. You must draw blood, you understand, but not too much.'

George took hold of his master's finger. Poirot shut his eyes and leaned back. The valet stabbed at the finger with the scarf pin, and Poirot uttered a shrill yell.

'*Je vous remercie*, George,' he said. 'What you have done is ample.'

Taking a small piece of green chiffon from his pocket, he dabbed his finger with it gingerly.

'The operation has succeeded to a miracle,' he remarked, gazing at the result. 'You have no curiosity, George? Now, that is admirable!'

The valet had just taken a discreet look out of the window.

'Excuse me, sir,' he murmured, 'a gentleman has driven up in a large car.'

'Ah! Ah!' said Poirot. He rose briskly to his feet. 'The elusive Mr Victor Astwell. I go down to make his acquaintance.'

Poirot was destined to hear Mr Victor Astwell some time before he saw him. A loud voice rang out from the hall.

'Mind what you are doing, you damned idiot! That case has got glass in it. Curse you, Parsons, get out of the way! Put it down, you fool!'

Poirot skipped nimbly down the stairs. Victor Astwell was a big man. Poirot bowed to him politely.

'Who the devil are you?' roared the big man.

Poirot bowed again.

'My name is Hercule Poirot.'

'Lord!' said Victor Astwell. 'So Nancy sent for you, after all, did she?'

He put a hand on Poirot's shoulder and steered him into the library.

'So you are the fellow they make such a fuss about,' he remarked, looking him up and down. 'Sorry for my language just now. That chauffeur of mine is a damned ass, and Parsons always does get on my nerves, blithering old idiot.

'I don't suffer fools gladly, you know,' he said, half-apologetically, 'but by all accounts you are not a fool, eh, M. Poirot?'

He laughed breezily.

'Those who have thought so have been sadly mistaken,' said Poirot placidly.

'Is that so? Well, so Nancy has carted you down here – got a bee in her bonnet about the secretary. There is nothing in that; Trefusis is as mild as milk – drinks milk, too, I believe. The fellow is a teetotaller. Rather a waste of your time isn't it?'

'If one has an opportunity to observe human nature, time is never wasted,' said Poirot quietly.

'Human nature, eh?'

Victor Astwell stared at him, then he flung himself down in a chair.

'Anything I can do for you?'

'Yes, you can tell me what your quarrel with your brother was about that evening.'

Victor Astwell shook his head.

'Nothing to do with the case,' he said decisively.

'One can never be sure,' said Poirot.

'It had nothing to do with Charles Leverson.'

'Lady Astwell thinks that Charles had nothing to do with the murder.'

'Oh, Nancy!'

'Parsons assumes that it was M. Charles Leverson who came in that night, but he didn't see him. Remember nobody saw him.'

'It's very simple. Reuben had been pitching into young Charles – not without good reason, I must say. Later on he tried to bully me. I told him a few home truths and, just to annoy him, I made up my mind to back the boy. I meant to see him that night, so as to tell him how the land lay. When I went up to my room I didn't go to bed. Instead, I left the door ajar and sat on a chair smoking. My room is on the second floor, M. Poirot, and Charles's room is next to it.'

'Pardon my interrupting you – Mr Trefusis, he, too, sleeps on that floor?'

Astwell nodded.

'Yes, his room is just beyond mine.'

'Nearer the stairs?'

'No, the other way.'

A curious light came into Poirot's face, but the other didn't notice it and went on:

'As I say, I waited up for Charles. I heard the front door slam, as I thought, about five minutes to twelve, but there was no sign of Charles for about ten minutes. When he did come up the stairs I saw that it was no good tackling him that night.'

He lifted his elbow significantly.

'I see,' murmured Poirot.

'Poor devil couldn't walk straight,' said Astwell. 'He was looking pretty ghastly, too. I put it down to his condition at the time. Of course, now, I realize that he had come straight from committing the crime.'

Poirot interposed a quick question.

'You heard nothing from the Tower room?'

'No, but you must remember that I was right at the other end of the building. The walls are thick, and I don't believe you would even hear a pistol shot fired from there.'

Poirot nodded.

'I asked if he would like some help getting to bed,' continued Astwell. 'But he said he was all right and went into his room and banged the door. I undressed and went to bed.'

Poirot was staring thoughtfully at the carpet.

'You realize, M. Astwell,' he said at last, 'that your evidence is very important?'

'I suppose so, at least – what do you mean?'

'Your evidence that ten minutes elapsed between the slamming of the front door and Leverson's appearance upstairs. He himself says, so I understand, that he came into the house and went straight up to bed. But there is more than that. Lady Astwell's accusation of the secretary is fantastic, I admit, yet up to now it has not been proved impossible. But your evidence creates an alibi.'

'How is that?'

'Lady Astwell says that she left her husband at a quarter to twelve, while the secretary had gone to bed at eleven o'clock. The only time he could have committed the crime was between a quarter to twelve and Charles Leverson's return. Now, if, as you say, you sat with your door open, he could not have come out of his room without your seeing him.'

'That is so,' agreed the other.

'There is no other staircase?'

'No, to get down to the Tower room he would have had to pass my door, and he didn't, I am quite sure of that. And, anyway, M. Poirot, as I said just now, the man is as meek as a parson, I assure you.'

'But yes, but yes,' said Poirot soothingly, 'I understand all that.' He paused. 'And you will not tell me the subject of your quarrel with Sir Reuben?'

The other's face turned a dark red.

'You'll get nothing out of me.'

Poirot looked at the ceiling.

'I can always be discreet,' he murmured, 'where a lady is concerned.'

Victor Astwell sprang to his feet.

'Damn you, how did you – what do you mean?'

'I was thinking,' said Poirot, 'of Miss Lily Margrave.'

Victor Astwell stood undecided for a minute or two, then his colour subsided, and he sat down again.

'You are too clever for me, M. Poirot. Yes, it was Lily we quarrelled about. Reuben had his knife into her; he had ferreted out something or other about the girl – false references, something of that kind. I don't believe a word of it myself.

'And then he went further than he had any right to go, talked about her stealing down at night and getting out of the house to meet some fellow or other. My God! I gave it to him; I told him that better men than he had been killed for saying less. That shut him up. Reuben was inclined to be a bit afraid of me when I got going.'

'I hardly wonder at it,' murmured Poirot politely.

'I think a lot of Lily Margrave,' said Victor in another tone. 'A nice girl through and through.'

Poirot did not answer. He was staring in front of him, seeming lost in abstraction. He came out of his brown study with a jerk.

'I must, I think, promenade myself a little. There is a hotel here, yes?'

'Two,' said Victor Astwell, 'the Golf Hotel up by the links and the Mitre down by the station.'

'I thank you,' said Poirot. 'Yes, certainly I must promenade myself a little.'

The Golf Hotel, as befits its name, stands on the golf links almost adjoining the club house. It was to this hostelry that Poirot repaired first in the course of that 'promenade' which he had advertised himself as being about to take. The little man had his own way of doing things. Three minutes after he had entered the Golf Hotel he was in private consultation with Miss Langdon, the manageress.

'I regret to incommode you in any way, Mademoiselle,' said Poirot, 'but you see I am a detective.'

Simplicity always appealed to him. In this case the method proved efficacious at once.

'A detective!' exclaimed Miss Langdon, looking at him doubtfully.

'Not from Scotland Yard,' Poirot assured her. 'In fact – you may have noticed it? I am not an Englishman. No, I make the private inquiries into the death of Sir Reuben Astwell.'

'You don't say, now!' Miss Langdon goggled at him expectantly.

'Precisely,' said Poirot beaming. 'Only to someone of discretion like yourself would I reveal the fact. I think, Mademoiselle, you may be able to aid me. Can you tell me of any gentleman staying here on the night of the murder who was absent from the hotel that evening and returned to it about twelve or half past?'

Miss Langdon's eyes opened wider than ever.

'You don't think –?' she breathed.

'That you had the murderer here? No, but I have reason to believe that a guest staying here promenaded himself in the direction of Mon Repos that night, and if so he may have seen something which, though conveying no meaning to him, might be very useful to me.'

The manageress nodded her head sapiently, with an air of one thoroughly well up in the annals of detective logic.

'I understand perfectly. Now, let me see; who did we have staying here?'

She frowned, evidently running over the names in her mind, and helping her memory by occasionally checking them off on her fingertips.

'Captain Swann, Mr Elkins, Major Blyunt, old Mr Benson. No, really, sir, I don't believe anyone went out that evening.'

'You would have noticed if they had done so, eh?'

'Oh, yes, sir, it is not very usual, you see. I mean gentlemen go out to dinner and all that, but they don't go out after dinner, because – well, there is nowhere to go to, is there?'

The attractions of Abbots Cross were golf and nothing but golf.

'That is so,' agreed Poirot. 'Then, as far as you remember, Mademoiselle, nobody from here was out that night?'

'Captain England and his wife were out to dinner.'

Poirot shook his head.

'That is not the kind of thing I mean. I will try the other hotel; the Mitre, is it not?'

'Oh, the Mitre,' said Miss Langdon. 'Of course, anyone might have gone out walking from *there*.'

The disparagement of her tone, though vague, was evident, and Poirot beat a tactful retreat.

Ten minutes later he was repeating the scene, this time with Miss Cole, the brusque manageress of the Mitre, a less pretentious hotel with lower prices, situated close to the station.

'There was one gentleman out late that night, came in about half past twelve, as far as I can remember. Quite a habit of his it was, to go out for a walk at that time of the evening. He had done it once or twice before. Let me see now, what was his name? Just for the moment I can't remember it.'

She pulled a large ledger towards her and began turning over the pages.

'Nineteenth, twentieth, twenty-first, twenty-second. Ah, here we are. Naylor, Captain Humphrey Naylor.'

'He had stayed here before? You know him well?'

'Once before,' said Miss Cole, 'about a fortnight earlier. He went out then in the evening, I remember.'

'He came to play golf, eh?'

'I suppose so,' said Miss Cole, 'that's what most of the gentlemen come for.'

'Very true,' said Poirot. 'Well, Mademoiselle, I thank you infinitely, and I wish you good day.'

He went back to Mon Repos with a very thoughtful face. Once or twice he drew something from his pocket and looked at it.

'It must be done,' he murmured to himself, 'and soon, as soon as I can make the opportunity.'

His first proceeding on re-entering the house was to ask Parsons where Miss Margrave might be found. He was told that she was in the small study dealing with Lady Astwell's correspondence, and the information seemed to afford Poirot satisfaction.

He found the little study without difficulty. Lily Margrave was seated at a desk by the window, writing. But for her the room was empty. Poirot carefully shut the door behind him and came towards the girl.

'I may have a little minute of your time, Mademoiselle, you will be so kind?'

'Certainly.'

Lily Margrave put the papers aside and turned towards him.

'What can I do for you?'

'On the evening of the tragedy, Mademoiselle, I understand that when Lady Astwell went to her husband you went straight up to bed. Is that so?'

Lily Margrave nodded.

'You did not come down again, by any chance?'

The girl shook her head.

'I think you said, Maemoiselle, that you had not at any time that evening been in the Tower room?'

'I don't remember saying so, but as a matter of fact that is quite true. I was not in the Tower room that evening.'

Poirot raised his eyebrows.

'Curious,' he murmured.

'What do you mean?'

'Very curious,' murmured Hercule Poirot again. 'How do you account, then, for this?'

He drew from his pocket a little scrap of stained green chiffon and held it up for the girl's inspection.

Her expression did not change, but he felt rather than heard the sharp intake of breath.

'I don't understand, M. Poirot.'

'You wore, I understand, a green chiffon dress that evening, Mademoiselle. This –' he tapped the scrap in his fingers – 'was torn from it.'

'And you found it in the Tower room?' asked the girl sharply. 'Whereabouts?'

Hercule Poirot looked at the ceiling.

'For the moment shall we just say – in the Tower room?'

For the first time, a look of fear sprang into the girl's eyes. She began to speak, then checked herself. Poirot watched her small white hands clenching themselves on the edge of the desk.

'I wonder if I did go into the Tower room that evening?' she mused. 'Before dinner, I mean. I don't think so. I am almost sure I didn't. If that scrap has been in the Tower room all this time, it seems to me a very extraordinary thing the police did not find it right away.'

'The police,' said the little man, 'do not think of things that Hercule Poirot thinks of.'

'I may have run in there for a minute just before dinner,' mused Lily Margrave, 'Or it may have been the night before. I wore the same dress then. Yes, I am almost sure it was the night before.'

'I think not,' said Poirot evenly.

'Why?'

He only shook his head slowly from side to side.

'What do you mean?' whispered the girl.

She was leaning forward, staring at him, all the colour ebbing out of her face.

'You do not notice, Mademoiselle, that this fragment is stained? There is no doubt about it, that stain is human blood.'

'You mean —'

'I mean, Mademoiselle, that you were in the Tower room *after* the crime was committed, not before. I think you will do well to tell me the whole truth, lest worse should befall you.'

He stood up now, a stern little figure of a man, his forefinger pointed accusingly at the girl.

'How did you find out?' gasped Lily.

'No matter, Mademoiselle. I tell you Hercule Poirot *knows*. I know all about Captain Humphrey Naylor, and that you went down to meet him that night.'

Lily suddenly put her head down on her arms and burst into tears. Immediately Poirot relinquished his accusing attitude.

'There, there, my little one,' he said, patting the girl on the shoulder. 'Do not distress yourself. Impossible to deceive Hercule Poirot; once realize that and all your troubles will be at an end. And now you will tell me the story, will you not? You will tell old Papa Poirot?'

'It is not what you think, it isn't, indeed Humphrey — my brother — never touched a hair of his head.'

'Your brother, eh?' said Poirot. 'So that is how the land lies. Well, if you wish to save him from suspicion, you must tell me the whole story now, without reservation.'

Lily sat up again, pushing back the hair from her forehead. After a minute or two, she began to speak in a low, clear voice.

'I will tell you the truth, M. Poirot. I can see now that it would be absurd to do anything else. My real name is Lily Naylor, and Humphrey is my only brother. Some years ago, when he was out in Africa, he discovered a gold-mine, or rather, I should say, discovered the presence of gold. I can't tell you this part of it properly, because I don't understand the technical details, but what it amounted to was this:

'The thing seemed likely to be a very big undertaking, and Humphrey came home with letters to Sir Reuben Astwell in the hopes of getting him interested in the matter. I don't understand the rights of it even now, but I gather that Sir Reuben sent out an expert to report, and that he subsequently told my brother that the expert's report was unfavourable and that he, Humphrey, had made a great mistake. My brother went back to Africa on an expedition into the interior and was lost sight of. It was assumed that he and the expedition had perished.

'It was soon after that that a company was formed to exploit the Mpala Gold Fields. When my brother got back to England he at once jumped to the conclusion that these gold fields were identical with those he had discovered. Sir Reuben Astwell had apparently nothing to do with this company, and they had seemingly discovered the place on their own. But my brother was not satisfied, he was convinced that Sir Reuben had deliberately swindled him.

'He became more and more violent and unhappy about the matter. We two are alone in the world, M. Poirot, and as it was necessary then for me to go out and earn my own living, I conceived the idea of taking a post in this household and trying to find out if any connection existed between Sir Reuben and the Mpala Gold Fields. For obvious reasons I concealed my real name, and I'll admit frankly that I used a forged reference.

'There were many applicants for the post, most of them with better qualifications than mine, so – well, M. Poirot, I wrote a beautiful letter from the Duchess of Perthshire, who I knew had gone to America. I thought a duchess would have a great effect upon Lady Astwell, and I was quite right. She engaged me on the spot.

'Since then I have been that hateful thing, a spy, and until lately with no success. Sir Reuben is not a man to give away his business secrets, but when Victor Astwell came back from Africa he was less guarded in his talk, and I began to believe that, after all, Humphrey had not been mistaken. My brother came down here about a fortnight before the murder, and I crept out of the house to meet him secretly at night. I told him the things Victor Astwell had said, and he became very excited and assured me I was definitely on the right track.

'But after that things began to go wrong; someone must have seen me stealing out of the house and have reported the matter to Sir Reuben. He became suspicious and hunted up my references, and soon discovered the fact that they were forged. The crisis came on the day of the murder. I think he thought I was after his wife's jewels. Whatever his suspicions were, he had no intentions of allowing me to remain any longer at Mon Repos, though he agreed not to prosecute me on account of the references. Lady Astwell took my part throughout and stood up valiantly to Sir Reuben.'

She paused. Poirot's face was very grave.

'And now, Mademoiselle,' he said, 'we come to the night of the murder.'

Lily swallowed hard and nodded her head.

'To begin with, M. Poirot, I must tell you that my brother had come down again, and that I had arranged to creep out and meet him once more. I went up to my room, as I have said, but I did not go to bed. Instead, I waited till I thought everyone was asleep, and then stole downstairs again and out of the side door. I met Humphrey and acquainted him in a few hurried words with what had occurred. I told him that I believed the papers he wanted were in Sir Reuben's safe in the Tower room, and we agreed as a last desperate adventure to try and get hold of them that night.

'I was to go in first and see that the way was clear. I heard the church clock strike twelve as I went in by the side door. I was half-way up the stairs leading to the Tower room, when I heard a thud of something falling, and a voice cried out, "My God!" A minute or two afterwards the door of the Tower room opened, and Charles Leverson came out. I could see his face quite clearly in the moonlight, but I was crouching some way below him on the stairs where it was dark, and he did not see me at all.

'He stood there a moment swaying on his feet and looking ghastly. He seemed to be listening; then with an effort he seemed to pull himself together and, opening the door into the Tower room, called out something about there being no harm done. His voice was quite jaunty and debonair, but his face gave the lie to it. He waited a minute more, and then slowly went on upstairs and out of sight.

'When he had gone I waited a minute or two and then crept to the Tower room door. I had a feeling that something tragic had happened. The main light was out, but the desk lamp was on, and by its light I saw Sir Reuben lying on the floor by the desk. I don't know how I managed it, but I nerved myself at last to go over and kneel down by him. I saw at once that he was dead, struck down from behind, and also that he couldn't have been dead long; I touched his hand and it was still quite warm. It was just horrible, M. Poirot. Horrible!'

She shuddered again at the remembrance.

'And then?' said Poirot, looking at her keenly.

Lily Margrave nodded.

'Yes, M. Poirot, I know what you are thinking. Why didn't I give the alarm and raise the house? I should have done so, I know, but it came over me in a flash, as I knelt there, that my quarrel with Sir Reuben, my stealing out to meet Humphrey, the fact that I was being sent away on the morrow, made a fatal sequence. They would say that I had let Humphrey in, and that Humphrey had killed Sir Reuben out of revenge. If I said that I had seen Charles Leverson leaving the room, no one would believe me.

'It was terrible, M. Poirot! I knelt there and thought and thought, and the more I thought the more my nerve failed me. Presently I noticed Sir Reuben's keys which had dropped from his pocket as he fell. Among them was the key of the safe, the combination word I already knew, since Lady Astwell had mentioned it once in my hearing. I went over to that safe, M. Poirot, unlocked it and rummaged through the papers I found there.

'In the end I found what I was looking for. Humphrey had been perfectly right. Sir Reuben was behind the Mpala Gold Fields, and he had deliberately swindled Humphrey. That made it all the worse. It gave a perfectly definite motive for Humphrey having committed the crime. I put the papers back in the safe, left the key in the door of it, and went straight upstairs to my room. In the morning I pretended to be surprised and horror-stricken, like everyone else, when the housemaid discovered the body.'

She stopped and looked piteously across at Poirot.

'You do believe me, M. Poirot. Oh, do say you believe me!'

'I believe you, Mademoiselle,' said Poirot; 'you have explained many things that puzzled me. Your absolute certainty, for one thing, that Charles Leverson had committed the crime, and at the same time your persistent efforts to keep me from coming down here.'

Lily nodded.

'I was afraid of you,' she admitted frankly. 'Lady Astwell could not know, as I did, that Charles was guilty, and I couldn't say anything. I hoped against hope that you would refuse to take the case.'

'But for that obvious anxiety on your part, I might have done so,' said Poirot drily.

Lily looked at him swiftly, her lips trembled a little.

'And now, M. Poirot, what – what are you going to do?'

'As far as you are concerned, Mademoiselle, nothing.

I believe your story, and I accept it. The next step is to go to London and see Inspector Miller.'

'And then?' asked Lily.

'And then,' said Poirot, 'we shall see.'

Outside the door of the study he looked once more at the little square of stained green chiffon which he held in his hand.

'Amazing,' he murmured to himself complacently, 'the ingenuity of Hercule Poirot.'

Detective-Inspector Miller was not particularly fond of M. Hercule Poirot. He did not belong to that small band of inspectors at the Yard who welcomed the little Belgian's co-operation. He was wont to say that Hercule Poirot was much over-rated. In this case he felt pretty sure of himself, and greeted Poirot with high good humour in consequence.

'Acting for Lady Astwell, are you? Well, you have taken up a mare's nest in that case.'

'There is, then, no possible doubt about the matter?'

Miller winked. 'Never was a clearer case, short of catching a murderer absolutely red-handed.'

'M. Leverson has made a statement, I understand?'

'He had better have kept his mouth shut,' said the detective. 'He repeats over and over again that he went straight up to his room and never went near his uncle. That's a fool story on the face of it.'

'It is certainly against the weight of evidence,' murmured Poirot. 'How does he strike you, this young M. Leverson?'

'Darned young fool.'

'A weak character, eh?'

The inspector nodded.

'One would hardly think a young man of that type would have the – how do you say it – the bowels to commit such a crime.'

'On the face of it, no,' agreed the inspector. 'But, bless

you, I have come across the same thing many times. Get a weak, dissipated young man into a corner, fill him up with a drop too much to drink, and for a limited amount of time you can turn him into a fire-eater. A weak man in a corner is more dangerous that a strong man.'

'That is true, yes; that is true what you say.'

Miller unbent a little further.

'Of course, it is all right for you, M. Poirot,' he said. 'You get your fees just the same, and naturally you have to make a pretence of examining the evidence to satisfy her ladyship. I can understand all that.'

'You understand such interesting things,' murmured Poirot, and took his leave.

His next call was upon the solicitor representing Charles Leverson. Mr Mayhew was a thin, dry, cautious gentleman. He received Poirot with reserve. Poirot, however, had his own ways of inducing confidence. In ten minutes' time the two were talking together amicably.

'You will understand,' said Poirot, 'I am acting in this case solely on behalf of Mr Leverson. That is Lady Astwell's wish. She is convinced that he is not guilty.'

'Yes, yes, quite so,' said Mr Mayhew without enthusiasm.

Poirot's eyes twinkled. 'You do not perhaps attach much importance to the opinions of Lady Astwell?' he suggested.

'She might be just as sure of his guilt tomorrow,' said the lawyer drily.

'Her intuitions are not evidence certainly,' agreed Poirot, 'and on the face of it the case looks very black against this poor young man.'

'It is a pity he said what he did to the police,' said the lawyer; 'it will be no good his sticking to that story.'

'Has he stuck to it with you?' inquired Poirot.

Mayhew nodded. 'It never varies an iota. He repeats it like a parrot.'

'And that is what destroys your faith in him,' mused

the other. 'Ah, don't deny it,' he added quickly, holding up an arresting hand. 'I see it only too plainly. In your heart you believe him guilty. But listen to me, to me, Hercule Poirot. I present to you a case.

'This young man comes -home, he has drunk the cocktail, the cocktail, and again the cocktail, also without doubt the English whisky and soda many times. He is full of, what you call it? the courage Dutch, and in that mood he lets himself into the house with his latch-key, and he goes with unsteady steps up to the Tower room. He looks in at the door and sees in the dim light his uncle, apparently bending over the desk.

'M. Leverson is full, as we have said, of the courage Dutch. He lets himself go, he tells his uncle just what he thinks of him. He defies him, he insults him, and the more his uncle does not answer back, the more he is encouraged to go on, to repeat himself, to say the same thing over and over again, and each time more loudly. But at last the continued silence of his uncle awakens an apprehension. He goes nearer to him, he lays his hand on his uncle's shoulder, and his uncle's figure crumples under his touch and sinks in a heap to the ground.

'He is sobered then, this M. Leverson. The chair falls with a crash, and he bends over Sir Reuben. He realizes what has happened, he looks at his hand covered with something warm and red. He is in a panic then, he would give anything on earth to recall the cry which has just sprung from his lips, echoing through the house. Mechanically he picks up the chair, then he hastens out through the door and listens. He fancies he hears a sound, and immediately, automatically, he pretends to be speaking to his uncle through the open door.

'The sound is not repeated. He is convinced he has been mistaken in thinking he heard one. Now all is silence, he creeps up to his room, and at once it occurs to him how much better it will be if he pretends never to have been near his uncle that night. So he tells his story. Parsons at that time, remember, has said nothing of what he heard. When he does do so, it is too late for M. Leverson to change. He is stupid, and he is obstinate, he sticks to his story. Tell me, Monsieur, is that not possible?'

'Yes,' said the lawyer, 'I suppose in the way you put it that it is possible.'

Poirot rose to his feet.

'You have the privilege of seeing M. Leverson,' he said. 'Put to him the story I have told you, and ask him if it is not true.'

Outside the lawyer's office, Poirot hailed a taxi.

'Three-four-eight Harley Street,' he murmured to the driver.

Poirot's departure for London had taken Lady Astwell by surprise, for the little man had not made any mention of what he proposed doing. On his return, after an absence of twenty-four hours, he was informed by Parsons that Lady Astwell would like to see him as soon as possible. Poirot found the lady in her own boudoir. She was lying down on the divan, her head propped up by cushions, and she looked startlingly ill and haggard; far more so than she had done on the day Poirot arrived.

'So you have come back. M. Poirot?'

'I have returned, Madame.'

'You went to London?'

Poirot nodded.

'You didn't tell me you were going,' said Lady Astwell sharply.

'A thousand apologies, Madame, I am in error, I should have done so. *La prochaine fois* —'

'You will do exactly the same,' interrupted Lady Astwell with a shrewd touch of humour. 'Do things first and tell people afterwards, that is your motto right enough.'

'Perhaps it has also been Madame's motto?' His eyes twinkled.

'Now and then, perhaps,' admitted the other. 'What did you go up to London for, M. Poirot? You can tell me now, I suppose?'

'I had an interview with the good Inspector Miller, and also with the excellent Mr Mayhew.'

Lady Astwell's eyes searched his face.

'And you think, now – ?' she said slowly.

'That there is a possibility of Charles Leverson's innocence,' he said gravely.

'Ah!' Lady Astwell half-sprung up, sending two cushions rolling to the ground. 'I was right, then, I was right!'

'I said a possibility, Madame, that is all.'

Something in his tone seemed to strike her. She raised herself on one elbow and regarded him piercingly.

'Can I do anything?' she asked.

'Yes,' he nodded his head, 'you can tell me, Lady Astwell, why you suspect Owen Trefusis.'

'I have told you I *know* – that's all.'

'Unfortunately, that is not enough,' said Poirot drily. 'Cast your mind back to the fatal evening, Madame. Remember each detail, each tiny happening. What did you notice or observe about the secretary? I, Hercule Poirot, tell you there must have been *something*.'

Lady Astwell shook her head.

'I hardly noticed him at all that evening,' she said, 'and I certainly was not thinking of him.'

'Your mind was taken up by something else?'

'Yes.'

'With your husband's animus against Miss Lily Margrave?'

'That's right,' said Lady Astwell, nodding her head; 'you seem to know all about it, M. Poirot.'

'Me, I know everything,' declared the little man with an absurdly grandiose air.

'I am fond of Lily, M. Poirot; you have seen that for yourself. Reuben began kicking up a rumpus about some reference or other of hers. Mind you, I don't say she hadn't cheated about it. She had. But, bless you, I have done many worse things than that in the old days. You have got to be up to all sorts of tricks to get round theatrical managers. There is nothing I wouldn't have written, or said, or done, in my time.

'Lily wanted this job, and she put in a lot of slick work that was not quite – well, quite the thing, you know. Men are so stupid about that sort of thing; Lily really might have been a bank clerk absconding with millions for the fuss he made about it. I was terribly worried all the evening, because, although I could usually get round Reuben in the end, he was terribly pig-headed at times, poor darling. So of course I hadn't time to go noticing secretaries, not that one does notice Mr Trefusis much, anyway. He is just there and that's all there is to it.'

'I have noticed that fact about M. Trefusis,' said Poirot. 'His is not a personality that stands forth, that shines, that hits you cr-r-rack.'

'No,' said Lady Astwell, 'he is not like Victor.'

'M. Victor Astwell is, I should say, explosive.'

'That is a splendid word for him,' said Lady Astwell. 'He explodes all over the house, like one of those thingimyjig firework things.'

'A somewhat quick temper, I should imagine?' suggested Poirot.

'Oh, he's a perfect devil when roused,' said Lady Astwell, 'but bless you, *I'm* not afraid of him. All bark and no bite to Victor.'

Poirot looked at the ceiling.

'And you can tell me nothing about the secretary that evening?' he murmured gently.

'I tell you, M. Poirot, I *know*. It's intuition. A woman's intuition –'

'Will not hang a man,' said Poirot, 'and what is more to the point, it will not save a man from being hanged. Lady Astwell, if you sincerely believe that M. Leverson is innocent, and that your suspicions of the secretary are well-founded, will you consent to a little experiment?'

'What kind of an experiment?' demanded Lady Astwell suspiciously.

'Will you permit yourself to be put into a condition of hypnosis?'

'Whatever for?'

Poirot leaned forward.

'If I were to tell you, Madame, that your intuition is based on certain facts recorded subconsciously, you would probably be sceptical. I will only say, then, that this experiment I propose may be of great importance to that unfortunate young man, Charles Leverson. You will not refuse?'

'Who is going to put me into a trance?' demanded Lady Astwell suspiciously. 'You?'

'A friend of mine, Lady Astwell, arrives, if I mistake not, at this very minute. I hear the wheels of the car outside.'

'Who is he?'

'A Dr Cazalet of Harley Street.'

'Is he – all right?' asked Lady Astwell apprehensively.

'He is not a quack, Madame, if that is what you mean. You can trust yourself in his hands quite safely.'

'Well,' said Lady Astwell with a sigh, 'I think it is all bunkum, but you can try if you like. Nobody is going to say that I stood in your way.'

'A thousand thanks, Madame.'

Poirot hurried from the room. In a few minutes he returned ushering in a cheerful, round-faced little man, with spectacles, who was very upsetting to Lady Astwell's conception of what a hypnotist should look like. Poirot introduced them.

'Well,' said Lady Astwell good-humouredly, 'how do we start this tomfoolery?'

'Quite simple, Lady Astwell, quite simple,' said the little doctor. 'Just lean back, so – that's right, that's right. No need to be uneasy.'

'I am not in the least uneasy,' said Lady Astwell. 'I should like to see anyone hypnotizing me against my will.'

Dr Cazalet smiled broadly.

'Yes, but if you consent, it won't be against your will, will it?' he said cheerfully. 'That's right. Turn off that other light, will you, M. Poirot? Just let yourself go to sleep, Lady Astwell.'

He shifted his position a little.

'It's getting late. You are sleepy – very sleepy. Your eyelids are heavy, they are closing – closing – closing. Soon you will be asleep . . .'

His voice droned on, low, soothing, and monotonous. Presently he leaned forward and gently lifted Lady Astwell's right eyelid. Then he turned to Poirot, nodding in a satisfied manner.

'That's all right,' he said in a low voice. 'Shall I go ahead?'

'If you please.'

The doctor spoke out sharply and authoritatively: 'You are asleep, Lady Astwell, but you hear me, and you can answer my questions.'

Without stirring or raising an eyelid, the motionless figure on the sofa replied in a low, monotonous voice:

'I hear you. I can answer your questions.'

'Lady Astwell, I want you to go back to the evening on which your husband was murdered. You remember that evening?'

'Yes.'

'You are at the dinner table. Describe to me what you saw and felt.'

The prone figure stirred a little restlessly.

'I am in great distress. I am worried about Lily.'

'We know that; tell us what you saw.'

'Victor is eating all the salted almonds; he is greedy. Tomorrow I shall tell Parsons not to put the dish on that side of the table.'

'Go on, Lady Astwell.'

'Reuben is in a bad humour tonight. I don't think it is altogether about Lily. It is something to do with business. Victor looks at him in a queer way.'

'Tell us about Mr Trefusis, Lady Astwell.'

'His left shirt cuff is frayed. He puts a lot of grease on his hair. I wish men didn't, it ruins the covers in the drawing-room.'

Cazalet looked at Poirot; the other made a motion with his head.

'It is after dinner, Lady Astwell, you are having coffee. Describe the scene to me.'

'The coffee is good tonight. It varies. Cook is very unreliable over her coffee. Lily keeps looking out of the window, I don't know why. Now Reuben comes into the room; he is in one of his worst moods tonight, and bursts out with a perfect flood of abuse to poor Mr Trefusis. Mr Trefusis has his hand round the paper knife, the big one with the sharp blade like a knife. How hard he is grasping it; his knuckles are quite white. Look, he has dug it so hard in the table that the point snaps. He holds it just as you would hold a dagger you were going to stick into someone. There, they have gone out together now. Lily has got her green evening dress on; she looks so pretty in green, just like a lily. I must have the covers cleaned next week.'

'Just a minute, Lady Astwell.'

The doctor leaned across to Poirot.

'We have got it, I think,' he murmured; 'that action with the paper knife, that's what convinced her that the secretary did the thing.'

'Let us go on to the Tower room now.'

The doctor nodded, and began once more to question Lady Astwell in his high, decisive voice.

'It is later in the evening; you are in the Tower room with your husband. You and he have had a terrible scene together, have you not?'

Again the figure stirred uneasily.

'Yes – terrible – terrible. We said dreadful things – both of us.'

'Never mind that now. You can see the room clearly, the curtains were drawn, the lights were on.'

'Not the middle light, only the desk light.'

'You are leaving your husband now, you are saying good night to him.'

'No, I was too angry.'

'It is the last time you will see him; very soon he will be murdered. Do you know who murdered him, Lady Astwell?'

'Yes. Mr Trefusis.'

'Why do you say that?'

'Because of the bulge – the bulge in the curtain.'

'There was a bulge in the curtain?'

'Yes.'

'You saw it?'

'Yes. I almost touched it.'

'Was there a man concealed there – Mr Trefusis?'

'Yes.'

'How do you know?'

For the first time the monotonous answering voice hesitated and lost confidence.

'I – I – because of the paper knife.'

Poirot and the doctor again interchanged swift glances.

'I don't understand you, Lady Astwell. There was a bulge in the curtain, you say? Someone concealed there? You didn't see that person?'

'No.'

'You thought it was Mr Trefusis because of the way he held the paper knife earlier?'

'Yes.'

'But Mr Trefusis had gone to bed, had he not?'

'Yes – yes, that's right, he had gone away to his room.'

'So he couldn't have been behind the curtain in the window?'

'No – no, of course not, he wasn't there.'

'He had said good night to your husband some time before, hadn't he?'

'Yes.'

'And you didn't see him again?'

She was stirring now, throwing herself about, moaning faintly.

'She is coming out,' said the doctor. 'Well, I think we have got all we can, eh?'

Poirot nodded. The doctor leaned over Lady Astwell.

'You are waking,' he murmured softly. 'You are waking now. In another minute you will open your eyes.'

The two men waited, and presently Lady Astwell sat upright and stared at them both.

'Have I been having a nap?'

'That's it, Lady Astwell, just a little sleep,' said the doctor.

She looked at him.

'Some of your hocus-pocus, eh?'

'You don't feel any the worse, I hope,' he asked.

Lady Astwell yawned.

'I feel rather tired and done up.'

The doctor rose.

'I will ask them to send you up some coffee,' he said, 'and we will leave you for the present.'

'Did I – say anything?' Lady Astwell called after them as they reached the door.

Poirot smiled back at her.

'Nothing of great importance, Madame. You informed us that the drawing-room covers needed cleaning.'

'So they do,' said Lady Astwell. 'You needn't have put me into a trance to get me to tell you that.' She laughed good-humouredly. 'Anything more?'

'Do you remember M. Trefusis picking up a paper knife in the drawing-room that night?' asked Poirot.

'I don't know, I'm sure,' said Lady Astwell. 'He may have done so.'

'Does a bulge in the curtain convey anything to you?'

Lady Astwell frowned.

'I seem to remember,' she said slowly. 'No – it's gone, and yet –'

'Do not distress yourself, Lady Astwell,' said Poirot quickly; 'it is of no importance – of no importance whatever.'

The doctor went with Poirot to the latter's room.

'Well,' said Cazalet, 'I think this explains things pretty clearly. No doubt when Sir Reubens was dressing down the secretary, the latter grabbed tight hold on a paper knife, and had to exercise a good deal of self-control to prevent himself answering back. Lady Astwell's conscious mind was wholly taken up with the problem of Lily Margrave, but her subconscious mind noticed and misconstrued the action.

'It implanted in her the firm conviction that Trefusis murdered Sir Reuben. Now we come to the bulge in the curtain. That is interesting. I take from what you have told me of the Tower room that the desk was right in the window. There are curtains across that window, of course?'

'Yes, *mon ami*, black velvet curtains.'

'And there is room in the embrasure of the window for anyone to remain concealed behind them?'

'There would be just room, I think.'

'Then there seems at least a possibility,' said the doctor

slowly, 'that someone was concealed in the room, but if so it could not be the secretary, since they both saw him leave the room. It could not be Victor Astwell, for Trefusis met him going out, and it could not be Lily Margrave. Whoever it was must have been concealed there *before* Sir Reuben entered the room that evening. You have told me pretty well how the land lies. Now what about Captain Naylor? Could it have been he who was concealed there?'

'It is always possible,' admitted Poirot. 'He certainly dined at the hotel, but how soon he went out afterwards is difficult to fix exactly. He returned about half past twelve.'

'Then it might have been he,' said the doctor, 'and if so, he committed the crime. He had the motive, and there was a weapon near at hand. You don't seem satisfied with the idea, though?'

'Me, I have other ideas,' confessed Poirot. 'Tell me now, *M. le Docteur*, supposing for one minute that Lady Astwell herself had committed this crime, would she necessarily betray the fact in the hypnotic state?'

The doctor whistled.

'So that's what you are getting at? Lady Astwell is the criminal, eh? Of course – it is possible; I never thought of it till this minute. She was the last to be with him, and no one saw him alive afterwards. As to your question, I should be inclined to say – no. Lady Astwell would go into the hypnotic state with a strong mental reservation to say nothing of her own part in the crime. She would answer my questions truthfully, but she would be dumb on that one point. Yet I should hardly have expected her to be so insistent on Mr Trefusis's guilt.'

'I comprehend,' said Poirot. 'But I have not said that I believe Lady Astwell to be the criminal. It is a suggestion, that is all.'

'It is an interesting case,' said the doctor after a minute or two. 'Granting Charles Leverson is innocent, there are so many possibilities, Humphrey Naylor, Lady Astwell, and even Lily Margrave.'

'There is another you have not mentioned,' said Poirot quietly, 'Victor Astwell. According to his own story, he sat in his room with the door open waiting for Charles Leverson's return, but we have only his own words for it, you comprehend?'

'He is the bad-tempered fellow, isn't he?' asked the doctor. 'The one you told me about?'

'That is so,' agreed Poirot.

The doctor rose to his feet.

'Well, I must be getting back to town. You will let me know how things shape, won't you?'

After the doctor had left, Poirot pulled the bell for George.

'A cup of tisane, George. My nerves are much disturbed.'

'Certainly, sir,' said George. 'I will prepare it immediately.'

Ten minutes later he brought a steaming cup to his master. Poirot inhaled the noxious fumes with pleasure. As he sipped it, he soliloquized aloud.

'The chase is different all over the world. To catch the fox you ride hard with dogs. You shout, you run, it is a matter of speed. I have not shot the stag myself, but I understand that to do so you crawl for many long, long hours upon your stomach. My friend Hastings has recounted the affair to me. Our method here, my good George, must be neither of these. Let us reflect upon the household cat. For many long, weary hours, he watches the mousehole, he makes no movement, he betrays no energy, but – he does not go away.'

He sighed and put the empty cup down on its saucer.

'I told you to pack for a few days. Tomorrow, my good George, you will go to London and bring down what is necessary for a fortnight.'

'Very good, sir,' said George. As usual he displayed no emotion.

The apparently permanent presence of Hercule Poirot at Mon Repos was disquieting to many people. Victor Astwell remonstrated with his sister-in-law about it.

'It's all very well, Nancy. You don't know what fellows of that kind are like. He has found jolly comfortable quarters here, and he is evidently going to settle down comfortably for about a month, charging you several guineas a day all the while.'

Lady Astwell's reply was to the effect that she could manage her own affairs without interference.

Lily Margrave tried earnestly to conceal her perturbation. At the time, she had felt sure that Poirot believed her story. Now she was not so certain.

Poirot did not play an entirely quiescent game. On the fifth day of his sojourn he brought down a small thumbograph album to dinner. As a method of getting the thumbprints of the household, it seemed a rather clumsy device, yet not perhaps so clumsy as it seemed, since no one could afford to refuse their thumbprints. Only after the little man had retired to bed did Victor Astwell state his views.

'You see what it means, Nancy. He is out after one of us.'

'Don't be absurd, Victor.'

'Well, what other meaning could that blinking little book of his have?'

'M. Poirot knows what he is doing,' said Lady Astwell complacently, and looked with some meaning at Owen Trefusis.

On another occasion, Poirot introduced the game of tracing footprints on a sheet of paper. The following morning, going with his soft cat-like tread into the library, the detective startled Owen Trefusis, who leaped from his chair as though he had been shot.

'You must really excuse me, M. Poirot,' he said primly, 'but you have us on the jump.'

'Indeed, how is that?' demanded the little man innocently.

'I will admit,' said the secretary, 'that I thought the case against Charles Leverson utterly overwhelming. You apparently do not find it so.'

Poirot was standing looking out of the window. He turned suddenly to the other.

'I shall tell you something, M. Trefusis – in confidence.'

'Yes?'

Poirot seemed in no hurry to begin. He waited a minute, hesitating. When he did speak, the opening words were coincident with the opening and shutting of the front door. For a man saying something in confidence, he spoke rather loudly, his voice drowning the sound of a footstep in the hall outside.

'I shall tell you this in confidence, Mr Trefusis. There is new evidence. It goes to prove that when Charles Leverson entered the Tower room that night, Sir Reuben was already dead.'

The secretary stared at him.

'But what evidence? Why have we not heard of it?'

'You *will* hear,' said the little man mysteriously. 'In the meantime, you and I alone know the secret.'

He skipped nimbly out of the room, and almost collided with Victor Astwell in the hall outside.

'You have just come in, eh, Monsieur?'

Astwell nodded.

'Beastly day outside,' he said, breathing hard, 'cold and blowy.'

'Ah,' said Poirot, 'I shall not promenade myself today – me, I am like a cat, I sit by the fire and keep myself warm.'

'*Ça marche*, George,' he said that evening to the

faithful valet, rubbing his hands as he spoke, 'they are on the tenterhooks – the jump! It is hard, George, to play the game of the cat, the waiting game, but it answers, yes, it answers wonderfully. Tomorrow we make a further effect.'

On the following day, Trefusis was obliged to go up to town. He went up by the same train as Victor Astwell. No sooner had they left the house than Poirot was galvanized into a fever of activity.

'Come, George, let us hurry to work. If the housemaid should approach these rooms, you must delay her. Speak to her sweet nothings, George, and keep her in the corridor.'

He went first to the secretary's room, and began a thorough search. Not a drawer or a shelf was left uninspected. Then he replaced everything hurriedly, and declared his quest finished. George, on guard in the doorway, gave way to a deferential cough.

'If you will excuse me, sir?'

'Yes, my good George?'

'The shoes, sir. The two pairs of brown shoes were on the second shelf, and the patent leather ones were on the shelf underneath. In replacing them you have reversed the order.'

'Marvellous!' cried Poirot, holding up his hands. 'But let us not distress ourselves over that. It is of no importance, I assure you, George. Never will M. Trefusis notice such a trifling matter.'

'As you think, sir,' said George.

'It is your business to notice such things,' said Poirot encouragingly as he clapped the other on the shoulder. 'It reflects credit upon you.'

The valet did not reply, and when, later in the day, the proceeding was repeated in the room of Victor Astwell, he made no comment on the fact that Mr Astwell's underclothing was not returned to its drawers strictly according to plan. Yet, in the second case at least, events proved the valet to be right and Poirot wrong. Victor Astwell came storming into the drawing-room that evening.

'Now, look here, you blasted little Belgian jackanapes, what do you mean by searching my room? What the devil do you think you are going to find there? I won't have it, do you hear? That's what comes of having a ferreting little spy in the house.'

Poirot's hands spread themselves out eloquently as his words tumbled one over the other. He offered a hundred apologies, a thousand, a million. He had been maladroit, officious, he was confused. He had taken an unwarranted liberty. In the end the infuriated gentleman was forced to subside, still growling.

And again that evening, sipping his tisane, Poirot murmured to George:

'It marches, my good George, yes, – it marches.'

'Friday,' observed Hercule Poirot thoughtfully, 'is my lucky day.'

'Indeed, sir.'

'You are not superstitious, perhaps, my good George?'

'I prefer not to sit down thirteen at table, sir, and I am adverse to passing under ladders. I have no superstitions about a Friday, sir.'

'That is well,' said Poirot, 'for, see you, today we make our Waterloo.'

'Really, sir.'

'You have such enthusiasm, my good George, you do not even ask what I propose to do.'

'And what is that, sir?'

'Today, George, I make a final thorough search of the Tower room.'

True enough, after breakfast, Poirot, with the permission of Lady Astwell, went to the scene of the crime.

There, at various times of the morning, members of the household saw him crawling about on all fours, examining minutely the black velvet curtains and standing on high chairs to examine the picture frames on the wall. Lady Astwell for the first time displayed uneasiness.

'I have to admit it,' she said. 'He is getting on my nerves at last. He has something up his sleeve, and I don't know what it is. And the way he is crawling about on the floor up there like a dog makes me downright shivery. What is he looking for, I'd like to know? Lily, my dear, I wish you would go up and see what he is up to now. No, on the whole, I'd rather you stayed with me.'

'Shall I go, Lady Astwell?' asked the secretary, rising from the desk.

'If you would, Mr Trefusis.'

Owen Trefusis left the room and mounted the stairs to the Tower room. At first glance, he thought the room was empty, there was certainly no sign of Hercule Poirot there. He was just returning to go down again when a sound caught his ears; he then saw the little man half-way down the spiral staircase that led to the bedroom above.

He was on his hands and knees; in his left hand was a little pocket lens, and through this he was examining minutely something on the woodwork beside the stair carpet.

As the secretary watched him, he uttered a sudden grunt, and slipped the lens into his pocket. He then rose to his feet, holding something between his finger and thumb. At that moment he became aware of the secretary's presence.

'Ah, hah! M. Trefusis, I didn't hear you enter.'

He was in that moment a different man. Triumph and exultation beamed all over his face. Trefusis stared at him in surprise.

'What is the matter, M.Poirot? You look very pleased.'

The little man puffed out his chest.

'Yes, indeed. See you I have at last found that which I have been looking for from the beginning. I have here between my finger and thumb the only thing necessary to convict the criminal.'

'Then,' the secretary raised his eyebrows, 'it was not Charles Leverson?'

'It was not Charles Leverson,' said Poirot. 'Until this moment, though I know the criminal, I am not sure of his name, but at last all is clear.'

He stepped down the stairs and tapped the secretary on the shoulder.

'I am obliged to go to London immediately. Speak to Lady Astwell for me. Will you request of her that everyone should be assembled in the Tower room this evening at nine o'clock? I shall be there then, and I shall reveal the truth. Ah, me, but I am well content.'

And breaking into a fantastic little dance, he skipped from the Tower room. Trefusis was left staring after him.

A few minutes later Poirot appeared in the library, demanding if anyone could supply him with a little cardboard box.

'Unfortunately, I have not such a thing with me,' he explained, 'and there is something of great value that it is necessary for me to put inside.'

From one of the drawers in the desk Trefusis produced a small box, and Poirot professed himself highly delighted with it.

He hurried upstairs with his treasure-trove; meeting George on the landing, he handed the box to him.

'There is something of great importance inside,' he explained. 'Place it, my good George, in the second drawer of my dressing-table, beside the jewel case that contains my pearl studs.'

'Very good, sir,' said George.

'Do not break it,' said Poirot. 'Be very careful. Inside that box is something that will hang a criminal.'

'You don't say, sir,' said George.

Poirot hurried down the stairs again and, seizing his hat, departed from the house at a brisk run.

His return was more unostentatious. The faithful George, according to orders, admitted him by the side door.

'They are all in the Tower room?' inquired Poirot.

'Yes, sir.'

There was a murmured interchange of a few words, and then Poirot mounted with the triumphant step of the victor to that room where the murder had taken place less than a month ago. His eyes swept around the room. They were all there, Lady Astwell, Victor Astwell, Lily Margrave, the secretary, and Parsons, the butler. The latter was hovering by the door uncertainly.

'George, sir, said I should be needed here,' said Parsons as Poirot made his appearance. 'I don't know if that is right, sir?'

'Quite right,' said Poirot. 'Remain, I pray of you.'

He advanced to the middle of the room.

'This has been a case of great interest,' he said in a slow, reflective voice. 'It is interesting because anyone might have murdered Sir Reuben Astwell. Who inherits his money? Charles Leverson and Lady Astwell. Who was with him last that night? Lady Astwell. Who quarrelled with him violently? Again Lady Astwell.'

'What are you talking about?' cried Lady Astwell. 'I don't understand, I –'

'But someone else quarrelled with Sir Reuben,' continued Poirot in a pensive voice. 'Someone else left him that night white with rage. Supposing Lady Astwell left her husband alive at a quarter to twelve that night, there would be ten minutes before Mr Charles Leverson returned, ten minutes in which it would be possible for someone from the second floor to steal down and do the deed, and then return to his room again.'

Victor Astwell sprang up with a cry.

'What the hell – ?' He stopped, choking with rage.

'In a rage, Mr Astwell, you once killed a man in West Africa.'

'I don't believe it,' cried Lily Margrave.

She came forward, her hands clenched, two bright spots of colour in her cheeks.

'I don't believe it,' repeated the girl. She came close to Victor Astwell's side.

'It's true, Lily,' said Astwell, 'but there are things this man doesn't know. The fellow I killed was a witchdoctor who had just massacred fifteen children. I consider that I was justified.'

Lily came up to Poirot.

'M. Poirot,' she said earnesly, 'you are wrong. Because a man has a sharp temper, because he breaks out and says all kinds of things, that is not any reason why he should do a murder. I know – I *know*, I tell you – that Mr Astwell is incapable of such a thing.'

Poirot looked at her, a very curious smile on his face. Then he took her hand and patted it gently.

'You see, Mademoiselle,' he said gently, 'you also have your intuitions. So you believe in Mr Astwell, do you?'

Lily spoke quietly.

'Mr Astwell is a good man,' she said, 'and he is honest. He had nothing to do with the inside work of the Mpala Gold Fields. He is good through and through, and – I have promised to marry him.'

Victor Astwell came to her side and took her other hand.

'Before God, M. Poirot,' he said, 'I didn't kill my brother.'

'I know you did not,' said Poirot.

His eye swept around the room.

'Listen, my friends. In a hypnotic trance, Lady Astwell mentioned having seen a bulge in the curtain that night.'

Everyone's eyes swept to the window.

'You mean there was a burglar concealed there?' exclaimed Victor Astwell. 'What a splendid solution!'

'Ah,' said Poirot gently. 'But it was not *that* curtain.'

He wheeled around and pointed to the curtain that masked the little staircase.

'Sir Reuben used the bedroom the night prior to the crime. He breakfasted in bed, and he had Mr Trefusis up there to give him instructions. I don't know what it was that Mr Trefusis left in that bedroom, but there was something. When he said good night to Sir Reuben and Lady Astwell, he remembered this thing and ran up the stairs to fetch it. I don't think either the husband or wife noticed him, for they had already begun a violent discussion. They were in the middle of this quarrel when Mr Trefusis came down the stairs again.

'The things they were saying to each other were of so intimate and personal a nature that Mr Trefusis was placed in a very awkward position. It was clear to him that they imagined he had left the room some time ago. Fearing to arouse Sir Reuben's anger against himself, he decided to remain where he was and slip out later. He stayed there behind the curtain, and as Lady Astwell left the room she subconsciously noticed the outline of his form there.

'When Lady Astwell had left the room, Trefusis tried to steal out unobserved, but Sir Reuben happened to turn his head, and became aware of the secretary's presence. Already in a bad temper, Sir Reuben hurled abuse at his secretary, and accused him of deliberately eavesdropping and spying.

'Messieurs and Mesdames, I am a student of psychology. All through this case I have looked, not for the bad-tempered man or woman, for bad temper is its own safety valve. He who can bark does not bite. No, I have looked for the good-tempered man, for the man who is patient and self-controlled, for the man who for nine years has played the part of the under dog. There is no strain so

251

great as that which has endured for years, there is no resentment like that which accumulates slowly.

'For nine years Sir Reuben has bullied and brow-beaten his secretary, and for nine years that man has endured in silence. But there comes a day when at last the strain reaches its breaking point. *Something snaps*! It was so that night. Sir Reuben sat down at his desk again, but the secretary, instead of turning humbly and meekly to the door, picks up the heavy wooden club, and strikes down the man who had bullied him once too often.'

He turned to Trefusis, who was staring at him as though turned to stone.

'It was so simple, your alibi. Mr Astwell thought you were in your room, but *no one saw you go there.* You were just stealing out after striking down Sir Reuben when you heard a sound, and you hastened back to cover, behind the curtain. You were behind there when Charles Leverson entered the room, you were there when Lily Margrave came. It was not till long after that that you crept up through a silent house to your bedroom. Do you deny it?'

Trefusis began to stammer.

'I – I never –'

'Ah! Let us finish this. For two weeks now I have played the comedy. I have showed you the net closing slowly around you. The fingerprints, footprints, the search of your room with the things artistically replaced. I have struck terror into you with all of this; you have lain awake at night fearing and wondering; did you leave a fingerprint in the room or a footprint somewhere?

'Again and again you have gone over the events of that night wondering what you have done or left undone, and so I brought you to the state where you made a slip. I saw the fear leap into your eyes today when I picked up something from the stairs where you had stood hidden that night. Then I made a great parade, the little box, the entrusting of it to George, and I go out.'

Poirot turned towards the door.

'George?'

'I am here, sir.'

The valet came forward.

'Will you tell these ladies and gentlemen what my instructions were?'

'I was to remain concealed in the wardrobe in your room, sir, having placed the cardboard box where you told me to. At half past three this afternoon, sir, Mr Trefusis entered the room; he went to the drawer and took out the box in question.'

'And in that box,' continued Poirot, 'was a common pin. Me, I speak always the truth. I did pick up something on the stairs this morning. That is your English saying, is it not? "See a pin and pick it up, all the day you'll have good luck." Me, I have had good luck, I have found the murderer.'

He turned to the secretary.

'You see?' he said gently. '*You betrayed yourself.*'

Suddenly Trefusis broke down. He sank into a chair sobbing, his face buried in his hands.

'I was mad,' he groaned. 'I was mad. But, oh, my God, he badgered and bullied me beyond bearing. For years I had hated and loathed him.'

'I knew!' cried Lady Astwell.

She sprang forward, her face irradiated with savage triumph.

'I *knew* that man had done it.'

She stood there, savage and triumphant.

'And you were right,' said Poirot. 'One may call things by different names, but the fact remains. Your "intuition", Lady Astwell, proved correct. I felicitate you.'

ALSO BY AGATHA CHRISTIE

The ABC Murders

A is for Andover – and Mrs Ascher battered to
death.
B is for Bexhill – and Betty Bernard is strangled.
C is for Sir Carmichael Clarke clubbed and killed.

Beside each body lay a copy of the ABC Railway
Guide – open at the relevant page. The police were
baffled. But the murderer had already made a
grave mistake. He had challenged Hercule Poirot
to unmask him . . .

'The acknowledged queen of detective fiction'
Observer

ISBN 0 00 616724 1

Fontana

Fontana

Ngaio Marsh's Roderick Alleyn Mysteries

- ☐ A MAN LAY DEAD £3.50
- ☐ ARTISTS IN CRIME £3.50
- ☐ CLUTCH OF CONSTABLES £3.99
- ☐ DEAD WATER £3.99
- ☐ GRAVE MISTAKE £3.50
- ☐ OVERTURE TO DEATH £3.99
- ☐ PHOTO-FINISH £3.99
- ☐ SPINSTERS IN JEOPARDY £3.99
- ☐ SURFEIT OF LAMPREYS £3.50
- ☐ SWING, BROTHER, SWING £3.99
- ☐ TIED UP IN TINSEL £3.99
- ☐ VINTAGE MURDER £3.99

You can buy Fontana Paperbacks at your local bookshops or newsagents. Or you can order them from Fontana, Cash Sales Department, Box 29, Douglas, Isle of Man. Please send a cheque, postal or money order (not currency) worth the purchase price plus 24p per book for postage (maximum postage required is £3.00 for orders within the UK).

NAME (Block letters)_____

ADDRESS_____

_____